Praise for Kelly Moran's
The Dysfunctional Test

"Fresh, funny and heartwarming! A can't-put-down, laugh-out-loud romp of a read that'll touch your heart as well as your funny bone."

~ *Robin Wells, award winning author of* The Wedding Kiss

"Great escape reading!"

~ *Library Journal*

"Kelly Moran has written a novel worthy of "best seller" status and I could really see this book as a big screen romantic comedy. Fresh, funny and romantic, *The Dysfunctional Test* will have you laughing and smiling until the very last page!"

~ *Night Owl Reviews*

"This was by far one of my favorite romances of the year, if not of all time. The bond between the main characters, the wonderment of their developing love and the bright, brash humor that is laced through every scene are simply extraordinary."

~ *The Romance Reviews*

The Dysfunctional Test

Kelly Moran

SAMHAIN PUBLISHING

Samhain Publishing, Ltd.
11821 Mason Montgomery Road, 4B
Cincinnati, OH 45249
www.samhainpublishing.com

The Dysfunctional Test
Copyright © 2013 by Kelly Moran
Print ISBN: 978-1-61922-109-3
Digital ISBN: 978-1-61921-662-4

Editing by Tera Kleinfelter
Cover by Kim Killion

First Samhain Publishing, Ltd. electronic publication: September 2013
First Samhain Publishing, Ltd. print publication: September 2014

Dedication

This book is about family, love and all the quirks and idiosyncrasies associated. My father's side of the family is Serbian, which means I'm half-Serbian, and writing this book feels a long time in coming. I remember having three Christmases as a kid—Christmas Eve with one family, Christmas Day with the other, and Serbian Christmas (*Hristo se Rodi*). There are so many traditions that stayed with me through the years, and even though most of my "Covics" have passed on, the customs stayed with me. And so this book is dedicated to my Serbian side of the family.

In addition, I firmly believe that some families you are born into, and others you form along the way, not unlike my hero, Troy. So, this book is also dedicated to two of my "formed" families: The Biels—Dennis, Phyllis and Brian; and the Theurichs—Susie, Chris and Tommy. You guys made me believe I was worth something, and made me laugh more times than I can count. With love and thanks, always.

Big props to my critique partners and fellow writers: Anne, Jenafer and Linda for the insight and help. You guys are awesome. And to my editor, Tera, thanks for loving the story so much and helping to make it even better.

Chapter One

Life Lessons According to Camryn:
Some people are like Slinkies. They're only good for a smile
when you push them down the stairs.

The first sign that Karma was now in cahoots with the Devil Incarnate to ruin her existence should have been before sunrise and pre-coffee. Well, okay, she didn't believe in Karma. Like fate, Camryn believed people made their own destiny. Any inclinations otherwise were for those too idealistic to accept reality. Though, now she was beginning to wonder if there was any merit to naive notions.

When she opened her apartment door to get the *Chicago Tribune* she instead found a note from her landlord. They were not renewing her lease—anyone's lease for that matter. The building had been sold and the new owners wanted to convert it into high-end condos. Oh, please. Chicago needed more high-end condos like they needed another baseball franchise. She had thirty days to find another apartment.

The second sign should have been spilling the last of her lukewarm full-caff, half-fat freshly ground beverage over her crisp beige suit shirt while braking for the Neanderthal in front of her, who, according to his bumper sticker, *Brakes for nature.* Someone should tell him there was no nature in Chicago. She had to resort to her emergency back-up shirt in the trunk—a hideous, orange garment her sister bought her for *Hristo se Rodi* last year—or risk being late into the office.

Seriously, could her sister, just once, get her a useful Christmas gift? Was that too much to ask?

The third sign should have been when, after arriving at the office, her secretary announced that Alicia St. John, Vice President, wanted to see Camryn in her office at nine fifteen sharp. The pointed pain-in-the-ass woman never summoned someone as low as a marketing director like herself unless things were about to get ugly.

At first she thought these nothing more than nuisances, a crappy start to what was proving a bad day. But as Camryn Covic stood in the doorway to her boyfriend-slash-boss's office, she had a niggling feeling this was not a bad day at all, but rather a screeching halt preceding a twelve car pile up.

And she was at the bottom of the wreckage.

Maxwell Orton, the Third, blinked at her from across his desk. Camryn blinked back. She waited for him to give her a heads up on what Alicia wanted. He worked a lot more closely with her on their projects than Camryn did. He'd know what the succubus wanted. Instead, he fidgeted with a stack of papers on his desk, arranging and rearranging them into a clusterfuck.

Camryn sat down in a chair and folded her hands in her lap, illustrating the calm she didn't feel. "What's going on, Maxwell?"

He stood, popped a Tums from his candy dish into his mouth, and walked behind her to close the door while he chewed. When he returned to his desk, he sighed so heavily she could smell the cherry antacid. He took several seconds straightening his blue striped tie into obedience, which was interesting because it wasn't askew to begin with.

"Camryn," he said in that tone reserved for a street urchin, not that he knew any street urchins. "I don't think this is going to work out between us."

Though her gut sank like Nana's three-day-old *slavski kolac* bread, she didn't flinch. By "this" she assumed he meant their fifteen-month relationship. The entire department knew about them dating, and though it was against policy at Davis, Davis, and St. John Advertising to fraternize within the company, no one said anything. Could this be what Alicia wanted to see her about?

"Is this about Alicia?"

His middling brown eyes popped from his head like he'd accidently swallowed a tamale. "You know about that? About the two of us, I mean? I wanted to talk to you privately before you heard about the relationship from someone else. I regret not calling you last night, then."

The relationship? Her intestines churned to the point she should've heard "Auntie Em!" blaring from her belly button. He was boinking the bitch. Behind her back.

Maxwell was good looking in a corporate, never-saw-the-light-of-day kind of way. He seemed suited for Camryn, both of them being the kind of people one would pass on the street and hardly take notice of. Not for Alicia. Alicia was...

"I see," she said. "Can I at least have the decency to know why?"

His lips curled, his obvious tell of disgust. When had she started disgusting him? She was no Alicia, but she wasn't disgusting. Was she? "This is why," he said, as if that explained anything. "You," he muttered, pointing at her as if scales grew over her arms. "You're a robot. You have no emotion whatsoever. Sex with you is like sleeping with a fish..."

Okay, that hurt. A lot. Camryn had thought because they'd been dating so long, had actually talked about marriage, maybe Maxwell had seen past what she showed others. Yeah, she was dull sometimes, but they were adults. Fun was for kids. They had a comfortable routine together, a mutual conformity and future outlook. The same goals. Get married in the next year, buy a condo, have one child, hire a nanny. Live happily ever after with a retirement fund and mutual stocks.

"You don't even laugh..."

She looked at him and realized he was still talking. Rather, still listing the many ways why she was an inferior, boring person. He was leaving her for beautiful, thin and fun Alicia St. John. Everything she wasn't. The harsh tickle of tears clogged her throat, but she cleared them.

Out of the perfect part of Maxwell Orton—*the Third's*—hair, horns began to grow. White ivory with ringed indents pushed through his scalp, barely disturbing the orderly comb of his dark brown strands. The lenses on his glasses cracked. Blisters formed over his skin. His hands morphed into hooves.

"Alicia and I are so good together..."

She blinked away the image before her, and the normal Maxwell returned. Her creative imagination always worked well as a defense mechanism. In her head, aliens could be invading the Upper West Side, using poodles as body cavities and laced Twizzlers for mind control. But on the outside, she was the pillar of calm. It was the only power she'd had growing up in a large, crazy Serbian family. In adulthood, it helped her hide feelings. Control. It was all about control.

She wasn't oblivious to how others saw her. The receptionists called her *The Ice Queen.* If only they knew what lay under the surface. How insecure and normal she was. Not so very different from them, really. But she thought Maxwell was different. If someone like Maxwell didn't want her, she *was* destined to be a spinster, just like her family thought. *Insert twelve cats here.* She didn't have charm and humor like her married younger brother. She didn't have good looks and a great body like her soon-to-be married younger sister.

Oh crap.

"What about my sister's wedding next week?" she asked him, cutting off his rant about her clothes not having any color. It would probably be argumentative to point out she was wearing a shirt the color of ripe cantaloupe. "I was supposed to introduce you to my family. We leave for Colorado in four days."

Camryn's family lived two hours north in Milwaukee, but her sister's fiancé, Justin, was from a well-to-do Boulder family. When they got engaged, his family wanted the wedding on their estate. They were flying the entire nut farm to Colorado for a week-long pre-wedding hurrah.

Maxwell's mouth snapped closed. "Obviously I won't be attending." He rose. "You have your meeting with Alicia now, and I think we're done here." Dismissed.

She looked at him a second more, bitter words on the tip of her tongue, then stood. "I believe you're right. I regret it happened this way. I...appreciated our time together." *You sack of monkey poo!* "I'll stop by later so we can discuss what team you want for the Fenzer account."

He sniffed. "That won't be necessary. Alicia and I have a team ready. You're being put on the Wholesome Foods account. Possibly."

Sign number five.

"I see," she said. *Good luck landing Fenzer Footwear without me.* "I'm sure the campaign will be stellar." *Stellar crap. And Fenzer's money will go to our competitor.*

She opened the door to find the entire department staring at her. She raised her brows when she really felt like yakking. "Good morning, everyone," she said, pulling out her Blackberry and pretending to check messages as if a giant hole hadn't just swallowed her.

She headed toward the elevator, texting her sister, Heather, along the way.

May come home a day early. Will explain later.

She pushed the button for the twentieth floor, where all the bigwig exec offices were. When the doors closed, shutting out the din, she leaned against the wall and exhaled. Her hand fluttered to her stomach, trying to keep the contents inside. She swallowed, sucked in a harsh breath, and straightened just as the doors opened with a ding.

The receptionist greeted her with a cool smile. "Hello, Ms. Covic. Miss St. John is expecting you. You can head straight back."

Camryn nodded and walked down the hall, passing advertising posters for their many accounts. Pet food, breath mints and, her personal favorite, tampons. She knocked and entered the first door on the right.

Alicia St. John, bitch extraordinaire, motioned her inside with a wave of her manicured hand. "No, I want it by Friday," she barked into the phone.

Camryn waited inside the doorway, watching Alicia pace the floor behind her mahogany desk. The click of her black heels matched time with a clock the company gave her last year for excellence. Or was it two years ago? Either way, she wasn't excellent at anything but bitchery. Her black suit resembled Fifth Avenue, but her pink camisole underneath whispered Victoria's Secret. Her coifed blonde hair fell to her shoulders in a smooth, shiny bob.

Camryn wondered if her perfect hair and her perfect makeup ruffled at all when she had her legs wrapped around Camryn's boyfriend. She was probably a screamer too. If Camryn were to claw Alicia's eyes out, would Maxwell still want her?

"Fine," Alicia said, slamming the receiver down. Without missing a beat, she looked at Camryn and pointed to a chair. "Sit, Camryn."

Do I get a treat if I do? Maybe she should wag her tail.

Alicia handed her a manila envelope before sitting herself. Camryn knew better than to open it before Alicia told her, in detail, what was inside. All hail the queen when she had something to say. Hell's fury erupted when full attention wasn't on her.

"We lost two big accounts this quarter. We have to make some cuts," she said before sipping from her Starbucks cup. She was probably the type to drink that chai tea crap instead of real coffee. "Your position is one of the cuts needed. The art director can do what you do without us having to pay the extra salary."

Uh, what? "My accounts weren't the two you lost. I also got you the Fenzer Footwear account."

Alicia stared at her. Just stared through her ice-blue eyes like Camryn just fell out of the stupid tree.

Pens and paper flew off of Alicia's desk and spiraled around the room. Files swirled out of the filing cabinet, slicing paper cuts into Alicia's face. When the stapler took flight, Camryn envisioned it landing solidly on Alicia's forehead.

"Am I being fired?" she asked, trying to hide the tremor in her voice with the clipped question.

"I prefer to say 'let go'. In that envelope is a letter of recommendation and a small severance package. It should get you through a few months."

Outside the massive twentieth floor window, the skyline of downtown Chicago lit up like a Roman candle. Helicopters buzzed between the skyscrapers and plummeted down. The office window shattered, blowing shards of glass inside.

Not my job too. What will I have left?

"I see," Camryn said. It was beginning to sound like a mantra. "I'll collect my things, then."

"Security will have to escort you out..."

Camryn stopped hearing anything but the steady hum of her heartbeat drumming her ears. Autopilot kicked in. She stood, walked out of the office, and straight to the elevator. She rode down in silence, exiting when the ding told her to. She walked directly to her office, collected her purse, and strode back to the elevator again.

Only then, while waiting for the elevator to return to take her to the bottom, did she notice Bill standing next to her. The security guard crossed his arms as if daring her to be difficult. Did they think she'd steal a laser jet copier on her way out by stashing it in her purse? *No, no. Never mind the huge bulge. That's just my day planner, Officer.*

Alarmed, she turned to find the whole department staring

at her again. Her heart thumped once and then gave up.

Everyone knew.

Several seconds ticked by. Staring, staring. Some had the courtesy to look away in shame, pretending to read a file or talk on the phone.

Chelsea, her secretary—make that her *ex*-secretary—hurried over with a box in her arms. "These are the things from your office, Ms. Covic. I'm so sorry."

She wasn't sorry. None of them were. They probably had a "ding dong, the witch is gone" party planned in five minutes by the water cooler.

Camryn nodded, taking the box from her with numb fingers just as the elevator door opened. Such a small box for the eight years she'd been employed there. Security Bill stepped onto the elevator with her and rode down. Down, down. She bit her tongue hard enough to draw blood; she'd be damned if anyone would see her cry. If she had nothing left—and that would appear to be the case—she had her pride.

Chin up. Act like you don't care.

Walking across the lobby, she kept her head high as she exited the front door, still high as she crossed the parking structure, and right up until she got to her car. Only when she got behind the wheel and slammed the door did she drop her head. Her eyes pinched closed as she sucked air through her nose.

Not here. Not here. Just get home.

Starting the car, she pulled out of the structure and headed toward her soon-to-be nonexistent apartment. There she'd cry like a darn baby in private until none of it mattered. Please. Who was she kidding? Of course it mattered.

Her life was over. Apartment? Gone. Job? Gone. Boyfriend? Double gone.

The banana and rye toast she'd had for breakfast started battling to the death on who'd escape her stomach first. She concentrated on the traffic and street lights just to survive the trip home.

Heck, she hated Chicago anyway.

"Damn and hell are bad words. We're not supposed to say them."

Camryn looked at her three-year-old niece standing in the doorway to her apartment, then at her sister. "I see Auntie Heather has been corrupting you again."

"Nonsense," Heather said, swishing past her and inside. "I cannot be expected to control my tongue in Chicago traffic. Seriously, it's a crime what you people call driving."

She had her there. Camryn looked down at her niece, Emily, again. "They are bad words. That's why we shouldn't repeat them, no matter who says them."

Wide, blue eyes stared back at her. "Shit too. Shit is a bad word."

Camryn sighed. "Yes." She closed the door behind them. "Heather, our dear brother is going to kill you if he hears his daughter cursing."

Heather plopped onto the sectional and crossed her feet on the coffee table. "Naw, he's driven here too. He'll understand."

"Speaking of Chicago, what are you doing here anyway? Don't you have wedding stuff to do?"

"Wedding stuff is all done. We just have to get on the plane Friday. I took Emily to the Shedd Aquarium today to celebrate." Heather deposited her red heels back on the floor and straightened, causing her matching red dress to plummet way past the recommended neckline. She surveyed the coffee table and then Camryn.

Had she known her sister would be dropping by, she would have hidden the Ben & Jerry's. And the wine. And probably would have gotten dressed. Camryn cinched her robe closed.

Heather merely lifted her brows. Camryn sighed and sat on the other end of the couch. It didn't matter what Camryn wore, or didn't wear, Heather was always the star of the show. Having inherited their father's high cheekbones and lean body, and their mother's thick, dark brown hair and flawless skin, Heather was conceived at the deep end of the gene pool. So was their brother, Fisher.

Camryn, on the other hand, got Dad's combination skin and ginger hair and Mom's curves. Whereas Heather and Fisher could eat whatever they desired, Camryn had to count each calorie. Not so easy in a Serbian family where one bite of a traditional dish was enough to get her kicked out of Jenny Craig for life. And probably maimed on the way out.

"What happened yesterday that made you want to come home early? Or eat the store out of ice cream?" Heather held up the pint in question. "Aw, man. And it's Chunky Monkey. My favorite. You could've saved me some."

Emily appeared distracted, having found her stash of crayons, and was now coloring on the floor. Camryn looked at Heather. As different as they were, Camryn had always been close with her sister. Heather may not always understand, but she was sympathetic.

"I got fired yesterday. And my landlord gave me an eviction notice." Camryn reached for her wineglass and drained the contents in one swallow. "Oh, and Maxwell broke up with me."

Heather leaned forward. "Shit."

"That's a naughty word, Aunt Heather." This from Emily, who apparently *was* listening. She had also stuck several crayons into her curly brown pigtails, making her resemble a cartoon version of Medusa.

Camryn wanted to toast to that, but instead said, "Why don't you go color in my bedroom, honey? We'll be done talking in a while."

Once Emily was out of earshot, Heather dive-bombed her with an interrogation similar to a WWII fighter pilot. "What happened? From the beginning. Don't leave anything out."

"This is my life, Heather, not soap opera gossip."

Heather snorted. "I don't know, this sounds like *Days of Our Lives* to me. Sure you don't have a brain tumor? Or an evil twin?"

Either might solve her problem. Alas, no. She told Heather about Alicia the bitch, and her eviction notice. When she told her about Maxwell, Heather flew off the couch.

"He said what? The jerk! I say we go back there and teach those assholes..."

"That's naughty too." This from the bedroom.

Heather sat back down. "Talk about injury to insult."

"I think you mean insult to injury."

"Whatever," she huffed. "What are you going to do?"

To avoid the question, Camryn stood and walked into the kitchenette to start a pot of coffee. Heather followed.

Once the brew was going, Camryn turned to her sister. "I'll probably move back home. I have a few days before we need to leave for Colorado. I'll get my resume out. Try interviewing after the wedding and look for an apartment." She opened the fridge to remove creamer. "There's no real advertising agencies in Milwaukee. I'll have to settle for Human Resources or something."

"There's other agencies here."

"I don't want to stay here. I only stayed this long because the company offered great money. Right out of college the opportunity was perfect for me."

"What about the wedding, though? Mom and Dad think you're bringing this guy with you."

"That's the least of my problems." *Liar!*

"Camryn, this is me you're talking to. I know you. You were

relieved to finally have met someone to bring home. To have Mom and Dad off your back."

True. If one thing was hammered into her skull her whole life, it was to find a mate and procreate. It never mattered to them how successful she was in her career if she didn't have someone to share her life with. Family was everything. And hers was a walk-in closet full of romantics. Very old school. It was shameful to her family that her younger brother married first. Downright disgraceful that her baby sister was marrying before her.

She was supposed to be next. She had chosen someone well suited to her. Someone even her family couldn't chase away. Her parents hadn't even asked his name. They were just relieved she was serious with someone. Prerequisites at this point were a living male.

Being alone never bothered Camryn, not really. In the end, the only person she could rely on was herself. No one else seemed to understand her, or understand her need for independence. It mattered not how she preached to her family about the modern woman, how she didn't need a man to make her happy. They just saw her singlehood as one more let down. If they could, they probably would have traded her for a mule in an arranged marriage.

Camryn could all but feel their disappointment now. The pity stares. The clicking tongues. *Poor, poor, Camryn. All alone. No one wants her.*

At least she'd bought her own plane ticket. Her family wouldn't know Maxwell's would go to waste.

She poured herself a cup of coffee and went back into the living room before the tears could come. Heather would see through her in a heartbeat.

"Why don't you hire someone? An escort or something."

Camryn gave her the best "shut-up" face she had in reserve. "Someone's been watching too much Lifetime again."

"I'm serious. Hire someone to be Maxwell, then explain the breakup later. They won't spend the entire wedding obsessing over that then. You never brought him home. They don't know what he looks like."

She didn't know what was sadder, the fact her sister thought the only way she could get a wedding date was to hire one, or late last night she'd thought up the same crazy idea.

"No. Mom and Dad will get over it. Eventually." She took a sip of coffee. "I'd never be able to pull it off with a stranger anyway."

"They're already upset we're not doing an Orthodox ceremony at church. They're going to spend the entire trip obsessing over that, never mind your spinsterhood. They're going to try to set you up with Justin's distant cousins or something. It'll be embarrassing."

Ah ha. The truth. Heather was more worried about her wedding day getting ruined than about Camryn's welfare. Though she did have a point. One Camryn had already considered.

"Heather, even if this wasn't absurd, this guy is going to be in your wedding pictures. I've been dating Maxwell for over a year. Mom and Dad know we were discussing marriage. I can't explain away not wanting my date in photos."

"You need someone we know," Heather said.

Camryn rolled her eyes as the gears turned in her sister's head. She was surprised there wasn't smoke. "No."

Her sister wasn't listening, though. She was on a roll. "Someone we wouldn't mind in photos."

"No."

"What about Troy?"

Camryn flinched. "Troy Lansky? As in our brother's best friend? He doesn't have enough fingers and toes to count the women he's been with. This year."

Heather was undeterred. "Exactly. He never brings a date

to family functions. He's not serious about anyone."

"No."

"Think about it, Cam. He knows you. Really well."

"No."

"Cam..."

"No."

Heather stood. "Cam, he'd pass the test."

Camryn snapped her mouth shut before another no could pop out. Heather was right about that. Troy would pass the test.

Back when they were teenagers, Camryn and her siblings had contrived what they called the dysfunctional test. If anyone they dated could survive a span of time with their family and not go clinically insane, *and* also be approved by the family, then they'd be the one for them. Her brother's wife, Anna, had passed the test. They had joked about it at their engagement party, letting Anna in on the secret. When Justin passed and proposed to Heather, they let him in on it too.

Camryn had never found someone to even try to pass. As time went by, she figured it didn't matter if she brought a paranoid schizophrenic with a toenail fetish home, he would suffice. Maxwell probably wouldn't have passed, but in the eyes of her parents, he would do. Living, breathing male.

Troy, however, passed the test at age ten, when he was first introduced to the family as their foster child. He never talked about it much, but his father was an abusive alcoholic. Having been in and out of their home for foster care until he turned eighteen, Troy had always been an honorary member of the family.

He also belonged on the cover of *Playgirl*. And knew it. Troy had sandy blond hair which lightened considerably in the summer and was always just south of needing a cut. His eyes were a deep, rich brown, and his lashes were a criminal waste on a man. Just shy of six feet tall, his body was the result of hard work and discipline. But his smile was the kicker. No woman had ever resisted that smile when the wattage cranked.

No one would believe they were a couple. Men like him didn't date women like her. It went against the balance of nature. The world would implode.

One more thing her family would blame her for.

Emily came running into the room waving a piece of paper. "I made a picture of you, Auntie Cam."

"Oh yeah? Let's see." Camryn looked down at the primitive etchings of her young niece. "Not bad, honey. But why do I have a big frown on my face?"

"Because you never smile."

This must be *make Camryn feel like crap* week. Camryn looked at Heather, who was too busy texting to notice. To prove the three-year-old wrong, Camryn plastered a big smile on her face. "Thank you. I love it. Maybe next time I can wear a smile?"

Heather laughed. Camryn thought it was at her until Heather turned the cell screen so she could see it.

Heather: What time do you get off work tomorrow?

Troy: 3. Why? Change your mind about the wedding? Wanna run away with me?

Heather: Lol. No, Cam will be at your place at 3:15 to discuss an important proposal.

Troy: Cam, huh? Must be serious.

Heather: Always is with her. Think about it before saying no.

Troy: Oh no. You're not sending her to arrange my wardrobe, are you? I can iron my own underwear.

Heather: Lmfao. Be home by 3:15.

Troy: K.

Camryn ground her teeth and stood. She was halfway to the kitchen before Heather spoke.

"What? You didn't say *no*."

When Camryn turned, Heather was wearing a pink baby doll dress and pigtails. Large black freckles spotted her nose. Some of the tension drained from Camryn before the image dissolved.

"I'm saying it now. No."

"Come on, sis. It'll work."

No, it wouldn't. Troy would never go for this charade. And even if he did, this would be one more joke to him. Contrary to popular opinion, her life was not a joke.

It may be sad and pathetic, but it wasn't a joke.

Chapter Two

Life Lessons According to Camryn:
Family trees full of nuts have nothing on me.
My family is temperamental.
Half temper, half mental.

The second her sister unlocked the front door to the family home, Emily barreled inside the door, pigtails bouncing. "Grandma, Grandpa, Auntie Cam started a fire at work. And she got an erection!"

Camryn stepped inside the door and dropped her suitcase at her feet. She pinched her eyes closed seconds after her eighty-five-year-old Nana spit coffee out of her mouth faster than the recorded speed of light.

Heather rushed over to Nana's recliner and smacked her on the back to dissolve her coughing fit. "Jeez, Emily. You're worse than the iPhone spell-check. Auntie Cam didn't *start* a fire, she *got* fired. And it's not an *erec*tion, it's *evic*tion."

Her father's bald head gleamed from the sun shining through the window as he shook his head in shame.

Her mother waddled into the small living room from the kitchen, rollers in her hair and a towel slung over her shoulder. "You started a fire at work? And what's this about an erection?"

Camryn walked over to Nana and kissed her cheek. "You okay? Need a heart pill?"

Nana waved her hand. "Stop fussing. I'm old, not dead. An erection is how I conceived your mom, you know."

"TMI, Nana," Heather said.

"It's an MRI, you twit!" Nana professed. "And my hip is fine. The doctor said so last week."

"No, Nana," Heather said, exasperated. "TMI means too much information."

"Why did you ask about the results then?"

Welcome home.

Camryn sighed and sat next to her father on the only thing older than the carpet—the couch. It was a shade lighter than the dark brown shag carpet. According to old family photos, it used to be white. Nothing ever changed at home.

"Camryn Covic, you answer me," her mother demanded.

She thought of responding with the first line of "Who's on First", but changed her mind. Her family didn't appreciate the ironic similarities between them and Abbott and Costello.

"I got let go from work on Monday. And my apartment building was sold. I have to move."

Her mother's eyes narrowed to slits. Her hands fisted on her hips. Camryn waited for steam to billow out her nostrils and her foot to stomp. Any second now she'd charge like a mad bull. Too bad the drapes weren't red. She could tear them down and divert her stampede.

Instead of charging, Mom harrumphed. "What's that got to do with an erection?"

"Nothing, Mother. Never mind."

"What did you do to get fired?" This from Dad.

"Budget cuts."

"Where are you going to live?" her mom asked, anger gone from her face and worry replacing it. Worry was worse than anger.

"She's not sharing my room," Nana claimed. "She snores."

"Mother, please," Mom said. "Camryn got herself into another mess. It doesn't matter if she snores or not."

Another mess? "I don't snore."

Nana slapped her hand down on her thigh, causing her knee-highs to drop to ankle-lows. "How do you know? You're asleep."

Heather, ever the peacemaker and good child, said, "Camryn is staying here until we leave for Colorado. Then she'll stay with Justin and I until she finds an apartment." A halo popped over her sister's head.

"In Milwaukee?" Mom asked. "You're coming home for good?"

Camryn prayed she'd remembered to pack a Valium. "It was Chicago, Mom. Not a third-world country."

Her father took a drink of beer. "Could've fooled me. Shitcago, I say. You're not a Bears fan now, are you? 'Cause you're not staying here if you are."

"Never mind that," Nana interjected. "How is Heather supposed to have marriage sex with this one snoring in the next room?"

Mom covered Emily's ears. "Don't listen, sweetie pie."

Camryn dropped her forehead in her hands. "Too late for that."

"Wait a minute," Mom said, an epiphany blooming. "What about your boyfriend? Won't he miss you in Chicago? He was supposed to escort you to the wedding. Where is he?" She figured her mom was looking around the room as if Camryn had hidden him somewhere.

Camryn was glad her head was still buried in her hands, 'cause all the imagination in the world wouldn't have masked her wince. "About that..."

"He lives in Milwaukee," Heather said, louder than necessary.

All eyes turned to Heather, including Camryn's. "Heather..."

"He'll be here Thursday night for dinner. He's still coming to the wedding. Don't worry."

Camryn stood, grabbed her sister by the arm, and dragged her into the kitchen. "What are you doing? I told you this wasn't happening."

Heather had the audacity to look upset. "Cam, if you don't do this for you, and God knows you should, then do it for me. Look at them." She pointed in the general direction of the living room. "That's only three family members. Add in the *yjakas* and *tetakas*, and it's a mess. They're going to embarrass me royally without trying to serve you up on a wedding martyr plate."

Great. Just great. She was playing the guilt card. Camryn pictured their *yjakas* and *tetakas*—Serbian translation, uncles and aunts—plus the *kumas* and *kumos*—godparents—and she could understand Heather's dismay.

"Troy hasn't even agreed to this yet."

And darn it, she was caving.

Heather removed her arm from Camryn's hold. "He will. You know he will."

Yeah, he would. Camryn sighed. What was one more humiliation in a long line? "Fine, Heather. I'll talk to Troy. But you owe me."

"You can have our firstborn," she joked.

"Oh no. I'll never hear the end of the single mother shame I bestowed on the family."

The front door squeaked open and Camryn's eyes rolled, wondering who else could add to this day. They went around the corner to find her brother, Fisher, and his wife, Anna.

Emily ran up to them and leapt for a big hug. "Auntie Cam started a fire, and got an erection. Nana had one for Grandma too. Auntie Heather can't have sex with Auntie Cam snoring. Oh, and shit is a bad word. We can't say it."

Fisher nearly dropped his daughter. "What the hell?" He looked around the room. "She was only with you for a day!"

Anna smiled but tried to hide it by pressing her mouth closed. Emily looked just like her with golden brown curls and massive blue eyes. But unlike her daughter, Anna knew when to shut her beautiful red mouth.

"Hell's a bad word too."

Right. Camryn picked up her purse from beside the couch. Even facing Troy with the proposal was better than this craziness.

"And I'm leaving. I'll be back later." Maybe.

Troy had just enough time to shower after work before Cam was due to show up for her so-called proposal. For a day and a half his mind geeked about what it could be. He couldn't think of a solitary thing he had that Camryn could want.

If Camryn was nothing else, she was punctual. He had the next ten days off work for Heather's wedding, so his boss didn't mind letting him out early. They had finished the road construction on South 84th Street by lunch anyway.

Cam was not the type of woman you met covered in asphalt and sunscreen. Even if she was like a sister.

Even if she was the only woman on Earth who could make him nervous.

He stripped out of his jeans and T-shirt in the bathroom, dropped them to the floor, and stepped under the spray of cold water. It had been a damn hot one today, even for June. In seconds, his body cooled down. He'd just finished rinsing the soap off when the doorbell rang.

He wrapped a towel around his waist and ran to the front door. "Cam, you're early."

She stood on his doorstep wearing a pair of pressed khakis and a white blouse. She surveyed him through those huge hazel eyes of hers. "Troy, you're naked."

"Not completely. I do have a towel." He stepped out of the way to let her inside. "Have a seat. I'll go get dressed."

After pulling on a T-shirt and shorts in his bedroom, he walked down the short hall to the kitchen. Knowing her answer, he asked anyway. "Want a beer?"

"No, thank you."

He grabbed a bottle of Miller Lite and sat across from her on the futon. "How's Chicago treating you?"

She took her eyes away from their family portrait to look at him. "I'm moving back home after the wedding."

With Camryn Covic, someone had to look very hard to see emotion. She had feelings, buried way deep under all the crap she piled on top. For Troy, his tell was her eyes. She had the same look now she had twenty years ago when the social worker first brought him to her parents' house. He'd gone to bed without dinner, by choice, and she brought him a PB&J with the crust cut off.

She didn't ask about his bruises. Didn't ask about his torn clothes. In fact, she didn't say anything except...

"You wanna talk about it?" he asked her now, mimicking the question she'd asked him so long ago.

She searched his face for several long beats, and then a smile traced the corners of her mouth. A sad smile, but a smile. She remembered. "No, but thank you."

That was his response back then too. Troy took a swig of beer to dislodge the lump. Camryn was also the only person who could make him feel sentimental.

"I haven't seen the house since you bought it. I like what you've done."

"Thanks," he said, glancing around. He'd painted the living room walls a burnt sienna. His furniture was black. Everything else screamed bachelor pad. "Heather says it needs a woman's touch."

"Well, then it wouldn't be yours."

Man, she always did understand him. Even more than her brother, his best friend. She understood how important it was, after a childhood like his, to own something of his own. She'd framed the family portrait of them from one Christmas as a housewarming gift. She'd also bought him a jar of peanut butter.

"So, Cam, what's this proposal? Is it at least indecent?"

Her posture turned rigid. "It's indecent all right. It's not really a proposal though..."

"Damn," he said, trying to lighten her mood. Futile. "Is it bigger than a..."

"I need a date for Heather's wedding."

Troy snapped his mouth shut, totally not expecting her to say that. Did she want him to set her up or something? 'Cause he didn't know a man who could handle her. "And?"

Her eyes closed briefly. "Would you be my date for the wedding?"

He almost laughed until he remembered she didn't have a sense of humor. He glanced around the room for a hidden camera anyway.

"What are you doing?"

"Um, nothing," he said. "What about your very serious boyfriend? Fisher said..."

"It didn't work out," she said impatiently, cutting him off and swallowing. "Look, long story short, I'm alone. You know Mom and Dad. Heather's worried about the family embarrassing her. I just need someone to be the guy I've been dating long enough to get through the trip. We'll break up right after."

He got up and looked under the couch. There had to be a hidden camera somewhere. A microphone. Something. Because Camryn Covic was stoically sitting in his living room, asking him out.

"Troy, what are you doing?"

"Did Heather wire the house? How'd she get you to do

this?"

When she didn't answer, he looked up from where he kneeled on the floor. Her hand fluttered to her mouth and her gaze darted to the window.

She wasn't kidding. He was an ass. He sat back down with a measure of control. "I've seen this movie, you know. It always ends with them falling in love."

"Won't happen."

She was right on that account. "You can get any guy you want. Why me?"

The way she looked at him had even his inner child cowering. "There's no need to make fun of me. I know you don't usually date women like me, but..."

"Women like you?" he repeated.

"Yes, we're vastly different. I'm not you're type."

Now he was interested. "And what's my type?"

She rubbed her forehead. "Thin, bottle blonde, and a bust size bigger than their IQ."

"Ouch, Cam. Now who's insulting whom?"

At least he'd succeeded in frustrating her as much as she did him. Not easily done with regards to Cam. The woman could handle anything, make any person feel like an imbecile. She let out a harsh exhale and looked away.

"Why wouldn't I date you?" Not that he didn't know the answer, but he was curious what her reasoning was.

"Christ, Troy. You look like you've been digitally enhanced from the moment you get out of bed."

"Was that a compliment?" It kinda sounded like a compliment.

She just stared at him, so he looked back. Really looked. Camryn was more cute than hot. More girl-next-door than girl-on-stripper-pole. She had a cherubic face slightly offset by a button nose. Her complexion was paler than her siblings, making her shoulder-length, cinnamon brown hair an emphasis. She wasn't a twig like Heather, having more of an hourglass curve he could always appreciate in a woman. But her eyes... It was like she never grew into them. A cosmic mix of green and blue and brown.

If she wasn't Camryn Covic, he probably would be attracted to her.

"You know me, Troy," she said quietly, finally breaking eye contact. "I know what doing this will mean for you. But, please, I don't want Heather looking back on her wedding day and only remembering how I ruined it."

She couldn't ruin something if she tried. More importantly though... "They'll hate me. Your family is the only one I have. After this supposed breakup, they'll hate me."

She shook her head. Stared into her lap. "No, they won't. They'll think you temporarily lost your mind. They'll hate *me*. For letting you go, or hurting you, or messing up another relationship."

No way did she believe that. Except the defeat in her face said she did. Her lips pressed together as if trying not to cry. The Cam he knew didn't know how to cry.

"Are you even attracted to me?"

Her mouth popped open. Her head whipped up. "Excuse me?"

"The family is going to expect us to act like a couple. Holding hands, kissing, public displays of affection."

"I don't do public displays of affection."

He wondered if she did private ones. He scooted next to her and draped an arm behind her back.

She flew off the couch. "What are you doing?"

He didn't think her eyes could get any bigger. How wrong he was. "Kissing you."

"Why?"

Standing, he took a step toward her. She stepped back.

They did this dance until she backed herself solidly against his entryway table. He pinned her by placing his hands on either side of her waist. When he leaned in, not to kiss her but to whisper in her ear, his cheek brushed hers. The rough rasp of his day-old growth grazed her pale, soft cheek. She sucked in a breath and grabbed his T-shirt, bunching it in her hand.

And just like that, he didn't know who was playing the trick on whom. Had no idea what his original point was in doing this. He closed his eyes and inhaled, smelling lemongrass. Light and clean and distinctly her. He couldn't tell if it was her heart or his pounding. Either way, it wasn't a good sign. For balance, he opened his eyes.

"Can you fake this kind of attraction, Cam? Because if you can't, this won't work." He took a step back, not enough to free her, but enough to look down at her to see if she was as ruffled as he.

She stared at his chest. Swallowed. "This was a mistake. I'm sorry." As if just noticing her grip on his shirt, she dropped her hand. "Pretend I never said anything." She brought her arm up and brushed by him.

Was that a tremor in her voice?

With his back to her, he could hear her walking to the couch to grab her purse, and then turning the knob on his front door. In the twenty years he'd known Camryn, he'd never known her to ask for anything, even help. Especially help.

Not then. Not now. Not ever.

It had to be so humiliating for her coming to him, particularly about something like this. And he'd just embarrassed the crap out of her. After all she'd done for him...

"I'll do it, Cam." He turned and looked at her when she paused. "I'll do whatever you need. I promise."

She gazed at her hand on the knob and nodded, but said nothing before leaving.

He stared at the door. Ran a hand over his hair. Stared at the door some more.

Finally, he pulled out his cell. "A little warning would have been nice, Heather!" His voice came out way harsher than he'd intended, but he'd just been rattled three times in the course of twenty minutes.

"I know, I know. But Cam would've killed me." She paused for him to speak. He didn't. "Are...you going to do it?"

He looked at the door again. "Yes."

"Thank you, Troy."

Heather's voice had gotten weepy, so he plopped on the couch and drank from his beer.

"That guy she was seeing, Maxwell, he kinda did a number on her."

No one ever did anything to Camryn. She'd never allow it. "How so?"

"Don't tell her I said anything, okay. She just..."

Troy set his beer down and leaned forward. "Just what, Heather?"

She paused long enough to have him worried. "She got let go from the firm and found out she has to move in the course of a day. She's moving back home. It's probably killing her."

Yeah, he could tell. Strip Camryn of control and independence and she was nothing. "What does that have to do with the ex?"

"He broke up with her right before she got fired. Said some things..."

Troy stood, tension wringing his jaw tight. If it was bad enough to have Heather upset, he could only imagine what it was doing to Camryn. "What did he say?"

"I just think she needs a morale boost, okay. Tell her she's pretty. Make her feel special. If anyone can do that, you can."

Camryn was not one of these women men had to placate.

Say empty, meaningless things to. He was pretty sure Cam would've punched him if he did. Heather knew that too. And they definitely weren't real a couple, so what in the hell had happened for Heather to want to intervene?

"Heather, what did he say?"

She paused. Sighed. "He called her a robot. Compared her to a fish in bed." Troy ground his teeth. "He was sleeping with someone behind her back."

Troy looked at the futon like Camryn was still sitting there. That look on her face and the things she'd said started making more sense now. If Camryn was anything, she was confident. When she came over today, she seemed the same. He didn't bother to try to understand, delve deeper.

No. He cracked jokes and...

"I'll talk to you later, Heather. Thanks for letting me know."

Chapter Three

Life Lessons According to Camryn:
Laughter is only the best medicine if you're the one laughing.

After the house was asleep, Camryn poured herself a glass of wine and went to sit out on the back deck. She could smell the dandelions and fresh-cut grass. This was the only peace and quiet she used to get as a kid, sneaking outside at night to breathe. Only now she felt less guilty about it. It was also the only time she didn't have to pretend to be fine. The small quarter-acre lot in her parents' subdivision was quiet except for the crickets.

She was pretty sure that's all she and Troy would hear tomorrow at dinner after the family found out they were "dating".

Earlier, she'd had a plan before heading over to Troy's. If he had agreed to this charade, they'd go over the details of their "relationship" to not trip over each other. Her family would demand details.

Except he'd tried to kiss her. Her mind had been a mess ever since. God, for a second there, she'd wanted him to kiss her too, proving insanity did run in the family.

Her cell rang from inside the house. She set her wine down and went to get it before it could wake anyone, answering while sitting back down on the deck.

"Did I wake you?" Troy. He'd changed his mind.

"No. I'm glad you changed your mind, though..."

"I didn't change my mind."

Oh. Then why was he calling?

"You wanted me to do this, Cam. I said I would." When she didn't respond, he cut in. "Look, I'm sorry for how I acted earlier. You just...surprised me."

She took a sip of wine. He surprised her too, so they were even. "We probably should go over some things."

"That's why I was calling," he said, his voice low. He was probably lying next to a beautiful blonde and trying not to wake her. "When did we, um...start dating?"

God. He couldn't even say it. "January of last year."

"And how?"

Huh. She wasn't sure on that one. "I don't know. Maxwell and I met at work." She swallowed. Her stomach churned. "Maybe you came to Chicago for the weekend and stopped by? Something happened?" If that wasn't the biggest crock of...

"Okay." Silence. "Are we discussing marriage?"

Maxwell's rejection cut her all over again. "We were, yes. But we can play that casually. I know you don't want to get married..."

"I never said that." He didn't have to. If Troy ever got married the depression rate for the population of single women would skyrocket. Troy would also have to be heavily medicated just to get down the aisle. "One must find the right person first."

Huh. She didn't remember him being this good a liar. Surprised, she said, "You just seemed like the type to not settle down." Resting her head against the back of the chair, she let a soft breeze cool her off as she closed her eyes.

"What color underwear are you wearing tomorrow?"

Luckily she hadn't been drinking just then. "Excuse me?"

"I know Nana. She's gonna want proof we're for real."

Yeah probably. She tried to rub the tension from her forehead. "I don't know, Troy."

He laughed. *Laughed.* "Oh yes you do, Cam. You probably pick your clothes out a week in advance. I'll bet you even know..."

Darn him. He did know her. "Blue, okay? They're blue."

"Do you still sleep in boxers and a white tee?"

She looked down at herself and pursed her lips.

"I'll take your silence as a yes. We grew up together. I know more than you think." He paused, waiting for her to say something. When she didn't—or rather, couldn't—he said, "I sleep in the nude, by the way."

As if he was in front of her, she slapped a hand over her eyes. He must have heard because he laughed again. She cleared her throat, hating how he was the only person who could ever get past her defenses. "Anything else, Troy?"

"Yeah, move in with me." Air wheezed from her lungs. "Until you get a place. You won't have to stay in the nut house." Pause. "I have a guest room. I'll wear pajamas. Promise."

Her grip tightened around the phone. No one had ever been that considerate. At least, not in recent memory. Then again, Troy had always been a nice guy. A flirt, naughty as hell, and with an uber dark past he hid from the world. But nice.

"Just think about it," he said quietly. Too quietly. "Oh, and Cam?"

"Yeah."

"You looked really nice today."

She expected "see you tomorrow", not that. Troy had never told her she looked nice. No one had ever told her she looked nice. She had her mouth open to say an awkward "thank you" when she realized why he must have uttered the compliment.

Heather told Troy the things Maxwell said when they broke up.

Troy wasn't being nice. He pitied her.

There was nothing more embarrassing or pathetic than

knowing Troy had this information. This was why he agreed to this fiasco. He felt sorry for her.

She pulled the phone away from her ear and disconnected. Before she could hold back, hot tears fell down her cheeks. Pressing her hands to her chest, she rocked, trying to sob quietly enough so no one could hear.

Something else she used to do often as a kid. Back then she'd sob into her pillow.

One day back home and she was already crying. This was going to be the week from hell.

Troy watched Camryn out of the corner of his eye as she drove them over to her parents' house. She had insisted on picking him up for dinner. He had a feeling it was to escape the house. A full Covic family could be...overwhelming. If she gripped the wheel any harder it was going to pop off.

"You're quiet," he said, just to get some conversation going.

"I don't have anything to say."

He'd bet there was enough going on in her head. "Why did you hang up on me last night?"

"I thought we were done."

"You don't say good-bye when you're finished with a conversation? Most people do." She stared straight ahead. "It was just a compliment, Cam."

"Well, you don't have to give me compliments."

Now he wanted to. "Boyfriends say nice things to their girlfriends."

"You're not my boyfriend."

She needed a team of massage therapists and a stiff drink. "I thought we were supposed to break up *after* the wedding."

She glanced over at him with a look of pure Pittsburg steel.

"Look, Cam, I'm nervous as hell too."

Her shoulders tensed as she pulled into her parents' drive and cut the engine. She stared at the house like it was going to eat her. "Last chance, Troy. You might need to be committed after this."

He needed to be committed now. But after learning what that ex of hers did, he was going to make this fake relationship work for the next week even if he had to literally propose to her. "You look nice."

She did too. She had her hair back in a ponytail, rare for her, 'cause it showed off her cute face. A knee-length white sundress hugged her waist and hips.

"Stop it, Troy."

He got out after her. Lord, the woman could not handle a compliment. "I mean it, Cam. I don't say things I don't mean."

She stopped at the front door and turned. He couldn't see her eyes behind her sunglasses. "Did you mean it before or after Heather told you the things Maxwell said?"

He stopped. Grabbed her arm. "Camryn..."

"Enough," she ground out. "Let's go."

And she opened the damn door to hell before he could even rebut. He sucked in a breath and stepped inside too. The entire clan was there, including her two aunts and uncles. It smelled like Nana's *sarma* recipe was cooking, stinking up the house with cabbage and minced meat. He hoped they'd made something else too, 'cause his stomach couldn't handle that now. Camryn stopped just inside the doorway to close the door behind him.

Mom rushed over and patted his cheek. "Oh, Troy. You made it." Her apron showed she was probably making cucumber soup in addition to sarma. Disgusting. Cucumbers belonged in salad. Give him another twenty years and he'd still hate Serbian food.

Mom looked around him. "Camryn, where's your

boyfriend?"

Now or never. "That would be me," he said, loud enough for the living room to hear so he wouldn't have to repeat it. If the statement bore repeating, he may bust out into hysterics.

The Covic house had never been that quiet. He was sure of it. Damn. If this was all it took to shut them up he should've done it sooner.

Her mother looked from Camryn to Troy to Camryn again. "No really. Where is he?"

He plastered the stupidest grin on his face he could muster without making his teeth hurt. He wanted to run home like the scared kid he used to be. He kissed Mom's cheek and took Camryn's hand, only to find it shaking, so he kissed her hand too.

Her mom backed away from them as if they were plagued by leprosy. Any second now she'd whip out the Clorox and make the sign of the cross.

Troy led Camryn by the hand deeper into the living room and found an empty chair. After sitting, he pulled her into his lap. The fact she let him said wonders about her anxiety level.

He looked around the room. Yep, everyone still staring— check. "Come on, guys. It's not *that* shocking." It totally was. If he were one of them and someone had told him they were a couple, he'd react the same way. He looked up at Cam's profile. She was intently staring at Heather to save her. Who'd save him? "I told you we should have said something sooner."

Her eyes darted to him. "Yes, perhaps we should have."

"Cam here wanted to wait until things were more serious before announcing it to the world."

Yjaka Mitch laughed. All eyes shifted to him. Then he laughed again, his round belly jiggling worse than the Easter Jell-O mold. By the time he was done, Troy was tempted to find a respirator.

Nervous laughter followed from the rest, like a hazardous

contagion. Camryn's shoulders sank. Troy brought his hand up to rest on her back.

"You had us going there for a minute," Kuma Viola said. "How'd you get Camryn there to do that? Too funny. I thought she was born without a funny bone. When do we eat?"

Tetaka Myrtle belched, then hiccupped, patting her chest as if that's ever helped her digestion in the last thirty years.

Nana came into the room from the kitchen, leaning more heavily on her cane than when he last saw her. "Dinner in ten minutes." Her gaze focused on Troy and Camryn when no one stampeded to the dining room. "Camryn, get off that boy's lap before you break him."

Obediently, she stood, but he pulled her back down.

Mom glared at Heather and Justin. "You said to act normal. You said to be open-minded. Is this funny to you?" Mom obviously didn't think it was a joke. "You knew about this, you two?"

Justin put up his hands in surrender. The lucky guy still had a chance to escape the family. He wasn't married in yet. "I found out yesterday. Don't blame me."

Dad stared at Troy and Cam, shaking his head in disappointment. It's not like they robbed a damn bank. "This *is* just a joke, right? The real boyfriend's coming later?" He looked too hopeful for Troy to break his bubble.

Fisher stood slowly and handed Emily off to his wife, Anna. Troy was expecting any variety of responses, but anger wasn't one of them. Fisher's hands fisted and flexed.

Troy'd had enough. It was time to get past shock and on to the interrogation or they'd be going in circles until their flight tomorrow. Standing abruptly, he caught Cam by the waist before she could fall, bent her over, and smacked his mouth right over hers. Her eyes flew wide, panicked. It was, unceremoniously, the least romantic thing he'd ever done. It was no way to properly kiss a woman, even if it was Camryn. He had warned her yesterday, after all. At least now they got the first awkward kiss out of the way.

And awkward it was.

"Oh, God. My eyes are burning," Justin declared. Jerk.

Troy tilted Cam back upright, held her arm to be sure she wouldn't pass out in shock, then sat back down with a plop. Camryn remained standing, eyes focused on the Orthodox crucifix on the wall above the fireplace.

Even Jesus was crying.

Nana sat down in her recliner, assessing the situation. "Why did Troy just kiss Camryn? He can't be that hard up."

Troy's jaw dropped as he looked at Camryn, who had finally snapped out of her haze. She looked at Nana and swallowed. To any lame person, she looked just like she always did, poised and calm. But her fingernails were digging into her palm.

Troy spoke when no one else did, ready to defend. "That was not a nice thing to say, Nana." It was downright cruel, actually. He loved Nana, all of them, but her tongue could be sharper than a sword.

Yjaka Harold piped in before Nana could retort. "It would appear that Troy is Camryn's boyfriend." He scratched his head, his thinning black comb-over not moving an inch.

Nana's gaze sharpened as she looked between the two of them. "My hearing must be going."

"No, Nana," Heather said. "It's true. I think they make a lovely couple. It's about time."

Everyone looked at Heather as if she'd just done the Electric Slide butt-naked. Including Justin, who tried to cover up his shock with a nod. Hell, even Troy couldn't mask his doubt.

Fisher stormed out the front door.

Nana laughed. Laughed some more. "Heather, what in Sam's Hell are you going on about? Your eyes must be going, you twit. I mean, look at her." She pointed to Camryn, and the room commenced in unison to stare at Camryn. "My granddaughter is...pretty, but she's not in *his* league."

Troy sucked in a breath. Through the years, he'd grown used to the family teasing him about his good looks. Teasing Heather about hers. Teasing each other for one thing or another. Yjaka Harold's comb-over. Tetaka Myrtle's constant indigestion. Kuma Viola's purple lipstick. Fisher's dimple. Mom's overuse of salt. Dad's bald head. And Camryn...for, well, everything.

He never noticed until now just how hurtful their words could be. Camryn was the smart, logical one. More of a mother to them in a sense. He never thought to wonder if all this bothered her, because nothing seemed to bother her. Camryn protected those she loved, but who protected her?

As he looked at her now, spine straight and chin up, it would appear the same old, same old. Except the corners of her glazed eyes were down, and her eyebrows were ever so slightly drawn together. Her jaw ticked as she swallowed.

They were ramming home everything her ex said.

From his position in the chair, he took her hand and squeezed. She didn't respond, and her hand was cold, probably having lost circulation twenty minutes ago. Had any of them bothered to tell her all her redeeming qualities? "She is pretty, Nana. And too good for me."

If there was any truth to the lie they were telling, it was that.

Her gaze dropped to the floor as she removed her hand from his. After clearing her throat she said, "Give me a minute to wash up for dinner, and then I'll help you set everything out."

Calm as ever, she walked to the staircase across the room, proceeded up the stairs, and only after he heard a door close did the chatter start. Troy rose and glanced out the window to see Fisher pacing in the front yard. His gaze dropped to

Heather, who was chewing on her lip.

Troy shook his head and addressed the room. "Camryn and I are together now. It's not a joke, or up for discussion."

Before they could piss him off anymore, make him say something he'd regret, he walked out the front door to face Fisher. Trying for the nonchalance he didn't feel, Troy sat on the top step of the porch and waited Fisher out.

Fisher whirled on him in seconds, his dark brown eyes narrowed to slits.

Before his friend could throw a punch, Troy raised his hands. "No black eyes for the wedding, man."

Fisher's wide jaw slackened as he stood erect. He ran a hand over his short, wavy brown hair. "How could you not tell me, Troy? How?" He paced to the curb and back again. "Camryn? Really?"

There was no logical or safe way to respond, so Troy wove his fingers together and looked down.

"Did you run out of women in Milwaukee? You had to fuck with her now?"

Troy ground his teeth. "You were given a very big surprise today, so I'm going to let that go. But even I have a limit, Fisher."

"She's not just some girl. Not a toy. Dating isn't a game to her."

"I know that!" he roared, standing. He dropped his hands on his hips and focused on a planter with begonias to avoid saying anything more.

"How..." Fisher blew out a breath, crossed his arms. "How long has this been going on?"

Troy pulled the information Cam gave him from memory. "Since last January. I was in Chicago and stopped by to say hello. Things...evolved."

"Evolved," Fisher dully repeated. "Evolved."

Troy ran a hand down his face. "I'm sorry I didn't tell you sooner." Not that he could have, seeing as he just found out himself yesterday.

"This is not okay." When Troy started to argue, Fisher raised his hand. "This is *not* okay with me."

"I'm good enough to be your best friend, but I'm not good enough for her. Is that it, Fisher? She deserves better than a construction worker with a drunk convict father."

Fisher closed his eyes and dropped his head. Troy thought he'd deny it, but he didn't, proving the real truth. He wasn't good enough. He'd never be good enough. He wasn't really family, not by blood. They'd always side with her. They would when the wedding was over. He'd be alone.

"This is Camryn for God's sake," Fisher said. "She doesn't get attached easily. When you leave her, and you will, it will kill her."

He couldn't tell Fisher the truth, including how Camryn was going to end their fake relationship, not Troy. Fisher had been his best friend nearly his entire life, as much a brother as blood would have tied them. He didn't know anything about what was really going on, so his words cut so much deeper than anything his drunk of a father ever said.

"Give me some credit, Fisher. Cam's different. This is different." It was all he could say.

Fisher shook his head and stared at him. "So help me God, you better think very hard about what you're doing. And while you do, keep clear of me for a while."

Troy watched him walk around the side of the house and out of view.

Then he breathed.

Forks scraped against plates. Lips sipped against cups. The chewing was so loud it was giving Camryn a headache. She almost preferred the interrogation to the silence.

Yjaka Mitch shoved a bite of sarma into his mouth and spoke around his food. "So, are you two sleeping together?"

And she was wrong. Silence was better. Much, much better.

"Of course they are," her mother said. "Right?"

"A gentleman never tells," Troy said.

"Ha," Kuma Viola said. "You're no gentleman, Troy Lansky."

Camryn set her fork down very carefully, even though she hadn't eaten a thing. "Some things are private. Even in this family."

Kuma Viola shrugged and looked down at her plate. "Bet Cam recites sales figures during sex."

Yjaka Harold coughed. "Good one."

Nana had yet to eat a bite. "I, for one, am not convinced they are dating."

Great. What now? Their sex positions?

Nana's eyes narrowed, and it took all Camryn's skill not to run from the room. "Does she snore, Troy?"

The humor in Troy's eyes didn't quash her nerves. He had a fifty-fifty chance of getting the answer right.

"No."

"See, I told you it's a lie," Nana said, throwing her hand in the air for dramatic flair. "She snores louder than a rhino in heat."

Heather placed her hand on Nana's arm. "I don't want to know how you know what a rhino in heat sounds like. And I hate to tell you this, but it's you who snores. I shared a room with Cam for sixteen years. She doesn't snore."

The cabbage rolls stood up from the baking pan and started dancing a waltz on the dining room table. Camryn watched them twirl around the butter dish until Nana opened her mouth again.

"What color underwear is she wearing today, Troy?"

The sarma flopped back down.

Yjaka Mitch laughed. "She wears white cotton panties. She's too conservative to buy the sexy kind. Am I right, Cam?"

He looked at her as if she'd actually respond to this question.

"If you must know, they're blue." Troy looked at her, full wattage smile in place as if to say, *See, told you they'd ask.*

"Prove it," Nana challenged.

The table looked at Camryn. "I am not showing you my underwear."

"Aw, c'mon, honey," Troy drawled.

She was very tempted to stick a fork in the center of his forehead. "No."

Fisher dropped his utensils onto his plate. The clanking sound lasted longer than his silence. "Can we stop talking about this?" he yelled, more an order than a question.

"My panties have *Beauty and the Beast* on them," Emily said, all innocence.

Anna stood. "Cam, could you help me in the kitchen for a minute?"

Anna had just become her favorite person on the planet. Camryn was going to dedicate a shrine to her on the front lawn. "Of course." She rose and followed her sister-in-law out of the room.

While Anna stood over the cake, cutting it into small slices, she shook her head. "I've been quiet about this until now, but I have to ask. Are you sure you know what you're doing?"

Cam passed her the plates so she could dish out the cake. "I thought so. I'm not so sure now."

Anna smiled and looked at her, her expression one of understanding. "They are a crazy bunch, but they'll come around." She walked over to her side of the counter to wrap an arm around Camryn's shoulders. "You know what will shut them up faster?"

Before Camryn could dare to ask, Anna fluffed the hem of Camryn's dress, peered underneath, and dropped it back down in less time than it took Camryn to blink.

"Dear God, they are blue."

Camryn sighed. "I can't believe you just did that. You've been in this family too long. They've corrupted you."

"Relax," she said, handing her two plates of cake. "I'm doing this for you."

"Is nothing sacred in this family?" she muttered, not expecting a response.

Anna picked up two plates. "Are you kidding? When I got pregnant with Emily, I prayed every day and night that I wouldn't go into labor with the family around. And what happened? Labor during Sunday dinner. Do you know how horrifying it was giving birth with ten people in the room?" Anna smiled despite the memory. "But when she was born, it was worth it, Cam. Troy doesn't have anyone. Can you imagine that? As mean and crazy as your family can be sometimes, I'd take that over no one."

Leave it to Anna to be the voice of reason. To put her in place. "You're right. You're totally right. Thank you."

Anna's smile never faltered. "Let them get used to the idea. This too shall pass."

They walked back into the crowded dining room to hand out dessert. Once everyone had a mouthful, Anna said, "For the record, her panties *are* blue. I checked."

On the drive home, Troy pulled out his cell and smiled at the incoming text.

"What are you smiling about? That was a disaster."

Aside from Fisher getting pissed off, Nana insulting Cam to the point where he was pretty sure she cried upstairs, and Troy possibly losing his best friend for life, he'd say it was a complete success. "It wasn't that bad. They believed us."

"Only after Anna forced me to flash her in the kitchen."

He would've loved to see the look on her face for that. "Heather just texted me. She put your suitcase in the trunk so you can stay in my guest room."

She said nothing.

Troy started playing with his ringtones. Grinning, he played the demo for "I Will Survive". "What do you think of your new ringtone?" She didn't respond. "No? Okay, how about this?" "Crazy" by Patsy Cline chimed through the car.

"I don't need my own ringtone. And you're not funny."

"I'm a little funny." He cued "My Life" by Billy Joel.

"What was my ringtone before?" she asked.

He fished through his downloads and played the "Imperial March" instrumental from *Star Wars*, the music used whenever Darth Vader entered a scene.

"Very funny."

"Told you I was," he said. At least she was smiling now. He found "When I See You Smile" by Bad English, and hit "Save."

She pulled into his driveway and looked at him out of the corner of her eye. "Are you sure it's okay I stay here? I could scar your reputation."

She was trying to be funny, but he wasn't buying it. "Your family was wrong, Cam. What Nana said back there, it was mean and completely not true."

Her gaze returned to the windshield. Her index finger drummed the steering wheel. "Fisher was pretty upset."

Yeah, and he didn't want to think about it. He exited the car, took her suitcase from the trunk, and unlocked the front door for them. "Go get your pajamas on. We're drinking beer and watching *Night of the Living Dead."*

She was going to laugh if it was the last thing he did tonight. The second time he'd been placed in foster care with the Covics, Camryn and himself, along with Fisher and Heather, had snuck downstairs to watch the movie on television. Heather had run upstairs crying and Fisher had fallen asleep. He and Cam had spent the whole movie laughing at the absurdity.

She smiled and took the suitcase from him. "Make mine wine instead of beer, and you're on."

Camryn stepped into her pajama boxers and stared at the sleeper sofa, then at the pool table. Who had a pool table in their guest room? No way was the bed going to pull out with the table that close.

"Um, Troy?"

She heard his feet pad down the hallway. "I'm coming to get you, Barbara," he said in a gloomy drone, mimicking the line from their movie.

She almost smiled.

Troy leaned against the doorway and crossed his arms over his bare chest. Bare chest. Muscled biceps. Six pack abs. Or maybe twelve pack. All the moisture left her mouth. Her gaze darted down to his pajama bottoms and stopped.

He followed her gaze down. "What?"

"You're wearing SpongeBob SquarePants pajamas."

"Yeah. And?"

"Do you have on Batman underwear too?" God. Even he could make SpongeBob sexy.

He grinned, causing her face heat. "Nope. Plain tighty whities. Wanna see?"

Her skin was going to burn off her face. "No." Yes.

"What's wrong with SpongeBob?"

She stared him down. "Aside from the fact you're thirty years old, you mean?"

His eyebrows lifted. "I knew I should've worn the Scooby Doo ones. These don't turn you on, do they?"

She sighed. He laughed. He had a great laugh. An uninhibited sound meant to dissuade unease and born to light every nerve in her body.

"Where's your shirt?" she asked, irritated that he could get to her just by doing nothing. He did nothing better than anyone she knew. He shrugged. "You promised me pajamas. That includes a shirt." *Please, for the love of all humanity, put on a shirt!*

He nodded. "So I did." He left the room and came back seconds later wearing a Kermit the Frog tee. "Better?"

Dear God, she was going to be sharing a house with a man who just stepped off a preschool choo-choo train. "Do you own anything without a cartoon character on it?"

"Technically, Kermit's a Muppet."

"Never mind, Troy."

He took a step closer. "Why does it bother you?"

"You're an adult."

He shrugged again. "One should embrace their inner child."

"Or the outer child in your case."

He stared at her a moment, letting a slow, easy grin form. Curse him. "Even you were a child once, Cam. Don't you ever wake up early on a Saturday morning, just for the hell of it, and eat a bowl of cereal while watching cartoons?"

He was hopeless. "No."

"What a shame." He was watching her again, like he wanted to laugh at her. Or start a pillow fight. "Emily bought me these. Every Christmas Anna takes her shopping for my gift. I wear them because they remind me of her."

"Oh." Oh. Now that was really sweet actually.

She tore her gaze away and glanced around the room to avoid looking at him anymore. The vision of him without a shirt would be permanently etched in her brain forever, combined with the sweet sentiment of him wearing something his goddaughter bought him. What right did he have to flaunt his sexiness anyway? It was even more charming he cared that much for Emily.

And what did she call him in here for?

Bed. Right. "I can't pull out the sleeper sofa with the pool table so close."

He came up behind her, pressing his chest against her back. Something strange happened to her insides at his touch. She froze. Pinched her eyes closed. He had her boxed in now. He smelled so good, like the outdoors in early summer. And soap. His breath fanned the back of her neck. Mentally, she told herself to close her mouth. Physically, she couldn't even swallow. Leaning forward, he slid his hand over her belly and pulled the handle on the sleeper in front of them. His arm brushed hers as it hung limp at her side. He had such dark, tanned skin compared to hers.

The springs creaked as he pulled. Half the bed emerged. She looked over her shoulder, realizing the bed *would* clear the pool table. Barely.

"Oh. I guess it does fit. Never mind," she said, feeling like an idiot. And flustered. Troy could always get under her skin so easily. "I got it."

He didn't move, still determined to help. The heat from his body had her temp mounting. They both reached for the bar to extend the bed, and while ensued in a battle of who could pull the bed out first, they flew backward. She landed on top of him on the pool table.

She paused, hands sprawled out. "This is awkward," she muttered.

"I don't know," he argued. His voice sounded strange. Deeper. "I've never had sex on this table. Might be fun."

She uttered a sound of distress and scrambled off of him, landing on the sleeper. "Would you be serious, Troy?"

She kinda wished he was.

"We *are* supposed to be dating," he answered, as if not disconcerted in the least.

"Not without witnesses." She pushed her hair away from her face.

His laughter filled the room for several seconds as he sat upright and hopped off the table. "Can I help you with anything else, Cam? Finding the shower? Using a blanket?"

Exhaling, her eyes narrowed. Infuriating man! "Does the neon Miller Lite beer sign turn off? It's a bit bright for a nightlight."

He pulled a string hanging under the sign on the wall, sending the room into near darkness. "Better?"

"Yes. Thank you." *Now get out before a fantasy pops in my head. Again.*

Troy stared at the pool table as if thinking the same thing she was. He blinked and looked back at her. "Why don't you take my room? I'll sleep in here."

"No, no. I'm fine." Sort of.

"You sure? I have Transformer sheets."

Swallowing, she looked him in the eye, wanting to know what he was really thinking. "Why are you doing this?"

A look of irritation crossed his face. "Doing what?"

Being nice. Making me want to know what's under the boy-child clothes.

She crossed her arms to block out the chill. "Agreeing to date me."

He stared at the pool table again. "I don't know, but I said I would." He looked back at her, his gaze roaming her face and

53

dropping to her mouth where it hovered for several seconds. "I'd do just about anything for you. You know that. And you know why."

Her mouth popped open. No, she didn't know.

He looked away and rubbed the back of his neck. "'Night, Cam."

"Troy." She struggled to stand. "Thank you."

He turned from the doorway. "No need to thank me."

Chapter Four

*Life Lessons According to Camryn:
Running late counts as exercise.*

The rush through General Mitchell Airport was something right out of the *Home Alone* manual. Yjaka Harold insisted on holding the tickets, Nana bitched about having to use a wheelchair, Kuma Viola was applying lipstick while attempting to go through security, and Emily made a guard spit his coffee out when she said he had a big stick.

The Covics never went anywhere without leaving a lasting impression.

Troy closed his eyes and lay his head back just as the fasten seatbelt light chimed off. Thirty thousand feet in an enclosed plane for three hours with the family. Good times. He grabbed a magazine and flipped through it.

Fisher walked past them to take Emily to the bathroom. He nodded at Camryn, avoided looking at Troy, and moved on.

"I don't understand why he's so mad," Cam said.

"You and I both know Fisher's temper."

"But why be mad at you? He should be angry with me. I'm his sister."

"He thinks I'm going to hurt you. My dating history doesn't bode well for changing his mind."

Deep down, Troy figured he and Cam were crossing a proverbial line in Fisher's opinion. A line they shouldn't cross and had. Or he thought they had. He wanted so badly to tell his best friend this was a lie. Knowing that would make Fisher feel better. But part of him liked this lie too. The part of him that still needed to prove he was worthy of something.

"Fisher must know that I'd be more likely to hurt you. I mean, I'm the reserved one here. I'd never let a man hurt me."

She had let a man hurt her. She may not realize it, nor acknowledge it, but this Maxwell jerk *had* hurt her. And Troy wasn't just any man. If this went wrong, everything would change, and he'd be the one left out in the cold.

He set his magazine down and looked at her. "You have feelings, Cam. I don't know why you find it necessary to hide them." She turned her head to stare out the window. "Go ahead, turn away. But I know you better than that. For the record, I'd never hurt you. Even if this were real."

She looked back at him, worry lines wrinkling her forehead. After assessing him, she shook her head. "This is pointless. No one's going to get hurt, because this *isn't* real. Fisher will get over it."

For once, she was more optimistic than he. "In a very dark way, this whole thing is funny. Fisher and I made a promise long ago to never fight over a woman."

One corner of her mouth quirked as her brows rose. "Not quite what you two had in mind."

Understatement.

Emily climbed over him to get to Camryn. Troy was the fun uncle, Heather the aunt who spoiled, but Cam was the little girl's favorite. Probably because she talked to her like an adult.

"You're wearing paint, Auntie Cam."

"Makeup. I usually wear makeup."

Emily gave Cam a calculated look while Troy smiled.

"Not this much makeup. Is it because the Hortons are better than us?"

The Hortons being Justin's family, Troy waited to see how Cam responded.

"They're not better than us, honey. Just different. So we have to be on our best behavior."

Emily leaned against her chest and sighed. "I know. Daddy told me already."

Troy wondered if Fisher had told the rest of the family to be on their best behavior.

"What's Colorado like?" Emily asked.

"Well, it was the thirty-eighth colony added to the States, the state bird is the lark, and the tree is the blue spruce."

Troy laughed. "She didn't ask for a history lesson."

Both Emily and Cam frowned at him, so he shut up.

Emily turned to face Cam. "Daddy said there's mountains."

"The Rocky Mountains. The city we're going to, Boulder, is just east of the mountains. You'll be able to see them. You should ask Uncle Justin about Colorado. He's from there."

Without further delay, Emily hopped down and walked to the back of the plane by Heather and Justin. Troy glanced around. Most of the family was seated in the back. They could talk without being overheard.

"So, tell me about this Max guy."

"Maxwell. He hates being called Max. What do you want to know?"

A lot of things he couldn't ask. "What did he get you for your birthday last month? You didn't come home. It must've been good."

Her glance darted to the window again. "We went out to dinner the next day."

"The next day?"

She turned her head back, but wouldn't look him in the eye. "We were in the middle of a big campaign. We worked late that night, so we went out to dinner the next day."

Code: he forgot. "Did you love him?"

She sighed. "I guess. Doesn't matter now, does it?"

"Love always matters," he said. And Cam deserved someone who didn't forget her birthday. Deserved more than the card he sent her, even if it did sing.

"What about you? What was your last girlfriend like?"

"Felicia. She was a closet opera fan. Never would've worked out."

Cam smiled, and his stomach did some kind of tilt he blamed on turbulence. "Uh huh. And what was the problem with the one before her?"

He'd only dated Felicia for a couple weeks. Same with the one before her, and the one before that. They all had something wrong with them. Or maybe it was him. Either way, they weren't important enough to discuss. "What did you love about Maxwell?"

Her smile fell, and he regretted asking. "We both loved our work." She shrugged. "He was stable. Reliable."

She sounded like she was car shopping, but he knew better than to say so. "Well, at least I'll show you some fun before you dump me for another boring guy." Those huge hazel eyes narrowed, so he grinned. "Even a fake boyfriend can be fun."

Emily barreled over his lap again and onto Cam's. "Uncle Justin says you're the smarty pants. I'm supposed to get a tutu from you."

Troy laughed until his side hurt and half the plane was staring at him. "I think you mean *tutorial*. And Auntie Camryn is the right person for that."

"Justin Horton, you didn't tell us you lived in a hotel!" Nana exclaimed.

Camryn rolled her eyes. Only Nana could make that sound like an insult. They exited the car the Hortons sent for them.

Scratch that, the *limo* they sent.

Justin rubbed the back of his neck and turned six shades of red. "Um, well...it's not *that* big."

It *was* that big. Camryn looked at the sprawling gray brick fortress in front of them. It took five minutes to get from the road to the front door, and past a ten-foot wrought iron security fence. Easily three floors high, the house had to be ten thousand square feet. The garage was bigger than her parents' house. The yard could've held a wedding three times the size of Justin and Heather's. And the Kentucky Derby. Around the side, she could just make out the edge of an in-ground pool.

Now she knew why Heather was so nervous.

A woman exited the front door and walked right to Justin. "It's so good to have you home!" she said. Justin looked just like her, with light brown hair and a thin, angular face. She wore a mint green suit that cost more than a month of Camryn's salary. "Oh, Heather. So good to see you again."

Heather introduced the rest of the family, who blessedly said nothing. Camryn hoped their shock lasted the whole week.

Bernice Horton squatted in front of her niece. "You must be Emily. I had the staff buy you a bunch of movies for while you're here, in case it rains."

Emily smiled. "With cockporn? Auntie Cam makes the best cockporn!"

Anna picked up Emily and set her on her hip as she giggled nervously. "She means popcorn. Popcorn. Camryn makes her popcorn, and...um."

The horrified look left Bernice's face as she patted her chest. "Of course. With popcorn, dear." She turned to Justin. "Your dad is in the study. Why don't you drag him out and give the family a tour of the house?"

A couple of staff came out to collect their luggage as the family walked inside.

Camryn and Troy stayed back, letting the others go ahead

first. Troy leaned over to whisper in her ear, "At least I'm sharing a room with the woman who makes the best cockporn. Honestly, the things you don't tell me."

She tried not to smile. "Shut up, Troy."

Justin's father seemed as nice as his mother. Once he saw them come inside, he rose from a desk and shook everyone's hand. As tall, if not taller than Justin, he had a wiry frame and a pear-shaped face hidden behind large black frames.

The house was amazing. Mahogany floors, ten-foot windows, open architecture. Complete with a library and media room, which Emily drooled over, it was something out of a Hollywood set. The entire east side had a beautiful view of the Flatirons and foothills at the base of the mountains. The north side had an in-ground Olympic-sized pool with a colorful perennial garden to accent.

The house had six bedrooms. Yjaka Harold, Kuma Viola, Uncle Mitch and Tetaka Myrtle were sharing a room on the second floor. Mom, Dad and Nana were across the hall. Fisher, Anna and Emily were on the third floor, along with Justin and Heather, and Troy and herself. Each bedroom had its own bath.

Left to their own devices until lunch, they opted to unpack and settle in. Troy flopped on the king-sized bed in their room. "I thought the family was very well behaved."

"Yes, aside from Nana complaining about getting lost."

The room was nicer than some of the four-star hotels she'd stayed in. The wallpaper was light blue with darker navy stripes. A border print of bluebells matched the bedspread covering the four-poster bed Troy lay on. On the same wall as the bathroom, a bureau held a forty-inch flat screen and DVD player. A set of glass French doors led to a balcony over-looking the mountain view.

She opened the closet to hang her clothes before they wrinkled. "I would kill for this closet at home."

"A woman and her wardrobe. No closet is big enough."

"My apartment is the size of this closet." She turned and stared at him, a thought looming. "We're going to have to share the bed."

Troy looked around the room. "The bed is big enough. No big deal. I hear you don't snore, so we should be fine." His smile was at full amp.

There may be a certain comfort level with Troy, but she thought she drew the line at sharing a bed, king-sized or not. Unless one of them took the floor, they were stuck. She couldn't ask him to do that, and she'd never walk upright if she slept on these hardwood floors. And what was with everyone's obsession on snoring?

"Relax, Cam. I won't touch you."

No doubt there. She couldn't handle him even if he did lose his mind and try. Last night at his house she'd nearly come undone at his touch. Troy didn't even mean anything by it. He was just trying to help pull out the bed. But it still had her skin heated.

She needed her mind off that. "What are you going to do while we have our final dress fitting this afternoon?"

"I plan on beating the crap out of Justin and Fisher at Grand Theft Auto. Should be fun in that media room."

Video games. Men.

He got up and walked to the French doors. "They're setting up lunch outside. Ready to head down?"

"Aren't you going to hang up your clothes?"

One eyebrow popped up in confusion. "Why?"

She sighed. It was a darn good thing they weren't really a couple.

They made their way downstairs and out a set of patio doors to where they thought the family was sitting, only to find themselves the length of the house away. "Wow, this house *is* big," she said.

She started to walk toward the tables when Troy grabbed her arm. She looked at him, confused. His blond hair was several shades lighter in the hot, dry sun, his brown eyes showing little golden flecks she never noticed before. She watched as his Adam's apple bobbed.

"What's wrong?" she asked, worried the heat or altitude was getting to him. When they first exited the car she noticed how much thinner the air was. Perhaps he hadn't adjusted yet.

"I have an idea, and you won't like it."

"Then my answer is no."

"You haven't heard the idea yet."

"I don't need to. If you think it's a bad idea..."

"I didn't say it was a bad idea. I said you wouldn't like it."

She crossed her arms. "Same difference."

He looked unamused. "Everyone is sitting across the yard over there. We can see them, which means they can see us. We need a public display."

She didn't like the sound of that. But before she could process fully, he slid an arm around her waist and drew her to him. Hard chest. Wall of hard chest. Now there was no air.

"Act like we've done this before," he whispered.

"Done what?"

"Kiss, Cam. Act like you've kissed me before."

"How am I supposed to do...?"

The words died in her throat as his mouth closed over hers. At first she froze, disoriented, but then their noses brushed, he tilted his head, and her eyes drifted shut. She grabbed his arms for balance. Muscled, firm arms that tensed beneath her fingers. She remembered the look of them from last night, but they felt so much better.

Troy had mad, mad skills. She knew he would. God in Heaven, did he ever. Camryn didn't think *she* had the ability to respond this strongly, though. A sharp, satisfying tremor rocked her center. His lips parted and he slid his tongue against hers. Once. Twice. As the kiss deepened, his hands came up to cup her cheeks and she leaned into him. She lost feeling from the neck down.

Troy. Troy Lansky was kissing her. With witnesses. Because he was pretending to be her...

He broke away, hands still cupping her cheeks, and stared down at her. "What in the hell was that?" he whispered, his voice harsh.

She thought it was a kiss. A darn good one. She may not have his experience, or his expertise, but she wasn't so daft she didn't know when she was just kissed. Properly.

His jaw ground as his mouth firmed into a thin line. He dropped his hands and stepped back. She'd never been a believer in spontaneous combustion, but by God she'd implode right now from embarrassment if he made fun of her. She wasn't beautiful like his other women. In fact, she was the South Pole of sexy. Her heart lurched, threatened to stop beating.

"You are *not* a fish," he ground out.

Maxwell's ultimate insult from Troy's lips sobered her. Except, did he say...?

Turning, he went to walk away, then must have remembered they came out together, because he came back, grabbed her hand and pulled her toward the awaiting tables.

"That looked like some kiss between you and Troy," Heather said, stepping out of her shorts and placing them on the bench in the dressing room.

Camryn ignored the statement and carefully removed Heather's wedding dress from the hanger. She unzipped the back and squatted down so Heather could step into it.

"Aren't you going to say anything?" Heather asked.

"Yes, get the dress on before it wrinkles."

Sighing, she did as asked. Camryn helped slide the garment up until it was in place, then turned her sister toward the mirror so she could zip the back.

"I mean, it didn't look like you two were pretending back there."

It didn't feel like it either, but Camryn lived in reality. "Of course it was pretending. We knew all of you were watching. It was nothing."

Nothing but a darn hot kiss that still had her shaking. Troy and his ideas could take a running leap off a very steep...

"C'mon. It was good though, right?"

"You're zipped. Turn around. Let's see."

Heather turned to the mirror and made a squeak, which Camryn knew in regards to her sister always preceded tears. "Oh, it looks great. Don't you think?"

Heather could wear a dust rag and look great, but she was right. She was going to be a lovely bride. The strapless off-white dress hugged her chest and waist before skimming to the floor in an elegant, sleek style. Woven into the satin of the train were tiny lavender pearls that matched the color of the bridesmaids' dresses.

"It's beautiful. So are you." Heather started to gush, so Cam quickly pulled a tissue from her purse. "Don't leak on the dress."

Emily stuck her head under the changing room door and assessed the situation. "Why are you crying, Auntie Heather? It's not as pretty as my dress, but it's not that ugly."

Camryn scooped her up and opened the door. "They're happy tears, honey."

"If she's happy, why is she crying?"

"I don't know. If you figure it out, let me know, okay?"

They stepped out and Mom started crying, which started a

chain reaction to Justin's mother, Bernice, and right on to Anna until stopping at Nana, who grinned through dry eyes.

"Are they happy crying too?" Emily whispered, as if scared out of her tiny skull by the female weeping display.

"Yes."

The store attendant held the train so Heather could step onto the block in front of a three-way mirror. "I think it fits okay. The length is fine. How does the waist feel?"

"Good," Heather said, pivoting to see every angle. "Cam and Anna, try yours on to make sure they're okay."

Camryn set Emily down and walked back to the dressing room. She handed Anna her dress and then stepped into her changing room. As far as bridesmaid dresses went, Heather had some taste. Lavender and strapless, the only pity was a thin white ribbon around the waist.

Camryn pulled the dress to her chest and reached behind her for the zipper. It wouldn't go up. Her stomach dropped. Twisting, she reached inside the seam and pulled the tag. Size twelve. Her size. Except it fit like a ten.

"How are they?" Heather asked from outside the rooms.

"I'm good," Anna said. Camryn heard Anna's door open and listened to them discuss the length. "It is a tad long, but with the heels I'll be fine."

Camryn put her hands on the wall and leaned into them, drawing in a deep breath. She'd obtained a fake boyfriend, was in the process of lying to her family about said fake boyfriend, and humiliating herself to boot, all to not ruin Heather's wedding, only to do so anyway by being too fat for her dress.

Opening her eyes, she turned the knob. "Mine doesn't fit. It's the right size, but it won't zip."

Silence. More silence.

Then a nuclear meltdown ensued. Mom pulled her to the mirror across the shop and onto the block. Heather started crying hysterically. Anna sat Emily in a chair and covered the little girl's ears. The wedding attendant pushed, pulled, and tugged until Camryn thought she'd drawn blood.

The zipper did not zip.

In the raging silence that followed, Nana sniffed. "No more goodies for you, missy. You starve until the wedding."

Camryn closed her eyes to the humiliation, pictured Nana as a leprechaun dancing a jig. It didn't help. Tears were clogging her throat too fast to shove them down.

Bernice knelt in front of her. "This dress is two inches too long. We can take some of the extra material and add it to the back by the zipper. You'll never be able to tell. These formal dresses run small. I should have warned you when we ordered them. This is my fault. I'm so sorry."

Camryn looked down at Justin's mother, lying through her teeth to make her feel better. It was working a little, though. The ache in her chest receded before a tear could fall.

"We can't get that done in five days," the attendant said. "That's too close to the wedding."

Bernice stood. "Then I'll do it. Camryn, go get changed. We'll take the dress home with us."

The room collectively looked at her as if senility was catching.

Bernice stared them down. "I know you all look at me as some kind of snob. The year Justin was born, my husband, Tim, made some good investments. Before then we lived paycheck to paycheck. The staff aren't permanent. We hired them to help get through the wedding. I made Justin's Halloween costumes until he was five, you know."

No one said a thing until Nana laughed. "Well, that's a relief. I hate rich people."

Heather wiped her eyes. "Can you really fix it?"

"Yes." She looked at Camryn. "Come on, I'll help you out of the dress."

Still shocked, Camryn let Bernice lead her back to the changing room and help her out of the dress. "Thank you. My family can be a little tactless sometimes, but they mean well. Don't hold it against Heather."

"Oh please. You haven't met my mother yet. Or my mother-in-law." She hung the dress while Camryn changed. "They're a little hard on you, your family."

"I'm the oldest. Goes with the territory, I guess."

Bernice nodded and smiled, reminding Camryn of Justin's smile. "I'm the oldest in my family. That man of yours likes you just the way you are, so don't you listen to them."

Camryn grabbed her purse, smile faltering. Most people didn't like her just as she was. Troy included.

Chapter Five

Life Lessons According to Camryn:
One must handle stress like a dog; if you can't eat it
or play with it, pee on it and walk away.

Troy stared at the golf ball on the green in front of him, then clear across the grounds to where it was supposed to land. No way was this going to end well. He'd never golfed a day in his life. Never wanted to. He aligned his club, reared back, and swung.

The ball bounced off a neighboring tree and straight at Justin's head. Justin ducked and looked at Troy as if they'd escaped a near-death experience.

Fisher shook his head. "Nice shot, man. At least you hit something. I can't find my ball."

Fisher was talking to him now. This was new.

Troy scratched his head. "Whose idea was it to go golfing anyway?" They were only on the fifth hole and collectively their score was higher than a basketball game.

Justin pointed an accusatory finger at his dad.

Tim shrugged. "You guys said sure when I asked."

Troy laughed. "I thought you meant golfing on the Wii. We're gonna kill someone out here."

Tim grinned and set a nine iron back in his bag. "Thank goodness. I hate golfing. Bernice bought these clubs for me thinking it would be good exercise. Want to have a beer in the clubhouse instead?"

They headed back to the clubhouse in silence. After ordering drinks at the bar and sitting at a table, they laughed, agreeing never to repeat the golfing experience.

"I still can't believe my son is getting married."

Fisher set down his beer. "I tried to warn him, sir."

Tim looked at Troy. "I guess you'll be next, then. You and Camryn seem like a nice couple."

Troy choked trying to swallow. Couple of what? After seeing Fisher's expression of confusion, Troy backpedaled. "One doesn't just propose to Camryn Covic. He must let her think it's her idea and give her the control."

A corner of Fisher's mouth lifted. It was a start. Problem averted.

Tim grinned and took a sip from his Scotch. "You know your woman well."

Camryn wasn't his woman, and he used to think he knew her well. Until that kiss today.

When Heather told him about what this Maxwell guy said to Camryn, his first instinct was anger. No matter how good a woman was or wasn't in bed, a gentleman never divulged the truth. After he got to thinking about it—and he'd tried really hard not to—he figured Camryn *was* wound too tight to ever let herself go and enjoy sex.

But after kissing her, he discovered Camryn had a whole other side to her. All cool and nice and controlled on the surface. Under that...

Well, she wasn't a damn fish, that's for sure.

He loved women. The way they smelled, laughed, felt. The way they looked first thing in the morning, the devious way they wrapped men around their finger. Women were the last great misunderstood mysteries to the world. Making love was one of life's true treasures. He'd been with a lot of women, and he wasn't ashamed of it.

None of them stopped his heart dead like Camryn had done

earlier. None of them had stunned him enough to render him speechless.

Hell, he'd be lying if he said he wasn't curious in exploring that more. This was Camryn, though. He wouldn't come out alive.

"Well," Tim said, "I'm just glad you all could come. Bernice has been so happy planning this wedding. She always wanted a daughter."

Justin drank from his bottle. "Thanks for the reminder, Dad."

Fisher lifted his drink. "Thank you for having us. This took a lot of...guts." Justin wanted to laugh, Troy could tell, but he somehow held back. "What do you guys say to horseback riding tomorrow? Jessie, my best friend growing up, has a farm at the edge of town. She's been on me to bring you by."

Fisher shrugged. "Sure. We can put the family in traction for the wedding."

Justin laughed. "I was thinking more along the lines of just us with the girls."

Troy tried to picture Camryn on a horse and couldn't. "FYI, Justin, we've never been this...rural."

"Oh relax," Fisher said. "It'll be fine. Emily wants a pony. She'd love riding."

Justin pulled out his cell. "Horseback riding it is," he said while texting. After a few moments, he got an incoming text. "Jessie says the day after tomorrow would be better. You guys will love her."

What Troy was going to love was the look on Cam's face when she found out he'd agreed to this. Moreover, watching her mount a horse. He shook his head and grinned. "Cam's gonna kill me."

Fisher eyed him speculatively. "Since when do you give a damn what a woman thinks? You can handle Cam."

Justin glared at Fisher. "Have you met your sister? Attila

the Hun is less intimidating."

Tim sat back as if enjoying the show. "This almost makes me miss being young."

"I haven't been on a horse since Girl Scouts," Camryn said and sat next to him on the bed, towel drying her hair from the family's after-dinner swim. "If I remember right, I couldn't walk for a week."

Troy set the remote down. One hundred channels and nothing on. "My concern exactly." He glanced at her out of the corner of his eye. "You're not mad?"

"Should I be?"

He was kind of expecting it, yeah.

She pulled the sheet up to her chest and leaned against the headboard, opening a book. He looked at the name on the back cover, noting his favorite author. She was holding the last book in the series. He wouldn't have pegged her as a horror fan. "Is that one any good?"

She kept reading. "It doesn't have pictures. You wouldn't like it."

"Ouch."

She grinned but didn't look up. His chest did some kind of strange constriction. Cam didn't smile much, especially like this. With no one watching, no one to impress, she seemed almost carefree. He wanted more.

Grabbing the book from her, he held it above his head. "I read books without pictures."

Her eyebrows rose, but she didn't make a move for the book. "Comic books don't count."

"For your information," he said, "I've read this whole series. Garrett Croft is supposed to die in this book, after the soul of his wife is freed."

Those crazy huge eyes of hers widened. "He does read."

"I'm literate too."

She laughed, a rustic, low sound born of sheer fantasy, and his heart all but ruptured. He could feel the smirk falling from his face, his arm lowering to the bed, but his gaze darted to her mouth. Small, pink. The bottom lip a little fuller than the top.

"Can I have the book back now?" she asked, smile still in place.

He wracked his brain for something else clever to say, just to hear that laugh again, but his mind drew a blank. He handed the book back. "You ever read King?"

"Sometimes. Not often. He goes off on too many tangents."

This time, he grinned. He felt the same way. "What about fantasy or romance? Might loosen you up a bit. Give you some wild ideas."

"I don't do wild ideas."

She didn't do public displays of affection either, but she'd kissed him in front of the family. Before he could look at her mouth again, remember that kiss, he reached behind his neck and pulled off his shirt. He clicked off the TV and flopped on his back.

"Do you seriously read romance books?"

He closed his eyes and smiled. "Good sex scenes."

"They're as bad as the movies. So unrealistic."

He opened one eye and looked at her. "And the demons in horror books are realistic?"

Turning on the bed to face him, she crossed her legs. "Well, no, but that's obvious fiction. Romance gives people the impression that love like that exists."

Not even she was that jaded. He leaned on his elbows. "Love like that *does* exist."

She whipped him a look of improbability. "Oh, come on. Happily ever after and dancing in the rain and one true love you can't live without?"

She *was* that jaded. It broke his heart a little. He sat up. "You don't believe in love?"

"Of course I believe in love. I love my family. I've been in love. But soul mates and other nonsense? No."

He couldn't believe his ears. What had happened to her that she couldn't believe in miracles and happiness? "Then you've never been in love, Camryn Covic. What a shame." Her lips pursed. He shook his head. "Have you never done anything silly in your life? Wished on a star, laughed until it hurt, fallen in love?"

She gave him a blank stare.

He rose and walked to the French doors on her side of the bed. There was no rain to dance in, but there were stars. "Come here."

She sighed. "Okay, Troy. I get it. You're a romantic. Never mind."

She didn't get it. He held out his hand. "Come here, Camryn."

After an epic stare down, she resigned herself and stood.

He opened the doors and stepped out onto the small balcony. He directed her to the railing to face the open expanse of the Hortons' yard. Standing behind her, he locked her in place with his arms and held the railing in front of her. Resting his chin on the top of her head, he breathed deep. Cool, clean air. Pine. The night was significantly cooler than the day. When a breeze came, he smelled lemongrass, reminding him of the moment with her in his house just a few days before.

"What are we doing, Troy?"

Being silly. His mouth dropped to her ear. "Pick a star."

"Why?"

"Just do it."

She must've sensed he wouldn't let her go until she

cooperated. She sighed and pointed above the mountains in the far distance. "That one. Can I go in now?"

"No," he said, smiling into her hair. So soft. "Make a wish. Out loud."

"No. This is stupid."

He grinned. "Make a wish, Camryn. For anything."

She crossed her arms over her chest, so he dropped his hold to her waist. Her T-shirt skimmed the elastic of her boxers, exposing a trace of skin beneath his thumbs.

"Fine," she said. "I wish I would find a job right away when we get back to Milwaukee."

Always work with her. Lemongrass filled his nose again, and it was starting to have an effect on him. He cleared his throat. "Pick another star. Make another wish."

"Troy..."

"Camryn," he shot back in the same dry tone.

She pointed to their right, and her hair brushed his collarbone. "That one. I wish my family behaves the rest of this trip."

None of these wishes were for her. Not for something she wanted deep down in that place even she forgot about. A wish for something crazy and unrealistic. "Find another star. Close your eyes and wish to yourself. Something you've always wanted but didn't think you'd get."

"Like world peace?"

He bit his tongue and shook his head. "For you, Camryn. Make a wish for you. And don't tell me what it is."

She looked up, exposing her neck, making her hair dance over his chest. His jaw clenched as everything south of his chest responded. To her. To Camryn of all people. His breath held. His thumbs brushed the soft, warm skin under her shirt.

"Done," she said after a few moments, and turned in his arms. "Can we go in...?"

"Camryn," he forced out, the thin strand of control tethering. Her eyes widened and looked at him. Hazel in a sea of blackness. He made a sound, part whimper, part moan. *God, no.* "I'm going to kiss you again."

"But no one's here to see. It's not necessary."

"No," he whispered. "It isn't necessary. Not at all."

Yet his mouth closed over hers anyway, and the faintness of her lips, the scent of her, had the insane part of him wanting more. More than he could give her. More than she would give him.

Nothing had changed from this afternoon. Like a punch to the gut, the kiss shocked him. She shocked him. The sheer pleasure and torture. Her lips parted against his, and as she deepened the kiss this time, he pressed against her. Her fingers dug into his biceps, riling hunger to a whole new plane. His fingers spread over her sides, her tummy, so soft under his calloused hands.

How could anyone think her cold? If he had less sense he'd take her right now. Right here under the moonlight with nothing but a breeze between them. If she hadn't been the first person in his life to make him feel worthy of love, back when he was an awkward, scared kid just wanting to be left alone...

He tore his mouth from hers and sucked in air. Grabbing the railing behind her, he dropped his head to her chest and tried to reason with his body to calm down. Her hand came down on his head, threaded his hair between her fingers. His eyes slammed shut.

This was not happening. Not. Happening.

He was not, could not, would not have feelings for Camryn.

Walk away. Walk away from her.

"Shit," he ground out and lifted his head, not daring to look her in the eye. He backed up right into the door and turned. "Good night, Camryn."

Shaking, Camryn shut the balcony door and walked inside their room to the adjoining bath without looking at Troy. She closed the door quietly and ran hot water in the massive tub before stripping to get in. Bringing her knees to her chest, she let the water warm her.

Troy had kissed her. No one was around this time, so it wasn't for show. So why, then? At first he acted like he wanted to. She wasn't an idiot, she could feel his response. But then he backed away, a look of pure horror on his face.

And her heart fell as hard as her mood. Like a slap to the face, reality came.

Maxwell was right. She had no passion, no appeal. As cold as a fish and just as unattractive.

She pressed a hand over her mouth to hide the cries and dropped her head to her knees. With Maxwell, the things he said hurt. But with Troy, just for a second, she wanted to be more. Wanted to be somebody he wanted. Someone fun and beautiful.

Someone she wasn't.

Served her right for wanting what she couldn't have. For thinking she could be like his other women. How could she face him now? How could she look him in the eye and pretend she hadn't been humiliated beyond recognition?

Pretend it didn't matter.

She'd been doing it her entire life. The black sheep, the ugly sister, the boring colleague. She'd been hiding pain from those around her long before Troy and this wedding. She could do it now. And would. Rising, she dried off and redressed. Drawing in a deep breath, she turned the knob and stepped out.

Troy was asleep in bed, his back to her. Padding across the hardwood, she slid under the sheets, and turned off the lamp quietly to not wake him.

Turning on her side, she stared out the French doors into the night. He'd made her wish on a star. She'd never felt so stupid in her life. As a kid she used to do that, until she realized wishes were frivolous, silly things. A waste of time. Wishes didn't come true, especially for her.

But when he told her to close her eyes and cast a wish out, she was eight years old again, wishing for things that would never come.

Wishing for someone like Troy to want her.

"Camryn," he whispered. He hadn't rolled over, so his back was still to hers. She barely heard him. When he didn't say anything again, she figured she imagined it until another, "Camryn," whispered out.

"Yes?"

"About what happened out there..."

No. No way was he going to add to her humiliation by apologizing. "It's okay, Troy. This is a long time for you to go without someone. I know it meant nothing."

Her chest felt like it was cracking open. She pressed a hand there to quell the pain. When he didn't confirm or deny her statement, she closed her eyes, hoping for sleep.

"What did you wish for?" he asked several moments later.

Her eyes opened and focused on the stars again. Why did he make her go out there and do that? To make fun of her, make her look as stupid as she felt? "You said not to tell you."

And I'm not telling you the truth. That's more embarrassment than even I can tolerate.

The bed shifted when he rolled to his back behind her. "I want to know. Please."

No, he definitely did not. She bit her tongue, forced her voice to sound normal. "Rain. I wished for rain."

Chapter Six

Life Lessons According to Camryn:
The old saying is wrong. Life is easy,
it's the darn people who make it difficult.

Around the breakfast table everyone chatted about making plans for the day. Camryn sat sipping her coffee, thinking about running away from the herd and going on a hike or taking a solitary swim in the pool. One of the staff came by and filled her cup.

Staff. She wasn't used to people waiting on her, even if they were silent and hardly noticeable. There were only a couple of women here now, unlike when they first arrived. One did the cooking, the other served and cleaned. Bernice said she wanted to be free to spend time with them instead of worrying about those things. More staff were coming later in the week for the rehearsal and wedding itself.

When the discussion of Mile High Gliding came up around the table, Cam tuned back into the conversation. She didn't know what that was, but it sounded like an ambulance would be required.

"Ha," Dad shouted, setting down the newspaper. "The Brewers beat the Rockies last night."

Justin was displeased. "I could've played for them if I hadn't blown out my knee. We would've beaten you then."

"That's right," Troy said. "You played ball in college."

Heather grinned and kissed Justin's cheek. "Full scholarship."

Troy leaned back and crossed his arms. "Fisher was on varsity in high school. Do you still have your equipment?"

Justin nodded. "In the garage, collecting dust."

Fisher bounced Emily on his knee. "What do you say, Em? Want to play baseball today?"

Around her colorful, no-nutrition-involved cereal, Emily nodded enthusiastically. "Yeah."

Bernice stood and cleared her place, only to have one of the staff take it for her. She obviously wasn't used to staff either. "I'll let you guys go ahead. I'm going to work on Camryn's dress."

Mom stood. "I'll help."

Troy looked at her. "What's wrong with your dress?"

Before Camryn could open her mouth, Nana interjected herself into the conversation. "Chubby here doesn't fit into her bridesmaid dress. It's a good idea to play ball today. She needs the exercise."

All aboard the humiliation train.

Heather stood, dragging Justin with her. "Let's go pull the stuff from the garage. We'll meet you all outside."

Camryn sighed and stood, averting Troy's questioning glare about the dress. Baseball had to be better than this Mile High nonsense. "I'll go get changed."

After running upstairs to put on a pair of shorts and a tee, she went outside to meet everyone. Raising her face to the sun, she breathed deep before heading over the hill. The humidity wasn't as heavy here as it was at home, but the altitude made up for it. Though the temperature was almost eighty degrees, the air smelled like snow.

Nana had parked herself in a lawn chair along the first base side to watch. They'd set up Frisbees as bases and had a stack of wooden bats behind home plate. Heather tossed her a glove.

Justin grinned. "Rules. Emily doesn't count as an out. Four balls, three strikes, no infield fly. Two fouls is an out. Yjaka Harold is ump and catcher."

Heather pursed her lips at Kuma Viola who was applying lipstick in a gruesome shade of plum. "This is baseball, Kuma. Put the makeup down."

She capped her lipstick. "I'm too old for this."

"As am I," Tetaka Myrtle agreed.

"Quit your belly-aching and play," Nana professed. "I'm not getting any younger."

Fisher and Justin called out teams.

"Troy," Justin said.

"Heather," Fisher countered.

"Anna," Justin challenged.

By the time they got through the dads, aunts and uncles, it was down to Emily and Camryn. "Emily," Fisher said.

Camryn sighed and put her hands on her hips. It was gym class all over again. "You picked Emily over me? Come on!"

Troy grinned and looked at Fisher. "We picked first, so you bat first."

They put Camryn in right field, which was for the best. No action out there. Heather stepped up to the plate and swung at the first pitch. Dad caught it from second base. Justin's dad hit a ground ball right back to Anna after she pitched it. Dad ran to first to get the out. At her turn, Kuma Viola swung so hard the bat flew from her hands, causing Yjaka Harold to hit the dirt. Err, grass. Nana laughed so hard she burst out in a two minute coughing fit.

"And you picked her over me!" Camryn yelled.

Anna walked Kuma on the next three pitches, probably to save the others from bodily harm.

Fisher stepped up to the plate, and hit the ball right to Camryn. She threw her hand up, going backward, running forward, until she completely lost sight of it in the sun. The ball landed on the grass next to her foot. She stared at it, and as everyone yelled at her, she jerked to react. She picked it up threw the ball to Anna. Well, nowhere near Anna, actually. It wound up closer to Nana. By the time the yelling stopped, Fisher and Kuma had scored. Yjaka Mitch struck the third out.

Camryn walked back to home. Halfway there, Nana shouted, "Move it, missy."

This was so not her idea of fun.

Anna and Tetaka Myrtle struck out in succession. Justin, Dad and Troy were all on base. Camryn walked to the plate, dragging her bat behind her. Heather pitched her two strikes. Camryn didn't swing at either.

From her lawn chair, Nana huffed. "You have to swing to hit the ball."

Is that how this works? she thought sarcastically.

As Heather brought her arm back to pitch Camryn her third strike, she decided she was going to swing no matter what. She brought the bat forward, connecting with the ball. Camryn pictured herself doing a happy dance until she realized the ball was flying foul. Not just foul, but toward Nana.

The ball sailed right into the center of Nana's forehead, propelling the eighty-five-year-old woman backward off her lawn chair and onto her back.

Everyone froze. Camryn dropped her bat.

After a long pause of disbelief, they rushed over to Nana, screaming a thousand things at once.

"Jesus, Cam. You killed Nana." This from Yjaka Mitch.

Well, it wasn't on purpose!

Anna pulled the collapsed lawn chair out from under Nana and set it upright. Troy and Justin helped Nana to her feet and set her back down in the chair. Someone sent Emily to go get ice. The little girl rushed inside.

Camryn stood back, shaking. The only thing she could see was Nana's deadly glare aimed right at her, and the large, reddened bump forming between her eyes.

"How many fingers am I holding up?" Yjaka Harold asked.

"She can't see that," Tetaka Myrtle insisted. "She's nearsighted."

"No," Kuma Viola argued. "She's farsighted."

Emily came running back out, cupping her hands. "Here's ice."

Anna looked down, picked up Emily, and walked toward the house. "Let's put that ice in a bag, sweetie."

"Get off of me!" Nana insisted. "I'm fine."

"Are you sure?" Heather asked. "You have a big bump."

Nana's hand flew to her head. "She hit me on purpose!" A wrinkled finger pointed at Camryn.

Everyone turned to look at her. "Oh, come on. I did not! It was a total accident."

Emily and Anna returned, Mom right behind. "Camryn Covic, you hit your grandmother with a baseball bat?"

Lord have mercy. "It was a ball, not a bat! And it was an accident."

Perhaps Mile High Gliding would have been a better idea.

Anna, voice of reason, crouched in front of Nana. She put the ice pack on Nana's forehead. "Does anything else hurt? Your hip? Your back?" Nana shook her head. "Do you feel sick? Blurry vision?" Nana shook her head again.

"Game over," Fisher declared. "Let's get her inside."

"But I didn't get a turn!" Emily squealed.

Justin took Emily over to home plate to let her have a turn before calling it a day, while the others walked Nana inside.

"I think she should go to the hospital," said Mom at the door.

"I think you should shut it and mind your own business," said Nana.

"Guys," Fisher interjected. "Camryn hit the ball. It couldn't have been that hard."

Camryn stood outside as the door closed in her face. For a few moments, she stared at it before deciding to take that walk after all. Maybe she'd complete this perfect day by getting bitten by a poisonous snake.

She walked past Justin and Emily taking batting practice. Emily hit the ball two feet in front of her and cheered. Figures. No wonder they picked the three-year-old over her.

"Where are you going?" Justin asked.

Camryn pointed west. "For a walk."

"Can I come?" Emily asked.

Camryn looked at her niece and agreed, figuring the hoopla inside would be best without *both* of them.

After dinner, Troy walked into the media room to pick out a movie for him and Cam to watch upstairs. Maybe the Hortons had *Major League*. Now that would be funny. Bernice and Cam were inside the room, Cam wearing a formal purple dress and Bernice standing behind her pinning the hem.

He stopped short. The strapless dress fit tightly around her breasts and waist before cascading to the floor, illustrating her hourglass curves. It was beautiful. So was she. Cam didn't wear much color, sticking mostly to shades of whites, beiges and black. She looked different in color.

After a few minutes of staring unnoticed, he cleared his throat. "Is this the bridesmaid dress?" he asked.

Cam looked at him, all surprise, then turned to Bernice. "I'll go change. Thank you for fixing it." She reached down to grab her clothes from a recliner. "What are you doing in here?"

His gaze skimmed down the length of her, then over to the twelve-foot shelves holding Blu-rays and DVDs by the huge flat screen. "Picking out a movie for us. Any suggestions?"

Her gaze was skeptical, but she shrugged. "Just make sure it doesn't have clowns in it."

She walked out and headed for the staircase. Troy grinned. He'd almost forgotten about Cam's fear of clowns. She'd been the butt of many jokes for that. It seemed a silly thing to be afraid of.

And then he got an idea. A quite dreadful and brilliant idea. Last night he'd gotten Camryn to wish on a star. Logical, composed Camryn did something impractical and frivolous. Maybe he could get her to do it again. A list of things, perhaps. Things not in her norm to bring out another side of her. Make her less tense. See the world for all its beauty.

"That's a wicked grin on your face, Troy."

He looked at Bernice. "Yes, it is. Do you have any Stephen King movies?"

Bernice looked at the shelves. "I'm sure we do. Try the second shelf."

Troy walked over and found what he was looking for. Tucking the DVD under his arm, he told Bernice thanks and headed upstairs.

Cam was just coming out of the bathroom wearing PJs when he walked into their bedroom. He put the disc in the player and sat on the bed. She joined him a second later, sitting and applying lotion to her legs.

He'd never noticed her legs before. Long, shapely...

"I can't believe I hit Nana with a baseball."

Snapping his eyes away, Troy swallowed. "She's okay. Besides, you didn't do anything the rest of us haven't wanted to do."

She shook her head and grinned, causing his stomach to flop.

"What movie did you find?" she asked, not glancing up from her task when the menu popped on the TV.

"Check it out," he said.

When she looked up at the menu for *It*, and the evil clown poking his head out of a sewer drain, she squeaked and fell off the bed. She crawled on all fours to the bathroom where she stood and crossed her arms, glaring at him.

Troy laughed so hard he thought his side had split open. He fell sideways on the bed, wiping tears, and holding his stomach.

"I'll have you know, Troy Lansky, that thousands of people suffer from coulrophobia. That's the official medical term for fear of clowns. An *official medical term.*"

He sucked in a breath and sat up. "Come over here, Cam."

"Absolutely not. Turn it off."

He picked up the TV remote and switched it off. She edged out of the bathroom doorway, peeked around the corner to ensure he did as asked, and then sat back down on the bed.

"That was cruel."

He shook his head. "Listen, Cam. I'm conducting an experiment. Last night you wished on a star. Tonight, you're going to do something that scares you. It's all part of a list I contrived."

"And what if I don't want to be part of your experiment?"

He smiled. "You don't have a choice. I have my reasons for the list."

"And that would be?"

"I'll tell you at the end of the week. Now, let's watch the movie."

She stood swift enough for the curtains to shift in her wake. "No."

She tried to flee to the bathroom again, but he caught her and dragged her back to the bed. He sat her between his legs and trapped her in a bear hold. "One thing, Cam. One thing that scares you."

"Why? There's no point to this."

"Oh, but there is. Trust me."

Her shoulders sagged beneath his grasp. "Not on your life." Pause. "How long is the movie?"

"Four hours."

"Four hours?" she repeated, her voice several octaves above normal. "That's cruel and unusual punishment, Troy."

He laughed. "Come on, Cam. Do something you've never done before. It won't hurt. I promise. We'll sit just like this the whole four hours if you want."

He waited her out. One minute, two...

"Fine. Play the movie."

He reached for the remote and clicked the TV back on, then hit Play. She was calm until the first sighting of Pennywise the Clown. In a surprising display of strength, she vaulted out of his grasp, over his shoulder, and behind his back to cower between him and the headboard.

Her face pressed against his back, her breath warm, tickling the hairs on his neck. Her legs hugged his sides. She was right. This was a very, very bad idea. Because he now wanted to turn the movie off, lay her out flat, and finish the kiss they started last night.

Instead, he ground his molars and held his position for the next fours hours until the movie ended and he didn't know which one of them got the worse end of the deal.

Chapter Seven

Life Lessons According to Camryn:
There's a lot of frogs to kiss before you realize they're all frogs.

Troy stared at the red-planked stables in front of them and then at the sky. Camryn might get her wish from the other night. The sky was threatening rain. The forecast was calling for an inch with storms through all afternoon and evening.

She'd wished for rain. He shook his head, disappointed. He'd hoped she had let go, been a little loose, even just a little. For him.

She also said their kiss was nothing. Right after she insulted him by assuming he couldn't go a week without sex. *This is a long time for you to go without someone.* Did she actually think the reason he kissed her was because of withdrawals?

He could still feel her against his back from last night. That wasn't nothing. Neither was the kiss the night before.

The wind blew, causing the long, wild grass beside the stables to swirl. It smelled like three-day old manure.

A woman came out of the stables—long, lean and naturally beautiful. Blonde hair cascaded down her back in waves. Full breasts demanded release from a blue-patterned flannel. Jeans hugged her thighs. She wore a pure, charming smile as she pocketed a pair of riding gloves.

Justin hugged her. "This is Jessie," he said to them.

She looked like a Jessie. And for once, he didn't feel a stirring in his gut, even in the presence of such beauty. A week ago he would have shifted to full magnetism mode to see where flirting got him.

Jessie's gaze took him in from head to toe like she wanted to eat her way through his clothes. Justin cleared his throat and started introductions. When he got to him, Troy interrupted.

"I'm Troy, and this is my girlfriend..."

Jessie darted a tongue across her lips, meant to moisten and tease, distracting him. Any basic male reaction he may or may not have had to the woman fled.

He said *girlfriend*, and she all but made a move. Jessie lost all her attractiveness in the blink of her green eyes. Eyes that were no match for Cam's.

"Camryn," Cam said, finishing his sentence while holding out her hand. "Thanks for letting us ride today." If she was irritated for his distraction or fumble she didn't look it.

"Sure," Jessie said, waving a hand to follow her.

Fisher eyed him. "Smooth, man."

He used to be.

Emily had been chatting the whole car ride here about riding a horse. She'd been so excited the car seat had barely restrained her. But once they entered the twelve-stall barn and she got a look at a real horse, she all but climbed up Anna's leg in fear. Troy couldn't blame her.

Jessie guided a white mare from the second stall. "You guys can pick whichever horse you want. They're all saddled and ready to go. This one here is for whoever rides with Emily. She's the most gentle of all."

Troy looked from Emily, face buried in Anna's neck, to the horse. "What's the horse's name?"

"Darby. She's eight years old."

Anna walked up to the horse and petted her nose. "Want to try, Emily?"

Emily shook her head, squirming against Anna's hold.

Troy stuck his foot in the stirrup and mounted Darby. He held his hands out for Emily. Anna handed her over, causing Emily to go into full meltdown. She arched back, screaming and flailing. Troy held her firm, swinging her legs across his lap so that she was facing him.

"Put your face against my chest," he said, guiding her. "There. You can't see anything. Let's try this for a minute, and if you don't want to ride, we won't."

Emily stiffened, then poked her face out from his chest. Slowly, Troy lifted the reins and directed the horse to step forward. Emily buried her face again, but didn't scream.

"Her hooves sound just like a heartbeat, right?" Fisher said to Emily, walking beside the horse as she took a few more steps.

Emily lifted her face to look at Troy. Troy smiled. "Kinda smells like your dad too." Emily laughed, much to the dismay of Fisher. "What do you say? Want to try?"

Emily nodded, so everyone picked out a horse, and Jessie led them out of the barn. "I thought we'd head out to pasture and then maybe through the wooded trails," she said, looking over her shoulder for a response.

"Sounds great," Heather said. "It is so beautiful out here."

Troy kept Emily close to his chest with one hand on the reins and the other around her as the little girl peered over his shoulder at Cam. Cam was riding a brown gelding named Sweet Tea. That had to be a good sign to the horse's temperament.

They made their way over a hill and to a flat meadow where wildflowers colored the tall grass. Far in the distance, the foothills at the base of the Rockies could be seen past a forest. The altitude made breathing heavier, but everything smelled fresh. Jessie turned and entered a path through the trees wide enough for two horses. Troy, being closest to her, pulled his horse next to hers. Anna and Cam followed.

Peat moss and soil heavily scented the air as the heat of the day lessened under the canopy cover. Not far from them a woodpecker banged away. It was quite relaxing, actually. Troy would rather ride a Harley through downtown Milwaukee, but this wasn't half bad.

"So, Heather," Jessie said over her shoulder. "What color are the bridesmaid dresses?"

"Lavender. I had Camryn in mind when I saw the color. It goes great with her skin tone."

Before yesterday, if Troy tried to picture Cam in anything but neutrals or white, he couldn't. Even now she had on khakis and a white tank top. But seeing that dress on her, the color against her skin...

Anna agreed with Heather. "It does look nice on her. What flowers are you having?"

"You know, I'm not sure," Heather said. "Justin's mom..."

Troy didn't hear the rest because Emily leaned over to check out the horse's legs. He tightened his hold on her. "Stay still, squirt. I don't want you to fall."

"What's on the horsey's feet?" she asked.

Jessie glanced over at Emily. "Those are horseshoes. They protect the horse's feet."

"They don't look like shoes."

"They're shoes."

"They don't look like shoes."

Troy grinned. "Horses only need protection on the bottom of their feet. Unlike little girl feet."

Satisfied, Emily nodded and looked away.

After about an hour of riding, his ass was killing him. He suggested a break when they arrived at a clearing. Jessie dismounted and tied her reins on a nearby branch. She came up beside his horse and plastered a grin of pure sex on her face as she took his reins.

The little vixen.

Emily leaned over again, and before Troy could adjust his hold, she slipped.

"Troy, she's going to fall!" Cam shouted, reaching out from next to him for Emily.

In the panicked millisecond it took to unwind the reins from his other hand, Cam had leaned too far, hauling Emily to her chest as she fell off her horse and flat on her back.

Anna dismounted before Troy could, and picked up the crying child. "Oh my God, are you okay?" She knelt on the ground and ran her hands over Emily's head. "Does anything hurt?" she asked.

Please, please, kid. Don't be hurt.

Troy looked her over, lifting her arms and running his hands over her back, seeing no scrapes or cuts. "I don't see anything. She slipped right out of my hands. I'm so sorry." He looked from Anna to Emily again. "Are you hurt?"

Emily shook her head, tears abating.

Heather placed a hand on his arm. "She's okay, Troy."

Fisher squat down next to them. "I think she's just scared. She fell on Cam."

Cam. From his knees, Troy turned and pushed Justin out of the way. She was flat on her back, arm sprawled out at her side. *Oh no. Oh God, no.* "Cam?"

Jessie knelt on the damp ground and held Cam's head still. "Justin, ride back and get help. Heather, tie up the horses."

"Shouldn't we use a cell and call?" Heather asked.

"No service out here. Justin knows how to ride. He'll get help fast. Go!"

Justin mounted his horse and rode off down the trail, kicking up mud in his wake as Heather jumped up to do as asked. Troy could hear her crying from across the clearing as she tied the horse reins to neighboring branches.

Air whooshed from his lungs, leaving him unable to draw a breath back in. He couldn't move, just stared at her, a thousand *I'm sorry's* careening through his brain. He scrambled over to her on his knees. "Cam?"

She opened her eyes, winced. "Not so loud."

When she tried to sit up, Jessie put a hand to her chest and eased her back down. "Lay still, just in case."

"In case of what?" she asked.

Heather came back from tying the horses, her face wet with tears. "Are you okay?"

"I'm fine. Just a headache." Cam looked around at the faces above her and stopped at Fisher. "Is Emily all right? I tried to grab her..."

"She's okay," Anna assured.

Cam tried to sit again, only to be held down by Jessie. One of her infamous glares darted to the woman holding her down, so Troy brushed Jessie aside and held Cam's head instead.

"Hold the side of her head," Jessie ordered. "Above the ears. If she has a neck injury you could do more damage."

"Let me up!" Camryn barked. Her face paled immediately after.

"Don't move, honey. Justin's getting help."

Honey?

Emily wanted to be by Cam, so Anna started walking around with her, bouncing her on her hip. When he looked back at Camryn, she looked mad as hell.

"I'll let you go if you promise to lie still."

"Fine. But there's nothing wrong with me an aspirin won't fix."

Fisher knelt next to her and took her hand as Troy pulled back and sat on his haunches. He looked down and saw blood covering his left hand. Cam's blood.

All that red.

"Fisher...she's bleeding," he said, his voice shaking half as violently as his hands.

This was darn near close to the most embarrassing thing to ever happen to her. And there were a lot of moments on that list. The family surrounded her ER bed, fighting and carrying on, her hospital gown left her rear end hanging wide open for the free world to see, and her doctor looked like he should be doing pelvic thrusts on a wet bar, not practicing medicine. Add in the fact that Troy refused to leave the room, including when they undressed her, and she had the cherry atop the ice cream sundae from hell.

They were awaiting x-ray results before discharge. Thankfully she didn't need stitches. The cut on the back of her head was small. The doctor assured them, Troy several times due to him freaking out, that the head bleeds a lot, even with minor injuries.

By the time Troy was on her very last nerve, he plopped in a chair in the corner and shut up. Next time she'd push him off a horse.

"You're lucky you don't need stitches, young lady." This from Mom. 'Cause she did this all on purpose. "What would your hair look like for the wedding?"

"At least something good came from this," Nana proclaimed. "Have you seen her doctor?"

Oh God. Nana was going to hit on the ER doctor. Perfect. Just perfect.

Kuma Viola opened a cabinet door and closed it. "Never mind the doctor. Have you seen those slipper socks they give you in the hospital? I just love those."

And now we can add in theft. Lovely.

The doctor came in the room holding her x-rays. He uncomfortably wove around the family to get to her bedside.

"Okay, nothing is broken. Pelvis, neck and spine are intact. You do have a minor concussion, so take it easy for the next twenty-four hours. Have someone wake you every couple of hours tonight. It would be a good idea to stay in bed tomorrow. No rigorous activity, like exercise..." Nana snorted, "...or sex."

Yjaka Harold laughed. "Hear that Troy? None for you tonight."

"Cam wouldn't know rigorous sex if it bit her in the ass," Nana said. "But her doctor on the other hand..." Nana pinched his butt, causing the poor man to jump.

Camryn closed her eyes as the ER staff spontaneously broke out into song and dance. The nurses climbed on top of the desk outside her room and kicked their legs in chorus. The doctors stripped off their white coats, twirling a stethoscope around their fingers and blinking the otoscope light lenses in harmony. Just as they were hitting the peak crescendo, her doctor interrupted.

"Ibuprofen is okay for pain. If you have any nausea or memory loss, come right back in. Do you have any questions?"

Are you sure you can't admit my family to the psych ward for observation?

"Nope. Can I go now?"

He nodded. "I'll get your discharge instructions ready." He glanced around the room, looking like a five-year-old who just wet himself. "You can get dressed now."

"Well, at least she won't be wearing a cast in the wedding photos," Tetaka Myrtle said.

Troy rose slowly, and before Camryn could open her mouth to intercept, he started yelling. "She could've been killed! She could've been paralyzed, and you're worried about wedding pictures? If not for her, Emily could've been a patient too."

Heather clapped her hands. "Out, everyone. Before Troy goes postal. Enough for one day. Come on."

A halo popped over Heather's head. The family exited the

room in silence.

Troy pinched the bridge of his nose and exhaled. He stared down at her, a look crossing his face she'd never seen before. After staring at her for several moments, he turned and flopped sideways on the foot of her bed.

"I thought I was going to kill them. How's that for wedding photos? No one would be alive. We'd have to prop them up like mannequins."

She grinned. "They were just worried. You know them. They treat everything like an apocalypse."

He turned his head and looked at her. "I've never been that scared in my life. I'm so glad you're okay."

Her chest swelled, making it hard to breathe. "I should have a T-shirt made: 'I visited a Boulder ER and all I got was this lousy T-shirt.'"

Frowning, he sat up and stared at her. "You pick now to grow a funny bone?"

If only he knew. She shrugged. "At least I saved you from having to ride the horse back to the stable."

"Dear God, you are trying to be funny. You hit your head harder than I thought." He shook his head. "If I ever see you on a horse again, it'll be too soon."

"May I remind you, if you hadn't been flirting with a pretty blonde farm girl, this never would've happened."

His gaze darted down to his hands as he swallowed. She'd gone too far. Her stomach sank. She reached for his arm, but he rose and stepped back.

"I'll leave you to get dressed. I'll meet you outside."

Shoot. "Troy, I was only kidding…"

But he was gone.

Troy stepped out into the Hortons' yard and drew a deep

breath. Still shocked at how much cooler it was here at night, he crossed his arms and glanced up. Thunder rolled in the distance. Moments later the western sky lit with lightning. The storm was coming later than forecasted, the humidity heavy. His and Cam's bedroom light blinked on above him.

He'd nearly lost it today. Seeing her on the ground, with Emily sprawled over her...

They'd been his family, his only true family, since long before he thought he needed one. He told himself the panic was for that reason. Even now, he still feared the Covics abandoning him. In the quiet of night, though, he knew that to be a lie.

Somewhere in the space between right and wrong, between family and friend, Camryn was becoming more. Warning bells went off in his house before they even left for Colorado when she backed into his table. When he touched her. Turning his head, he looked at the spot in the yard where they'd kissed.

He shook his head. Because of his inattention, Emily or Cam could've been hurt. There was no force on Earth that would've allowed him to forgive himself had that happened.

Ever since his father got locked away when he was eighteen, he'd made a pact with himself to never become the monster his dad was. Never raise a fist, never drink more than one beer, never hurt another person. Use humor when possible, smile freely, show those he loved how he felt.

In honesty, his pact was probably why he never allowed himself to truly fall in love. Love led to marriage, which led to kids... And though it sickened him, his father's DNA coursed through his blood. It only took a second to lose his patience and repeat the cycle of abuse.

A door closed behind him. He turned and looked at Fisher. "What are you still doing awake?"

Fisher shoved his hands in his pockets and stood next to him. "I could ask the same thing."

Troy looked out over the horizon. "I keep seeing them in my

head, laying there."

"Me too."

"I'm so, so sorry, Fisher. I should've been paying more attention."

Fisher turned to face him. "That's not why I came out. It was an accident, Troy. Nothing more. And thankfully not serious."

Fisher was more forgiving than he was. "What do you want to say, then? I know you. There's something on your mind."

Fisher looked up at their bedroom window and then at his feet. "Emily and Camryn aren't the only ones I keep seeing in my mind. It's you too. The look on your face when you saw her fall. The one you had at the hospital." He looked him in the eye. "You've never looked at a woman the way you looked at her today. So this thing with you and Cam, it's okay with me."

Troy closed his mouth and searched Fisher's face. Long, perfectly shaven, dimple on the right cheek. Eyes staring frankly into his, offering Troy the ultimate trust. If he was becoming that transparent for Fisher to see, what must Cam be thinking? Troy couldn't say anything through the lump in his throat, but his mind raced to spill the truth to his best friend.

No words would come. Truth be told, he'd rather have Fisher mad at him.

Fisher nodded. "Good night."

Troy stared at the door as it closed, and then up at the sky as it rained.

Chapter Eight

Life Lessons According to Camryn:
Most of the time, life doesn't pass me by, it tries to run me over.

Camryn sat on the bed alone, biting her thumbnail, waiting for Troy to return. She wanted to erase that look on his face she'd put there in the hospital. She'd always thought Troy was too laid back to take anything seriously. Maybe he hid his guilt as well as she hid her discontent.

Lightening flashed, illuminating the room brighter than the lamp did. She'd seen him outside and had turned on the light so he'd know she was awake. They hadn't been left alone since the hospital. What she had to say was for his ears only.

He came in a few minutes later, glanced at her, then pulled off his damp shirt. Every time he took his shirt off she wanted to run her hands over his chest to see what it felt like. All that hard muscle and smooth, tanned skin. As her skin heated, he stood next to the bed, staring at it like he didn't know what to do next.

"I didn't mean what I said, Troy." He didn't say anything, just kept staring at his side of the bed. "Look at me." When he did, she almost broke out into tears. "It wasn't funny, and I'm sorry."

In the seconds that ticked by, as they looked at each other, she remembered lying in bed one night as a kid, listening to Troy's cries through the wall. A stupid kid, she'd wracked her brain trying to think of a way to make him feel better. She'd never experienced that kind of sadness. Her parents were odd, but they'd never hurt her. How terrible it must have been to have the one person who was supposed to love you hate you so much.

She'd snuck into the bedroom he shared with Fisher and saw her brother was asleep. Troy had quickly wiped his face and sat up from the bottom bunk. Not wanting to embarrass him, she walked to the shelf and pulled out a blue Matchbox pick-up truck. She handed the toy to him. *Take this to remind you that one day you'll be old enough to drive away*, she'd whispered. *It's not your fault.*

She didn't think it helped him back then, and it probably wouldn't now either. "It's not your fault."

He flinched, then blinked and swallowed. His gaze whipped to the patio doors, and then over her. "How are you feeling?"

"Fine. I'm fine, Troy." He needed to know that, so she repeated it. "I'm fine."

"Does anything hurt? Do you need more meds?"

"No and no. I'm fine."

One corner of his mouth quirked. He looked at the doors again, probably remembering the kiss they shared the other night. Knowing Troy, he was most likely trying to take a scrub brush to his brain to forget.

"Are you dizzy or nauseous?"

She sighed. "Troy…"

He came around to her side of the bed and looked down at her. "Just answer the question."

"No, I'm…"

"Fine," he said. "Good."

Before she even knew what the heck happened, he picked her up and set her over his shoulder. Visions of him needing spine surgery flashed before her eyes. "Put me down. You're going to end up in the ER too."

He carried her to the patio doors, opened them, and deposited her on the balcony in the rain. She made a dash past him to get inside, but his arm snaked around her waist and set her right back. His palm came up as he filled the doorway, in his other hand he pushed buttons on his cell.

"I'm not amused, Troy. Let me inside."

"Singing in the Rain" began playing from his phone. He turned up the volume and set the phone on a nearby dresser. "Dance," he ordered.

By now, she was soaking wet and resembling a sodden sloth. "Excuse me?" He grinned, and her heart dropped solidly to her stomach. Damn that smile of his.

"Dance, Cam. It's on the list. I'm not letting you in until you do."

Her jaw dropped. He wasn't serious. First, wishing on stars. Then, scaring the ever-living crap out of her with that movie. Now this? "No. This is..."

"Stupid," he finished. "I know. Do it anyway."

She crossed her arms over her chest to hide her breasts. And to disobey. He stepped out into the rain with her and took her hand, wrapping his arm around her waist. Spinning in a dizzying waltz, he lead them around the tiny balcony while singing a terrible rendition of Gene Kelly's famous song.

Trying her best to hang like a limp noodle, she eventually gave up and started laughing. She wrapped her arms around his waist and danced. He was bona fide nuts. And she was getting there by allowing him to do this.

The song ended and he stopped, but her giggles couldn't be quashed. This wasn't only stupid, is was insane.

And God help her, it felt good.

Thunder cracked overhead as he looked down his nose at her. His hair was shades darker from the rain, his eyes darker yet. Rain poured off his face and onto hers. She stopped laughing and stared back. Stopped breathing.

That's when she realized her hands were trapped between her sopping shirt and his bare chest. Wet, bare, hard chest. She looked at her fingers sprawled over his skin, and just once, just to know what it felt like, she brushed her fingertips over his chest. His heartbeat thumped hard beneath her palm. Despite the heat radiating from inside her, he shivered as if he were cold, but he made no attempt to let her go.

Beneath her palm, his heart rate sped as they continued to stare at each other. A muscle ticked in his jaw. What was he thinking?

She was thinking they were going to catch pneumonia. Then her family could bitch about that. What she wanted was his mouth over hers again. She wanted that more than anything she ever wanted before. The impractical side she never let escape needed him to kiss her. To make her feel like she was a desirable woman worthy of kissing on a balcony in the rain. She'd never felt such a primal need before. In her past relationships, there had been attraction, but not like this. Troy wasn't her boyfriend. They weren't a couple.

She made an attempt to back away, but he held firm. He brought his hand up to brush a strand of wet hair from her cheek, and she watched as his Adam's apple bobbed.

Bending, he lifted her just enough to back her into the bedroom and set her down. Her heart rate sped, hoping he'd...

Drop his arms like she'd electrocuted him. No, that definitely wasn't what she had in mind.

"Check that off the list," he said. "You danced in the rain."

Turning around, he closed the balcony doors and walked to the bathroom. She didn't so much as blink until she heard his shower running.

Heat drained from her body, replacing the unfamiliar warmth and optimism with her usual emptiness.

Troy glanced at the bedside clock and flopped an arm over his face. Four and a half minutes until he needed to wake Cam again. The first time he had her count backward from twenty. He should have had her recite the periodic table, except he'd have no idea if she was right. Maybe this time he'd mix it up and have her list the state capitals.

She'd know what they were too.

He could listen to her voice longer then. The quiet, sleepy lull that was driving his libido mad. He was starting to contrive ways to irritate her just to hear his name from her lips.

He'd made her laugh. While dancing in the rain under duress, he'd made her laugh. His rib cage was still shaking from the way the sound made him feel. Like he was Superman. Like she was Lois.

Back at his house, when first discussing the plan, he'd joked that shams like this always ended with a backfire. The couple overcame the odds, couldn't live without each other, and declared their undying love with a musical interlude.

He turned and looked at the back of her head. Cam didn't believe in that stuff. Nonsense, she'd called it. But he believed. And he was digging his own grave by allowing himself even the idea that they could be more. What moron permitted himself to have feelings for a woman who didn't believe in magic?

He wondered if doing this list in his head would loosen her up.

He rolled on his side and tapped her back. "Cam, wake up. Concussion check." She moaned. His dick jumped. "What's your name and where are you?"

She shifted to her back, and the sheet fell, exposing her belly button below the hem of her tee. He gripped the blanket to stop himself from edging over and placing his mouth there.

"Alice, and we're in Wonderland."

He froze.

The bed shook as she laughed. His eyes narrowed. She rolled on her side to face him. When one eye peeked open and she saw his expression, she laughed harder.

Stopping abruptly, her hand flew to her head. "Ow."

"Serves you right," he said. "That wasn't funny."

Sighing, she dropped her hand and tucked it under her cheek. "You're losing your sense of humor, Troy."

And you're growing one. "Two items checked off in one night. I'm impressed." She sent him a questioning glare, so he elaborated. "Dance in the rain and laugh until it hurts. Check and check."

Her gaze roamed his face before she asked, "Are you trying to change me with this list? People don't change, Troy."

Yes, they do. At least some people did. And she didn't need changing. He liked her just as she was, uptight quirks and all. She'd had this whole other side to her once, she just lost it somewhere along the way. If no one else but him saw this side of her, he could live with that. Just so long as she knew she could expose it once in a while. Just so she knew there was nothing wrong with her.

"You're changing me," he said, and immediately regretted the slip. By the look on her face, she thought he'd insulted her. Which was probably for the best.

"You were good with Emily today."

"Before or after I dropped her off a horse?"

She smiled. "The way you handled her fear, it was amazing. You'll make a great dad."

And wasn't that the damndest thing she'd ever said. More than anything, being a father was his greatest fear. The thought of losing his temper and laying a hand on a defenseless child...

"You're not him," she whispered. His gaze shot to hers. "You're not your dad."

Holy damn. How hard had he fought to hide that part of himself? To bury it deep where no one could ever see the weakness? And in one sentence she spilled it all out there. Said every fear in three words. She'd been a lifeline back then. So had Fisher, but for different reasons. She told no one about seeing him cry. About the mean things he shouted at her while working through the anger. It all stayed between them. Every last private, humiliating moment.

"Tell me the state capitals."

She pursed her lips, and he wanted to laugh but refrained. "I don't need a quiz. My head is fine."

No comment. "Maybe so, but I can't sleep. State capitals should bore me enough."

She smiled and closed her eyes. "The capital of Wisconsin is Madison. The capital of Illinois is Springfield. The capital of Iowa is Des Moines. Wyoming's capital is..."

She trailed off and fell asleep before he could learn the capital of Wyoming. Shame too, because for some reason, he wanted to know.

At the smell of coffee, Camryn peeked one eye open hoping to see the caffeine fairy holding a fresh pot. Maybe a donut too, for good measure. Instead, Troy was standing next to the bed, staring down at her with a tray in his hands. Okay, he'd do.

"What are you doing?" she asked, sitting up. She pressed a palm to her throbbing head. So much for feeling better.

"Breakfast in bed," he said. "The doctor said to take it easy today."

She'd never taken anything easy. It was just a concussion. She'd had worse. "Got any aspirin to go with that coffee?"

He set the tray down on the bed in front of her and sat across from her. "Yeah, and some toast. If that stays down, I can get you some eggs. The cook made Denver omelets."

As soon as the room stopped spinning, and her stomach with it, she may try food. Swallowing the aspirin, she studied him. He stared down at her tray, and then around the room. He was feeling guilty. Still. Telling him the accident wasn't his fault last night didn't help.

"I may need to go back to the hospital. I think I have a brain bleed."

His gaze whipped to hers. "What?"

She laughed, causing her headache to split her skull wide open. "Relax, Troy. It's just a headache. I'm fine." She resisted the urge to press her hand to the pounding. Darn little elves in her head drilling holes.

He frowned at her. "You think that's funny? I'm worried sick and you think that's funny?"

She sobered. People didn't usually worry about her. "I'm not used to all this attention," she said, staring at him. "I'm sorry."

His features relaxed. "Get used to it, 'cause you're stuck with me all day."

She didn't like the sound of that. "Excuse me?"

His glare was intended for no breathing room. "You're not leaving this room today."

"I don't take orders."

Crossing his arms, he leaned against the bedpost. "You're taking this one." He crossed one foot over the other as if settling in.

"Troy..."

"Camryn..." he mimicked.

Huffing out a breath, she glared at him, trying to remind herself he did this out of guilt. "I realize you're upset for throwing me off a horse..."

"I didn't throw you off a horse."

Exactly. "And for giving me pneumonia by making me dance in the rain..."

"You don't have pneumonia..." He cut himself off and snapped his mouth shut, finally figuring out her motive. "Clever girl. No wonder Emily likes you so much. You have reverse psychology down to an art form."

She sipped her coffee. "You can stop feeling bad now. I'm not an invalid."

His tone softened. "Today, you're *my* invalid."

The way he said *my* had a possessive ring to it. One she didn't mind. Instead of making her feel dependent, it made her feel wanted. She'd never felt wanted before. However, she was not going to spend all day in this room doing nothing. What would the family think?

"I've never spent all day in bed, I'm not going to start now."

"You've never spent a day in bed? Just relaxing?"

"No. I live in the real world. People work, and have things to do."

His brows lifted. "And what do you have to do today?"

He was infuriating. There was no arguing with him. "The family..."

"Is off on a hike. They left an hour ago. They're going to grab lunch and head to the bakery afterward to try cake samples. We're alone all day."

She looked at the bedside clock. Ten a.m.? "I've never slept this late." She looked out the patio doors, seeing the sun near full blaze.

"There are benefits to staying in bed, you know." He wiggled his brows.

No way did he go there, even if he was only kidding. After those kisses, she was having a hard enough time not envisioning what it would feel like having Troy touch her. Do more than kiss.

"Bed sores?" she said, trying not to show her true thoughts.

"Ah, Cam. You disappoint me." He nodded at her tray. "Eat your toast."

She glanced at the tray before her. It was really sweet of him to bring this up, even if it was out of guilt. He'd laid a wild daisy from a patch she'd seen edging the yard next to the orange juice. "I've never had breakfast in bed either."

"Really? What's wrong with these guys you've been dating?"

Everything. Nothing.

When she didn't answer, he leaned forward. "Well, I'll add this to my Camryn list. Today will be a day of firsts. Sleeping in, breakfast in bed, and staying in said bed all day."

She didn't like the sound of that either. A day in bed with Troy. Okay, maybe not all bad, except Troy didn't have naughty fantasies in mind. And she was deluded for even thinking it. She picked up the flower and twirled the stem between her fingers, watching the petals spin and blur. She should feel stupid for liking the gesture. It was just a flower, and he didn't mean anything by it.

"Add giving me flowers to that list, then."

He was silent so long she glanced up from the daisy at him. Mouth open, he gaped at her. "Are you trying to be funny again? I can't tell."

Now she did feel stupid. She could feel her face heat. Troy was the only person on this planet who could make her lose her cool. She said things and admitted things she never would otherwise. For some reason, he not only frustrated her to no end, but he confused her too.

"Are you trying to have me believe no man has brought you flowers? Ever?"

Now he was making her sound pathetic. Something she could do just fine on her own. She certainly didn't need him for that. "No. What does that matter? They die fast and stink up the room," she justified.

He shook his head in obvious pity. "What else haven't you done?"

She hated pity most of all. "I haven't stood on my head and twirled either, but you don't see me upset over it."

His glance darted heavenward, and then back to her.

107

"Seeing as you have a concussion, perhaps something less active would be appropriate." She didn't answer. "Okay, Cam. Lay it on me. What's something you've always wanted to do, but never have?"

A lot, by his standards. But she could only think of one thing, and there was no harm in telling him, since they couldn't do it anyway.

"I always wanted to visit Paris."

"You?" he asked, like the statement was preposterous. "Camryn Covic in the most romantic city in the world?"

Romance had nothing to do with it. "Paris is considered one of the best cities in the world for innovation. I dealt with a few companies in Paris at my old job. Plus, the Eiffel Tower was supposed to be temporary for the 1889 Universal Exposition, but the tower was never dismantled. I find that fascinating."

"Uh huh," he said, staring at her as if she were an alternate life form.

"The food would be worth it too. Crepes, croissants, soufflés, espresso. I'm gaining ten pounds just thinking about it, but the weight would be worth the trip."

"Only you could take the romance out of Paris."

"Espresso's very sexy."

He laughed and stood. "All right, Cam. I'm going out for a bit. I left some stuff in the bathroom for you. Take a hot bath while I'm gone."

A hot bath sounded good. "Where are you going?"

"Eat your toast," he said. As if that was an answer. He stopped at the door. "And don't leave this room."

Just to defy him, she crossed her arms. "And what if the house is on fire?"

"Argue with the flames," he said dryly. "You'd probably win. It'll put itself out."

What a comedian.

After he left she drank the rest of her coffee and headed for the bathroom. On the side of the tub was a packet of scented bath salts and lotion. She'd never bought that kind of stuff before. The most frivolous female thing she used was her lemongrass shampoo, and that was only because she liked the brand. It tamed her hair.

Shrugging, she turned on the water and sat on the edge of the tub to read the directions.

Chapter Nine

Life Lessons According to Camryn:
Stress is when you wake up screaming before
you've fallen asleep.

Troy let himself back into the house and set the shopping bags on the kitchen counter. He'd been able to find just about everything he needed in town.

Paris. He shook his head. He hoped one day she'd make it there for real, but for now, his fake Paris would have to do. It would also keep her in their room resting without too much argument.

He hoped. If it was one thing Camryn did best, it was fight him. Stubborn woman.

Grinning, he climbed the stairs to check up on her. Upon entering their bedroom, the bathroom door was closed. He'd been gone almost two hours. Worried, he knocked on the door. "Cam, you okay in there?"

"Um, yes." Splashing. "I must have fallen asleep. I'll be out in a second."

Good, she'd rested. At least she'd listened to him on that account. He looked at the bed. The orange juice and toast were still on her tray. She'd finished the coffee. Well, hopefully she was hungry now.

"Actually," he said through the door, "take your time. I'll call you out when I'm ready."

Pause. "Ready for what?"

He rolled his eyes. She couldn't leave things be or sit back and enjoy life. She had to know everything, control everything. Which gave him an idea for his list.

"I have supplies for an Amazon mating ritual."

"Excuse me?" The door whizzed open, steam billowing out.

She stood there in a black robe, eyes popping from her sockets. Her hair was pinned up in a high ponytail, damp and curling at the ends. She smelled like the rose-scented bath salts he'd left for her instead of her usual lemongrass. Pity. He liked the lemongrass better. Suited her more. Light and fuss free, like her.

"I'm joking," he said. "No mating ritual, I promise. Stay in the bathroom. In fact, stay in your robe. Give me ten minutes to set up and I'll call you out."

She narrowed her eyes before she complied and shut the door.

Grabbing the breakfast tray, he ran downstairs to fetch the other stuff. He wound up having to make two trips. As fast as possible, so she didn't come out and ruin his surprise, he set up his mock Paris. Not bad for no notice. Nodding, he called her name.

She emerged from the bathroom and halted, staring at the red scarf around his neck and the black beret on his head. Then she laughed, the sound so soothing and rich he wanted to weep. God, he loved her laugh.

"You need one of those thin little mustaches," she said.

She stepped back into the bathroom and came out holding what looked like one of Emily's coloring tools. She drew a thin line under each of his nostrils and stepped back to examine her handiwork, only to laugh again. Hell, he'd dress like a mime and do parlor tricks if she kept laughing like this.

"Your table awaits, madame," he said in his best attempt at a French accent. Bowing, he gestured toward the balcony where he set up a TV tray and two chairs. It wasn't a cafe table overlooking the Seine, but it would do.

"Oh, that was a terrible French accent," she said, laughing. Her whole face lit up this time. "You mustn't do that again."

An unfamiliar pressure weighed his chest down as he straightened. He'd never seen her like this. Happy. Not concerned over what she said, not censoring her actions or responses. Just Cam. Free.

And he was wrong. Back at his house he'd thought she was cute. Attractive even, in a girl-next-door sort of way. But no, she was way more than that. She was beautiful. How had he not noticed this before?

"Here," he said, handing over another beret. She stared at it, so he placed it on her head.

"What's that out there?" she asked, walking toward the balcony.

He cleared his throat. "Crepes with cherry cream filling, croissants and cheese, and espresso. They didn't have soufflé. Sorry."

She stared down at the table. "It looks so good. Where did you find all this?"

"There's a bakery in town. My cholesterol skyrocketed just by smelling the pastries. Apparently cheese is very popular in France."

"It is. There are more than two hundred types of cheese. They're also protected by law, so no one can reproduce them. They have strict quotas placed on how much can be produced yearly, in order to prevent the value of a cheese decreasing."

He swore she said this stuff just to make others feel like idiots. It turned him on. "How do you remember all this stuff?"

She shrugged. "I'm a plethora for useless information. I remember most everything I read. Or hear."

"Well, that's just a sharp cheddar cheese. Pretend it's fancy or something."

Smiling, she sat down. He poured them both a cup of espresso from a carafe and stepped inside. He came back out with a framed poster of the Eiffel Tower, leaning it against the railing, and keeping his other hand behind his back.

She looked at him with raised brows. "Nice."

"Walmart," he said. "They have an excellent poster collection. If you like, I can go back and get a Justin Beiber one."

She laughed, sipping her coffee. "I'll pass."

Bringing his other hand from behind his back, he held out the bouquet of flowers. The smile fell from her face as she stared at them. Shoot. She didn't like them. "I didn't know what kind you liked, so I got a mix."

Slowly, she set her cup down and reached for the bouquet. "You got me flowers?"

"Every woman should get flowers. Even if they stink up the house, as you say."

One corner of her mouth quirked. "I don't have a flower preference."

"Every woman needs a favorite flower. Like a favorite color or candy. It's a must."

"I don't have a favorite color either. These are beautiful. Thank you."

"You're welcome. One more thing." He ran in, then back out holding DVDs. "You have your choice between *Forget Paris* with Billy Crystal, *Midnight in Paris* by Woody Allen, or *Beauty and the Beast.*"

She looked at the Disney movie. "*Beauty and the Beast?*"

He shrugged. "It's set in France. Emily made me watch it three times the last time I babysat."

Ah, there was the smile again.

"I'm not a Woody Allen fan. *Forget Paris*, I guess." She took a bite of the crepe and threw her head back, moaning. "This is fantastic."

He grew hard instantly. He sat down so she wouldn't

113

notice. "Better than sex?"

"Oh, most definitely."

He grinned. "Then you're doing it wrong." The smile disappeared again. Realizing what he said, and how she probably interpreted the comment, he called her name so she'd look at him. "Then *they* were doing it wrong," he corrected.

Acknowledging him with a nod, she broke off a piece of croissant and took a bite. "I used to feel sorry for your girlfriends, with you having so many, or how fast you go through them. But now I'm rethinking that. Do you do this sort of thing for all your women?"

No. Flowers, yes. Nice dinner, yes. Planning a whole afternoon to transport them to a European city just for the hell of it, never. "First, I only date one woman at a time, and she gets my sole attention. And two, we're fake dating. The rules don't apply here." Though he spoke the truth, that last part felt like a lie. He wasn't even sure if he said it for her benefit or his. Something was changing between them.

She studied him, the croissant in hand halfway to her mouth. His gaze dropped to that mouth, remembering just how well she used it for something other than trivia knowledge. If he kissed her now, he'd taste her, mixed with the buttery croissant.

After several elongated minutes, she looked away. "Well, either way, this was very thoughtful. Thank you."

"You're welcome."

She pulled the beret off her head, and set it on the table, then picked up a napkin. She leaned over and wiped the fake mustache off his lip. Having her that close again made him want to grab her wrist and yank her into his lap. He'd show her what Paris was really known for.

It wouldn't stop at a kiss then.

They were getting into dangerous territory here. At least he was. If this kept up, he wouldn't be able to control this want much longer. Then all hell would break loose.

He took a croissant and bit into it, just to have something to do with his mouth besides kiss her. And damn it, kissing her was much more preferable.

She finished her crepe, moan-free this time, and sipped her espresso. "I'm wondering how you expect me to sit through a movie after drinking espresso."

"They make decaf. Seems pointless to me. It's essentially a strong decaf brew slapped with the name espresso."

She stared into her cup. "I didn't know that. It tastes the same."

"Well, there you go. You don't know everything, smartypants."

At least Troy let her go downstairs for dinner after the movie when she said her headache was gone. As interesting and fun as the day was, she was going stir crazy in the room. The family chatted their way through dinner, not noticing her at all. Though a rarity, it was just the way she preferred it.

Jackie, one of the Hortons' staff, came up behind her. "Is something wrong, miss?"

Camryn glanced down at her plate, and then back to her. "No, I'm just not very hungry. I had a late lunch." After those crepes, nothing would be as good anyway.

Nodding, the woman took the plate of shrimp stir-fry away.

Troy smiled from the seat next to her, having eaten only half his dinner. He'd finished off the croissants and cheese during the movie.

Exhausted from their day, everyone excused themselves for an early evening. Camryn, however, was wired. After spending her day doing nothing, which she admitted was nice, she needed to get some energy out.

"I think I'll go for a walk," she told Troy once the family left the room.

"I'll come with you. Just give me a second to run upstairs."

The man had to leave her alone at some point.

She stepped outside to wait for him, and examined the property. A couple hundred yards east was a heavily wooded area. It wasn't too dark yet to check it out. Dusk was just settling in, the fireflies blinking. The humidity had faded, so a walk would be pleasant.

Troy came out moments later holding the red, silk scarf from before.

"Still in Paris?" she asked.

What he did earlier was single-handedly the nicest thing anyone had ever done for her. He fabricated a pretend Paris for her just so she'd rest. And rest she had. She could still smell the bouquet of flowers he gave her. The gesture shouldn't make her this happy. No wonder women fell at his feet.

"It's for an item on my list."

There he goes again. The list. "Planning on tying me to a tree and leaving me for the wolves?"

"Something like that."

She crossed her arms. He started walking.

After quite a few steps, he turned. "Coming?"

Resigned she walked next to him. "I thought we could head into the woods. See if there's a trail."

Nodding, he turned in that direction. When they came to the tree line, they discovered a hiking path. Under the canopy, the atmosphere changed. Though cooler, the humidity was heavier. Pine and moss hung heavily in the air as the small creatures stirred around them. A few rabbits, squirrels, and an owl just waking. She hoped to see a deer.

They walked in silence for a few minutes, their feet shuffling over the dried, fallen pine needles. Once around a bend, Troy stopped. "Here looks good."

"For what?"

He grinned, holding up the scarf by the ends. "My experiment. Come here."

When she refused, he stepped behind her, speaking over her shoulder. "You have to be in control of everything all the time. Sometimes it's good to let go of that. Not everything has to have an order or purpose, Cam."

And just how did he plan on releasing her supposed control?

She swallowed when he pressed flush against her back. He smelled like soap and sin. He felt better than sin. What was it with him? Why was she on hyper-alert whenever he was within two feet?

The red scarf came down over her eyes, and his mouth hovered over her ear. There was something so personal, so distinctly him when he talked to her. He didn't allow for any breathing room. Normally she needed that foot of personal space. There was no personal space around Troy.

"I'm going to put a blindfold on, and you're going to use your other senses. You're going to depend on me to get through."

She'd look like an idiot. Worse, feel like one. She didn't need anything else negating that. "No, Troy."

He paused. "Do you trust me?"

His breath fanned her neck, causing a ripple of need to pulse inside. Did she want him? God, yes. Did she know him well? Yes, more than anyone. But could she trust him?

"Yes."

"Be quiet, then." He tied the scarf behind her head, shutting out what little light was left. He stepped in front of her, sliding his hands up and down her arms. "I'm going to take a few steps back, follow my voice."

"Troy, this is stupid. What is the point of this?"

He took a full fifteen seconds to answer. "To liberate control."

Her head whipped to the right, where she heard his voice several paces away. Turning, she walked in that direction. Instinctively, her hands shot out to avoid crashing into anything. Though she couldn't see anything, she could hear the leaves rustling in the breeze, her footsteps padding on the soil.

Her hands touched something, so she stopped. Realizing it was Troy's chest, she dropped her hands.

He grabbed her wrists, bringing them back up to touch him. "What do you feel?" he whispered.

A hard, beautifully, muscled chest. "Your shirt."

"And?"

Turned on? "I don't know. Cotton?"

She swore she could hear him smiling. "Stay here. I'll move again."

She sighed. "Troy..."

"Over here," he said from her left. "Put your hands down this time. I'll direct you."

"If I fall on my face..."

"You won't."

Why in the heck had she agreed to this? She dropped her hands to her sides and walked ten steps. He sounded closer than before. For all she knew, he had left her.

"Stop," he directed. "There's a tree root. Step over it."

Pointing her toe, she dragged her foot along the ground until she felt the root jutting out. Stepping over it, she kept going. Going, going. An owl hooted from a tree above her. She should've reached him by now.

"Troy..."

She smacked solidly into his chest.

"What do you feel?"

"A bloody nose coming on? Jeez, you let me walk right into you, Troy."

His hands fell on her shoulders, so warm. So large. Oh, she bet he could do such great things with those hands.

"What do you feel?"

"Why do you keep asking me that? I feel ridiculous."

He sighed heavily, as if irritated with her. "Stay here." She could hear him walking ahead and stopping. "Okay, Cam. Over here."

This time, she walked without pausing, trying to imagine what it was he sought from her with his repeated question. If she answered correctly, maybe he'd stop this charade. Heck, she should just rip this blindfold off and head back to the house. Why the heck couldn't she say no to him?

Her left foot came down mid-step, landing on nothing but thin air. Off-balance, she propelled forward in a free fall. A scream caught in her throat. His arms came around her, jerking her to a stop against his solid chest.

"What do you feel? Right now. Answer without thinking."

"Scared. Helpless." She waited for her heartbeat to start again.

"Good."

"Good?" she repeated, grinding her teeth, ready to pound her fists on his chest. "You jerk! I fell."

She reached up to yank the blindfold off. His hands pinned hers down.

"Yes, good. I caught you, didn't I? Scared and helpless is how most of us stumble through life, Cam. Not like you, always in control. You can't control everything."

The temper drained out of her. If only he knew how scared she was. All the time. She didn't have near the control she pretended she did. "You made your point. Can I take this off now?"

"In a second," he muttered. His voice sounded strange again. Low.

He released her wrists and slid up her arms, over her shoulders, and cupped her cheeks. And there was her heartbeat. Still functioning. In hyper drive. She could hear the click of his swallow. Could feel the heat from his skin.

The air around them shifted, or maybe it was just her. But seconds ticked by, waiting for what he'd do. Wondering what he was thinking.

"Cam," he said, mere centimeters from her mouth. "I'm having a really difficult time not kissing you right now."

Did that mean he was feeling this shift too? That it wasn't only her?

His thumbs slid under the scarf at her temple, drawing it up and over her head. She blinked to adjust her eyes, only to find them surrounded by darkness. There was only him in front of her.

A look crossed his face, part pain, part guilt. His mouth popped open like he would say something, but instead he dropped his hands and backed away.

She shivered, suddenly, glaringly cold.

His gaze darted around them before landing at her feet. "That's enough for one night," he said, his voice hoarse. "Let's head back."

She followed him back to the house in silence, trying to logically categorize these strange feelings. She'd dated Maxwell for almost two years, and not once had she ever felt like she just did with Troy. Like if he didn't kiss her she'd die.

He was the one making her lose control. Forget his list and everything else. She wasn't herself around him. Even in her own head.

They stepped into the house, finding Fisher and Emily at the kitchen table.

Troy crossed his arms and leaned against the counter. "I thought you guys went to bed."

Fisher glanced down at Emily in his lap. "Emily wanted to see Camryn."

"Can I sleep with you?" her niece asked, pleading through huge, glassy eyes.

Fisher sighed. "I think the fall scared her. Then not seeing you all day today made it worse. Would you mind?"

Camryn shook her head. "It's okay with me if it's okay with Troy."

Troy nodded his consent. "I'll meet you upstairs. I'm going to take a quick shower."

Fisher watched Troy leave the room, then turned to her, studying her like an algebra equation she used to help him with in high school. "Did I interrupt something? Is everything okay between you two?"

No. Yes. "Nothing to worry about." She held her arms out for Emily. "Come on, honey. We can watch a movie and fall asleep."

As she climbed the stairs, Emily snuggled her nose against Camryn's neck. Perhaps Fisher was right. "Were you worried about me today? Did that fall off the horse scare you?" Emily nodded her head. Had she known, Camryn would have made an appearance downstairs today, Troy be damned. "I'm sorry about that. But I'm okay. The doctor told me to rest, so I did. I would tell you if something were wrong. I always tell you the truth, right?"

Emily lifted her head and nodded. "'Cause I'm not a baby."

"That's right."

She carried Emily into their room and set her on the bed. Camryn pulled on her pajamas just as Troy's shower turned off. After she set up the DVD player with *Beauty and the Beast*, Troy emerged from the bathroom. He flopped on his back on his side of the bed. Camryn hit Play and sat down on her side with

Emily between them.

Emily looked between her and Troy. "How come you sleep in the bed with Uncle Troy now?"

Troy grinned. "Yeah, Auntie Cam. How come?"

She narrowed her eyes. She opened her mouth and closed it again, wondering how to explain to a three-year-old, when Camryn wasn't even sure herself. "Um, well, Uncle Troy and I are dating now, so that's what people do."

"What's dating mean?"

"When two people are attracted to each other, they start dating. They go out together and spend time together."

Emily appeared to be mulling the information over as Belle in her movie started singing through a small French village. "So you and Uncle Troy attack each other now?"

Troy laughed. "Auntie Cam and I have been attacking each other for years."

Emily whipped him an irritated look. Troy snapped his mouth shut and focused on the movie instead.

"We're *attracted* to each other, yes," Camryn said, the statement holding more truth than she'd like.

Troy muttered a sound of duress.

Emily bore him down with a glare. "Be quiet," she ordered, then looked at Camryn. "So you kiss and stuff?"

It was the *and stuff* Camryn couldn't get out of her head. She really wanted the *and stuff*. "Sure. Let's watch the movie now. It's past your bedtime."

"What happens after dating?" she asked, undeterred.

"Well, if things go well, and you're lucky, you get married."

"Like Auntie Heather and Uncle Justin?"

"Yes," she said, pointing to the TV, hoping the barrage of questions would stop and she'd watch the movie. Camryn had never minded answering Emily's endless questions before, as her niece always was inquisitive. But this was getting severely uncomfortable.

Emily sat back and started watching her movie, so Camryn laid down and settled in.

After a few minutes, Emily turned to Troy. "Are you lucky?"

Troy looked up at her. "Lucky?"

"Lucky enough to get married?"

Troy's face went blank as he looked back at the TV. "Luck's never been on my side," he mumbled.

Chapter Ten

Life Lessons According to Camryn:
It takes a lot of effort to look this relaxed.

Camryn looked around the small boutique spa and quelled another sneeze looming. The place had baskets of cinnamon potpourri and several scented candles burning. Supposedly for ambiance. The walls were a hideous mint green, probably for a calming effect, but it only served to remind Camryn of a Shamrock Shake.

It had been Heather's idea for them to have a relaxing girls day out. Seated between Bernice and her mother, Camryn fidgeted with the white robe the staff made her put on, while Anna and Heather each paged through a magazine. This was not her idea of relaxing. They were waiting on their massages currently.

"That one," Heather said.

"Oh, I agree," Anna said.

Camryn sighed. "I told you I'm not getting my hair cut."

Heather turned the magazine around for her to see, as if that would change her mind. "This would only be an inch off, with a few layers. Some nice highlights..."

"No."

They were trying to be nice, but they were really trying to make her prettier. More attractive. A haircut and highlights wouldn't do that.

"Camryn Covic," her mother said in her infamous warning tone, "there's nothing wrong with a change."

Camryn rolled her eyes. What the hell. It couldn't be worse, right?

A team of people entered their room—two young men, two women, and what Camryn could only describe as a third woman who looked like she'd been personally trained in medieval torture.

One of the men looked at a clipboard. "Heather, you're with me."

Of course she was. Did they only breed hot people in Colorado? The other man took Anna, the two women for Mom and Bernice, leaving Camryn with Brunhilda the Tormentor.

Relaxing, my ass.

Brunhilda led her down a long hall and into a small, darkened room where ocean waves played softly from a CD player. More ambiance.

"You can hang your robe on the back of the door and get on the table, face down."

"Naked?" she asked, horrified. Camryn looked around for torture devices.

"You'll be under a sheet."

Brunhilda left the room, so Camryn quickly disrobed and flopped on the table before she could return. She had just pulled the sheet up when the woman re-entered. Brunhilda— she never asked her real name—stretched her arms above her head. Scratch that, stretched her tree trunks above her head. She was a solid mass of muscle.

"What's your name?" Camryn asked as a seagull cried out from the ocean waves CD. What next, a barge?

"Clarice," she said, cracking her knuckles. "Now, relax."

Great, she got the massage therapist from *Silence of the Lambs.* That was only one step up from Brunhilda the Tormentor. She wondered when Anthony Hopkins would show up.

An hour later, Camryn walked back into the waiting room feeling like she'd been plowed by a steamroller, scraped off the sidewalk, and run over again for good measure. Everyone else gushed about how wonderful their massages were as she dressed.

Moments later, Jeffrey the Hairdresser came in and called her name. Wanting to point to Heather, she instead raised her hand. He tapped his mouth with a finger while walking circles around her.

When finished with his third lap, he looked at Heather. "I see what you mean." He looked at Camryn. "Come with me."

Do I have to?

He seated her in front of a mirrored station and draped her. He did three more laps. "I think caramel highlights. They'll go nicely with that natural ginger color." It sounded like a meal. Two more laps. The guy must be in training for the Hairdresser Olympics. "A half-inch off the bottom, and two-inch layers. How does that sound?"

Having no idea what he just said, or what it meant, she shrugged.

"Fabulous," he declared and walked off.

Camryn eyed Heather in the chair next to her with a honed look meant to make her run screaming in fear. Heather beamed a nervous smile and quickly diverted her eyes. *Coward.*

The others waited in nearby seats as Jeffrey slathered and folded foil in her hair. While she sat processing, though the word she'd use was baking, Camryn wondered how far the radio signal from her head would reach. Perhaps if she tilted her head enough, alien beings could come abduct her?

Before long she was ordered to a shampoo chair, washed, rinsed, and placed back at the original station. Jeffrey's hands flew around her head, cutting, snipping. By that point she just hoped she had hair left. He pulled out a blow dryer the army would kill to have in their possession, and proceeded to dry her hair.

Eventually, he put his arsenal down and clapped his hands. "Ta da." He swiveled her chair around so she could look at the damage.

Just skimming her shoulders, her hair looked thicker than before. The highlights blended with her natural color, but seemed to make it appear lighter. Huh. It didn't look bad at all. She wouldn't need a paper bag in public.

"Oh, would you look at that," her mother said. "You look just beautiful, Camryn."

Camryn whipped her head around so fast she got whiplash. Never had her mother called her beautiful. If compliments were issued toward her, which were few and far between, they said things like nice, or on the rare occasion, pretty. Never beautiful.

"Thanks, Mom," she said awkwardly, waiting for the other shoe to drop. *Now, just lose some weight.* Or, *you're no Heather, but you'll do.*

Heather smiled. "I say we pick up Emily and go shopping. Get you some new clothes to go with your new hair."

"Oh no." She drew the line at shopping with Heather. By the time they were done, she'd look like Rainbow Brite had thrown up all over her.

"Oh yes," her mother said. "Imagine what Troy will think."

Troy. *Would he like it?* she wondered. And why would that matter? Three days until the wedding and then he'd finally be free of her. He could go back to his real women and not worry that others thought him insane for dating her.

Camryn stood and grabbed her purse. There was no sense in fighting the family. She'd appease them. No one said she actually had to *wear* the clothes.

But an hour later, after Heather had picked out five dresses and eight shirts, Camryn looked at herself in the changing room mirror. "I look like a watermelon."

Heather shook her head. "You do not. It looks nice on you."

Nice. They were back to nice.

The lime green monstrosity of a sundress was too snug around her waist and breasts, and cut an inch above the knee before the cotton flowed out in a loose skirt. It was a spaghetti strap too.

"What's going on with you and Troy?"

Camryn looked at her. "I don't know what you're talking about."

Heather crossed her arms, eyebrows raised. "Uh huh. Something's going on. You two actually act like a real couple."

"Wasn't that the point?"

Heather glared at her, looked straight into her eyes. Camryn wanted to shrink. "You like him. Really like him, don't you?"

"I'm calling the cable company to have them block Lifetime from your service."

"You're falling for Troy," she responded, as if not hearing her at all.

"And Hallmark for good measure."

She shook her head, gaze softening. "Be careful, Cam. You don't want to…"

"Get my heart broken?" she finished. Camryn knew well enough where this conversation was heading. "Because Troy won't return those feelings. I'm not someone who'd interest him. Don't worry, Heather. I know that."

"That's not what I was going to say," she whispered, the look in her eyes proving that a lie.

"I don't need a lecture, or your warnings. Nothing is going on between me and Troy."

Heather stared at her a second more, scooped all the clothes into her arms, and walked out.

Camryn pinched her eyes closed, sighed, and muttered to herself. "New hair and clothes don't change ugly."

Heather was right, whether she said so or not. Camryn needed that mental reality slap. No matter what she thought was going on, Troy would never return these feelings. She reached down to grab her old clothes from the bench, only to come up empty.

Heather had taken her clothes.

Camryn opened the changing room door to demand them back but found Emily instead. Camryn took her niece's hand and looked around the store for Heather, finding her at the register. Before she could say anything, Heather leaned over and cut the tag off the dress she had on, then handed the scissors back to the cashier.

"All paid for. You can wear it home."

"I don't want to wear it home. I want my clothes."

Heather picked up Emily and shrugged. "Too late. They're in the car." She looked at Emily. "Ready to go?"

Camryn glanced outside the window where the rest were waiting. No one had the bags, which meant they were already in the trunk. It was an ambush. Fine. She'd wear this home, sneak inside, and change before anyone saw her.

"Finally," Fisher said. "They're home. I'm starving."

From the patio chair, Troy glanced over to the driveway at the approaching car. They'd been gone all day doing girly stuff. Cam was going to be pissy. He looked out over the yard as the car doors closed.

"Oh my God," Justin said. "Look at all those bags. Who let Heather near a retail store?"

"What did they do to Camryn?" Dad said, setting his lemonade on the table in front of them.

Troy looked. Blinked. She was wearing green. Not white, not beige, not black. Green. And her hair was different. Lighter.

Shorter. The ladies walked over to them and set down their bags.

Justin eyed the goodies. "Did you buy out the mall?"

Heather grinned. "These are all for Cam. We bought her some new clothes."

Troy looked at her, hands on her hips, eyes cast down. Oh, she was not a happy camper. But damn, did she look good. Whatever they did to her hair made her eyes stand out. They were beautiful before, but now it was all he could see. His stomach did a slow roll as his hands flexed.

There had to be a way to stop this reaction to her. To stop this train from derailing in front of him. She was clawing her way under his skin.

"That's a nice shade of watermelon," Yjaka Mitch said, grinning like a cat for what he thought a clever tease.

Cam whipped her gaze to Heather, something close to accusatory.

Emily hopped over and pulled on his sleeve. "Aunt Cam isn't ugly anymore, right, Uncle Troy?"

His jaw dropped. He looked at Cam. Her eyes were closed, head down. "She was never ugly. Who said that?"

Camryn interrupted any response. "Bernice, I'll help you make dinner."

It wasn't just her body language that had Troy worried, her slouched shoulders and crossed arms, but her voice had gone flat.

Justin's mother nodded and they went inside.

Fisher came over to them. "Who told you Auntie Cam was ugly? We don't say mean things like that. You need to tell her you're sorry when she comes back out."

"But I didn't say it!" Emily insisted, lip quivering. "Auntie Cam said she was fixing her ugly. I didn't think she was ugly, honest."

Troy's chest constricted. If she did all this, her hair, her clothes, because she thought she was ugly, then why did she look so mad at Heather? Cam wasn't one of these females who spent hours in the bathroom primping. It's one of the things he found so damn charming about her. She was a refreshing change from the high maintenance women he surrounded himself with.

Nana came outside to join them and sat in a chair next to Troy. She looked at the faces around her. "What's the matter with all of you?"

Emily burst out into tears. "I hurt Auntie Cam's feelings." Anna rushed over and picked her up.

Nana huffed. "She doesn't have feelings. What's this about?"

Kuma Viola fluffed her hair. "Apparently someone called Cam ugly and Emily overheard."

This had Nana in a rage. "Who called my granddaughter ugly?" Her cane whipped up at her side like a light saber ready to defeat the dark force.

"I think Emily misunderstood," Fisher claimed, sitting back down.

"She must have misheard," Tetaka Myrtle said, hiccupping. "I mean, I'd kill for her cheekbones."

"I'd kill for her breasts," Heather said.

Troy pinched the bridge of his nose. "Perhaps you all should tell her these things? Maybe she doesn't know."

"Bull," Nana said. "That's a woman confident in her own skin."

Troy didn't think so. He was beginning to wonder if he'd pegged her wrong. If they all had.

"Emily will apologize when they come back out," Fisher said. "Won't you, honey? Even if you didn't mean it how it came out." Emily nodded her teary agreement.

"Well," Heather said. "If you think I should, I'll tell her I want her breasts."

Justin laughed. "I second that."

"No," Anna interjected, handing Emily over to Fisher. "You'll embarrass her. Just leave it alone."

An awkward silence ensued until Bernice and Camryn came back outside. He watched her as she set down a bowl of chicken salad and a plate of croissants. She looked calm, not at all hurt someone called her ugly.

Camryn was the furthest thing from ugly, but he wondered if she knew that.

Bernice set out a plate of fruit and a bag of chips. Everyone began to dig in.

He couldn't stomach the food, so he sat back and watched her. She didn't seem to notice until after several minutes, she glanced his way. Her eyebrows drew together in question. He shook his head, just slight enough for her to notice, and mouthed, *You look nice.* Her lips parted, then pursed.

Well, damn. There was his answer. She didn't believe him. It wasn't that she *couldn't* handle a compliment, rather she didn't *believe* it.

A look passed between them, his laced with guilt, hers with sadness. But over the course of a few seconds, it morphed into heat. Want. It was just her and him, finally acknowledging what shouldn't be said. Things between them had been building to this point. He'd tried fighting it.

"I don't want it!" Emily shouted. "I want chicken nuggets!"

Bernice placed a hand to her chest. "I'm so sorry, dear. I don't have any."

Fisher set his sandwich down. "We don't cater meals. She eats what we serve."

"She's just tired," Anna said. "Emily, you're being rude."

"I don't care! I want chicken nuggets."

"Mrs. Horton," Cam said, calm as a summer breeze. She set her sandwich down and brushed her hands together. "Do you have any baby food?"

Troy couldn't help but smile. His goddaughter always had a healthy appetite. Even when she was a baby. At least she was on table food now. He remembered being impressed the first time she ate peas. Any child who could keep down something even the Exorcist kid spit out had talent.

Bernice seemed to catch on to Camryn's tactic. "Now that I might have."

Emily stopped crying and stared at them. "I'm not a baby. I don't eat baby food."

Cam shrugged. "You don't eat big girl food either. I think we should get the baby food."

Bernice stood. "No problem. I'll be right back…"

"No!" Emily yelled and picked up her sandwich. After taking a huge bite, she said around her food, "See?"

Bernice sat back down. Troy grinned like an ass. Never mind him being a good father, as Cam indicated once. Cam had reverse psychology down to an art. No kid stood a chance. Now *she'd* be the great parent. They'd probably be little prodigies, playing Mozart by age two.

"I'm sorry that you're ugly."

And there went the mood.

Everyone stared at Emily, everyone except Cam, who examined the food on her plate.

Anna wiped her mouth on a napkin. "What you mean is, I'm sorry I called you ugly."

"Right," Emily said, popping a grape in her mouth.

"Oh, Cam, I'm so sorry. She misunderstood something and she just repeats everything she hears…"

Cam lifted her hand, cutting off Anna. "It's fine. She's a three-year-old."

"You're not ugly," her mom said, causing Cam to drop her head in her hands in obvious frustration.

"Yes, I know I'm not Swamp Thing. Can we move on now?"

Troy watched her, wanting to take her upstairs and show her just how ugly she wasn't. "You're several bars above Swamp Thing."

"Except in the morning," Fisher said, trying to lighten the mood.

Epic fail.

No one spoke until Emily again filled the silence. "What's a Swamp Thing?"

Chapter Eleven

Life Lessons According to Camryn:
Pretending to be a pleasant person all day is exhausting.

Troy turned on the bedside lamp and pulled his pajama bottoms from his bag. Camryn walked to her bag, pulled out her stuff, and proceeded to the bathroom without a word. He changed and sat on the bed. After a few moments, she walked to the closet and reached for a hanger.

"You looked nice today." With her back to him, he couldn't see her face, but she paused before slipping the dress on the hanger. "What's wrong?"

"Nothing. I'm just...beginning to hate that word."

"Nice? Okay, I'll use another. You looked pretty today."

Sighing heavily, she walked to her side of the bed and snatched her bag before returning to the closet. Guess pretty was out too.

"So, what sparked this change? Your hair, the clothes?"

She disappeared into the closet. "Heather made me." He heard some shuffling before... "And dammit, she took my clothes."

He got up and walked to the closet. There was more color in there than a Smurf village. She marched to him, past him, and right on her way to the bedroom door.

"Where are you going?"

"To kill my sister."

He ran over to her. "Whoa, not so fast." Grabbing her by

the waist, he picked her up and deposited her feet back by the closet. "It's not that bad."

"Not that bad?" she repeated, stepping into the closet once more. She pulled out a pink shirt. "Fuchsia. This shirt is fuchsia, Troy." She pulled another. "Turquoise, orange, yellow... It's a waste of money."

"Well, she bought them for you. Might as well wear them through the trip. You can get your regular clothes back at home. What's wrong with a little color anyway? That green looked...beautiful on you."

"Troy..."

And then it hit him. Wear neutral colors, no one notices. Wear those and... "You don't like the attention. That's it, isn't it? What's wrong with a little attention once in a while?"

She looked down at the clothes in her arms. "Because what happened down there at dinner happens, that's why."

He swallowed and softened his tone. "What was that about? This ugly business?"

Carefully, she hung the shirts on their hangers and deposited them on the rod. Closing her eyes, she took a few deep breaths. It was quite cute. And he could tell she wasn't going to answer his question.

"I've never seen you mad."

"Of course I get mad."

Uh, no. Not really. "Not like this. You raised your voice a second ago." Her eyes narrowed on him. "And you're not done. Hold on." He walked to the bed, grabbed a pillow, and stepped inside the closet with her. He shut the door and handed her the pillow. "Scream into that."

"Excuse me?"

He smiled. Most people just said *what*. Camryn, even confused or pissed off, said *excuse me*. "If you start screaming without the pillow against your face, the family will think I'm murdering you."

136

"I'm not going to scream at all."

His smile widened. "It's on the list, Camryn. You wished on a star, did something that scared you, danced in the rain, lost control, and laughed until it hurt. Now, get mad."

She ground her teeth and spoke through them. "Why does everyone find it necessary to change me? I've survived this long without help. I've lived with not being funny, or beautiful, or..."

"More on that later," he said, cutting her off. And he *would* revisit those lies later. But for now, she was losing her anger. "Scream, Cam."

Ah, it was back. "No."

"Do it, wimp."

Her nostrils flared. "No."

He backed her up against the wall and put the pillow to her face. "Scream, Cam."

Without further hesitation, she clenched the pillow, pressed it against her face and screamed into it. Loud, long and strong enough to make her tremble. When finished, she lowered the pillow and stared at it. Her face was an adorable shade of Chuck Berry red.

"Need to do it again?"

As an answer, she handed the pillow back.

"Feel better?"

She looked at him, one corner of her mouth curved before she nodded. "I don't suppose you'll forget those things I said."

Not a chance in hell. That was on the list too. To spill her guts. "No, but that's a talk for another night."

He draped an arm over her shoulders and squeezed. She winced and jerked back.

"I'm sorry. Did I hurt you? I thought you were better."

"It's not from the fall. It's from my massage."

"Huh?" His gaze raked over her. "Massages aren't supposed

to hurt."

She walked around him and opened the door. She plopped on the bed, rolling her shoulders. "Tell that to Brunhilda the Tormentor."

He wasn't sure if he should laugh or not. "Come again?"

"Never mind."

He kicked the closet door shut and went to sit next to her on the bed. Carefully, he lifted a finger and touched her shoulder. She cringed. "Oh, hell no. Are you that sore?"

As an answer, she stared straight ahead.

He looked in the direction of the bathroom, then over at her again. Rising, he grabbed her robe and a bottle of lotion from the bath. He was going to regret this. Until the day he died. Keeping his hands—and mouth—off of her had been a demanding and intolerable task the past few days. Even telling himself that she was Camryn Covic no longer worked.

"Put your robe on," he said. "I'll rub the kinks out."

She whipped him one of her attractive pissed off looks. "No. I have bruises on top of bruises."

"And I'll help."

"No."

"Camryn, put the robe on."

"I'm not getting...naked in front of you."

Oh, now that brought all sorts of naughty, pleasurable things to mind. He closed his eyes. "You don't have to get naked. Leave your shorts on, take your shirt off, and put the robe on backward."

When he opened his eyes, she looked like she was considering it.

"I'll wait in the bathroom," he said, rising. He shut the bathroom door and grabbed her two Tylenol. After waiting a few minutes, he reopened the door. "Are you ready?"

"Yes."

He stood next to the bed, holding the Tylenol. She took them and swallowed them. Before he could change his mind, he sat behind her and squeezed some lotion into his hand.

The second his hand touched her bare shoulder, she tensed. So did he. "Relax," he said, for both their benefits.

As he moved his hands over her shoulders, down her back, he found the trouble spots and worked them out. She had a small gathering of freckles just below her hairline on her neck. His gaze trained on them as he continued the massage. Her skin was so pale, so smooth. His hands were calloused from working in construction, his skin tanned from the sun.

How different they were, in every sense of the word. Yet touching her turned him on, made him want to lay her out flat and release her tension in other ways. If her lovemaking was anything like her kiss, he may never leave this bed.

If he were to kiss her neck, right there over those freckles, would she lay her head back and moan? If he closed his mouth over her ear, would she call his name? If his hands slid around her side, to her breasts, how well would they fit in his palm? There was something very different about how she turned him on compared to other women. Something he couldn't control himself to explore.

"What's wrong?" she asked.

He blinked, realizing his hands had stopped moving. "Nothing. I'm tired. Do you feel better?"

"Yes," she said, glancing over her shoulder. "Thank you."

He cleared his throat. "Go ahead and change."

She got up and disappeared into the bathroom. Sucking in a breath, he looked down at his lap and the painful erection. He hauled the sheet over his lap and rolled on his side.

No way in hell was he going to make it through the week.

After beaning Nana with a baseball, and Camryn's trip to the hospital, the family decided it was best to do some sightseeing around town and then go for lunch. Camryn couldn't hurt anyone by doing that.

As if either instance were her fault.

They went into several tourist shops, an Indian Heritage museum, and walked through an area of the Indian Peaks Wilderness, where Camryn learned what Mile High Gliding was. Apparently, people—being of sound mind—attached themselves to a cable wire and threw themselves off a perfectly good mountain. She was glad she'd nailed Nana with a baseball instead. Nana probably wouldn't agree, but her bump was disappearing and there had been minimal bruising.

No harm, no foul. Though, technically, she guessed it was foul.

After wearing themselves out, they sat down at a table in a bar and grill and ordered drinks. The place was straight out of a Paul Bunyan story. Complete with moose and deer heads above the bar. Dark wood planked the walls, making the place feel like a log cabin in the middle of a mountain.

Camryn glanced at the menu, wincing at the caribou steaks as the special. Her cell phone chimed, finally in an area of service. She hadn't had so much as one phone call since arriving in Colorado. She reached in her purse to check it. One voice mail and one text. She read the text first.

I miss you.

She gasped. Everyone at the table eyed her. She smoothed her features into a blank face. Maxwell missed her? Why? She thought she was a cold fish with no color coordination.

"Let's run to the bathroom," Heather said, standing.

Blindly, Camryn stood, still looking down at Maxwell's words on the way to the rest room.

"Okay, spill," Heather said.

Camryn clicked off the message and put the phone away. "I was told I couldn't maim anyone today. I'm assuming this means clothes too, so no spilling."

Heather's jaw dropped. "Was that a joke?"

Not really. "Maxwell sent me a text saying he misses me."

Heather turned the faucet on to wash her hands. "What's that mean?"

"I don't know," she said. "But I have a voicemail too. Hold on." Camryn pulled her cell out again and punched in the numbers to check her messages.

Hello, Miss Covic. This is Erin Bronson from Greyshaw Industries. We received your resume and would like to set up an interview. If you could please call us back as soon as you can, we'll get everything going. Thank you.

"Job interview," she relayed to Heather. "Thank God. That's the first hit I've had on my resume since sending it out last week. I was getting worried."

"That's great. What about Maxwell?" Heather reached for a towel to dry her hands. The towel dispenser had a stuffed squirrel mounted above it. Apparently Colorado loved their taxidermy.

"I don't know. You speak man language. What does it mean when your boyfriend sleeps with Barbie behind your back, dumps you for her, insults you on the way out, then texts to say he misses you? Is there a term for that?"

"Assholitis?" Heather threw her paper towel away. "Maybe he sent the text to you by mistake, or regrets the breakup."

The first seemed more logical.

"What are you going to tell Troy?"

Camryn looked at her phone again. "Nothing. It's not like we're a real couple."

"You should tell him."

Without answering her, she washed and dried her hands.

"Cam, he deserves to know."

"Heather, he won't care. This is not a real relationship. My personal life is none of his business." She held the door open for her sister.

"I don't know, Cam. I think he'll be upset if you don't say something and he finds out."

Troy had never cared who she dated before now, he wasn't going to start. They left the bathroom and returned to the table.

After she sat down, Troy leaned over. "Everything okay?"

She nodded. "Just got a hit on my resume."

"Ow," her dad bellowed from next to her, jumping a foot off his seat. He bent over, rubbing his shin.

"Sorry, Dad," Heather said, eyeing Camryn. "My foot slipped."

Troy eyed the two of them, then apparently decided to let it go. "I ordered for you."

Great. She hoped it wasn't the special.

Troy turned to Bernice. "May Cam and I borrow your car tonight?"

"Oh sure," she said, waving her hand. "Use the GPS so you don't get lost."

Camryn looked at Troy, not liking the grin on his face. "Why do we need the car? Where are we going?"

"It's a surprise."

"Aw," Mom gushed. "That's so sweet."

Bull. Her eyes narrowed. There was no sweetness involved here. Troy was up to something on his list. Something the opposite of sweet. Like...no good.

Chapter Twelve

Life Lessons According to Camryn:
What happens in Vegas never happens to me.

Troy drove the forest-lined, two lane road, paying extra attention on the sharp curves to not hit a deer, or bear, or whatever else might be out this time of night. Did they have moose in Colorado? At one point, about three miles back, there was a drop-off straight down an embankment. There wasn't even a guardrail.

He didn't need to glance at Cam to know she was stewing in the passenger seat. According to the GPS, the turn he was looking for was a half mile up the road.

"Where are we going?"

He grinned, keeping his eyes ahead. "To tell you would defeat the purpose."

"And what is the purpose?"

Clever girl. "We're doing something spontaneous."

"I don't..."

"Do spontaneous," he answered. "I know. That's the purpose."

"This is hardly spontaneous, Troy. You know where we're going and why."

"But *you* don't."

He almost missed the turn quipping with her. Slowing, he turned left and drove through the wooded park. If Justin's directions were right, they were almost there. After a few

Kelly Moran

minutes of driving, the road ended and opened into an unlit parking lot.

"Here we are," he said, cutting the engine. "Hop out."

She glared out the windshield. "What? You brought me to Camp Crystal Lake? Is a serial killer in a hockey mask going to slaughter us now? *That* would be spontaneous."

He sighed. "You take the fun out of everything." She turned her head to look out the side window. "I'm sorry. I didn't mean that."

"Yes, you did. And you're right, but I never claimed to be fun."

She *was* fun, she just forgot she was. "Officially, Jason's mother was the killer in the original *Friday the 13th*. She didn't wear a mask." She whipped him an un-amused glare. "Come on, let's go."

"Go where?"

He exited the car and crossed his arms, waiting on her. After several moments, she hesitantly got out. Taking her hand, he led her across the parking lot and over a short hiking trail, until a clearing emerged. A small, natural wading pool and waterfall lay before them, steam billowing out into the chilly night.

"Indian Head Hot Springs," he said.

He watched her eye the water, the trees surrounding them, and then she looked at him with raised brows. He grinned, and her eyes bulged.

"Get in," he said.

"Excuse me?"

"You're so predictable. You should change up your answers once in a while."

"I am not going swimming, without a suit, in the dark, surrounded by woods."

Oh yes, she was. "Where's your sense of adventure?"

She gave him an incredulous glare. "Where's your sense, period? Is this even legal?"

He shrugged. "Probably not. Let's do it anyway."

She crossed her arms, ever defiant. He was beginning to love that.

"You give me no choice, Camryn Covic."

He picked her up, walked to the water's edge, and flopped into the water still holding her. The shock of warm water was several degrees higher than the air. It was like jumping into a sauna. He let her go and rose to the surface. When he opened his eyes, she was glaring at him, literal steam pouring off her face from the cool air hitting the hot water.

"You're cute when you're mad."

She blinked as water ran off her hair, over her face. Her white dress molded to her breasts, and as he glanced downward, he could see all the way to her toes through the water. Those huge eyes of hers looked back at him, starlight reflecting off the water, and suddenly *he* wanted to do the spontaneous thing.

Lifting his hand, he traced a water droplet from her throat, to her collarbone, and over the swell of her breast. Her skin, so soft beneath his rough fingers. Warm, inviting. Like cream. She inhaled, shivered.

As they stared at each other, chest-deep in spring water, her expression changed from anger to surprise to heat. Her lips parted. Her gaze dropped to his mouth. And he knew he wasn't the only one feeling this kick in the gut. This crazy, impractical, could-only-end-badly, attraction.

Then again, when did he ever do the practical thing?

Cupping the back of her head, he pulled her to him. She melted instantly against his mouth, pressed her curves to fit the hard contours of his body. No woman had ever responded like Cam did. None of them had ever felt as good as she felt. His hand fisted in her hair, holding on, holding back, until a moan bubbled from her throat, and he lost it.

His hands gripped her waist, dove under her dress, grabbed her backside to haul her closer. She wrapped a leg around his hips, flush to the throbbing he thought would never cease. Her fingers bunched in his shirt, her head tilted for a deeper kiss, and...there were too many damn clothes between them.

A rustling sounded behind them. He broke away and turned to look, not seeing anything. Still panting from their mind-blowing kiss, he tried to listen for what he first heard, but far off in the distance he heard a growl instead.

Oh, shit.

"Cam, we need to go now."

Without waiting for her response, he hauled her over his shoulder, trekked through the water, and ran for the car. His legs dragged due to the extra weight of soaked clothes. She flopped over his shoulder with every step. Imaginable things clawed through his mind, like being ripped to pieces.

Go. Go. Go.

Finally reaching the car, he threw down the towels he'd brought to cover the seats, and dropped her. Slamming the door, he came around the driver's side and jumped in. Then he hit the door lock, just in case bears and wolves had evolved to opposable thumbs.

Leaning forward, he glared out the windshield, out the side window, the rear. "I don't see anything," he said, winded.

When he looked at her, she had her lips pressed together. Quickly, she covered them with a hand. Her shoulders shook, and she...laughed. Deep, thunderous laughter before she sobered and pointed at him, then burst out all over again. Her head flew back, exposing her throat.

He had a very strong urge to strangle that throat, then kiss it better.

"*Friday the 13th* is just a movie, you know," she said,

wiping her eyes and sighing. "Jason's not real."

"I heard a growl."

"Uh huh. Was it Bigfoot? 'Cause we need pictures of that."

She laughed again, and he just shook his head in awe. His skin heated, his pants shrank, and his heart stopped mid-beat. He'd never seen her like this. More importantly, he'd never felt like this.

"God, Camryn. You really need to laugh more often. It's a beautiful sound."

On a dime, her laughter stopped as she stared at him. Something in her eyes lost all humor, and a bitter sadness replaced the joy.

His heart cracked wide open inside his chest.

It was one thing to lie to the family and pretend they were dating. There was safety in that, knowing there was an end. A breakup coming. No harm done. It was another thing entirely to start acting on that lie with no one around but their conscience. If they did this, gave in to some strange attraction for each other, he would end up on the losing end.

Once upon a time, all he had was a broken home and a couple of trinkets as reminders of good memories. Good memories so few he could count them on one hand. They were all tied to her. The woman before him who had more inside her than she even realized. Through the years he got a family. Her family.

The kisses they shared before tonight were nothing in comparison to what almost happened back there in the spring. He'd almost... They'd almost...

Swallowing, his gaze flashed to the steering wheel. She was different. She was more. He started the car and backed out.

Troy had flopped on his back, his side, and to his back

again more times than Camryn could count, but she didn't dare move from her spot on the bed. Her legs were going numb, but she didn't care. For some reason, some idiotic and irritating reason, she couldn't hold her tongue, or her sanity, around him. Her defense mechanism threw up mental blocks whenever they were alone. Nothing worked.

She could smell his soap. He'd showered after her most recent humiliation, which actually turned out to be quite fun. And hot. Very hot. Troy and his list. She wondered if he called it *101 Ways to Make Camryn Look Like a Fool*. Worse, she wondered if there were one hundred and one things on his list.

The smell of soap shouldn't be sexy. In fact, it should be against the law…

"Camryn," he whispered.

Do. Not. Answer.

"Camryn, are you awake?"

Under any circumstances.

She sighed. The way he whispered her name had her insides turning into a combustible engine. "Yes, I'm awake." *Idiot!*

She rolled over and looked at him, seeing something in his expression that had her nervous. She'd hoped it wasn't for something else on his supposed list, 'cause for some reason, she couldn't tell him no either. Well, yeah she did. He was just more persistent than she was strong.

"I'm not going rock climbing in the middle of the night," she said. "Or tiptoeing through the tulips. Just for the record. I don't care if they're on your list or not."

His expression didn't change, but his jaw muscles tensed and loosened. "Why?"

Auntie Em was blaring from her stomach again. "What do you mean, why? Why what?"

"Why are you still awake?" he asked, his voice dangerously, deliciously low.

She didn't like where this was going. Or maybe she did. "I don't know, Troy."

As she said his name, his eyes closed as if in pain. "Yes, you do."

When he reopened them, she looked into his dark eyes, over his face. The inside of her mouth lost all moisture. "No, I don't." But she did. The tremor in her voice gave her away. And why was he baiting her?

In one swift, jarring move, he pushed her flat on her back, straddled her, and pinned her arms above her head. She wheezed in air. Her stomach brushed his. Skin to skin. Heat to heat.

"Yes, you do, Camryn. You're awake for the same reason I am. I need you to admit it. I went this far, meet me halfway. Make the next move."

Oh God, was this really happening? Was he really doing this? Everything south of her naval throbbed, wanting him inside her. His erection pressed against her belly, and that throb turned to a painful ache.

Please, please don't let this be another thing on his stupid list. An action to prove a point.

"Make a move, Cam."

His voice, barely above a whisper, pleaded. His eyes, so dark, demanded.

Don't think. For once in your miserable life, don't think.

She closed the distance between them and crashed her mouth to his.

Her head hit the pillow when he came down, pressing the full length of his body over hers. Arching, she deepened the kiss, opening to him. His tongue slid against hers, and everything inside her went mad. Her wrists fought his hold. Her legs wrapped around his waist.

Dropping her wrists, he reached for her tee, tugging it over her head without so much as a pause. It caught her hair before

149

he tossed it aside. He looked down at her breasts, her stomach, a determined eye examining what was before him.

No. No, don't look. Just touch.

When she crossed her arms over her chest to hide, he took her wrists again and held them at her side.

Every insecurity seeped out. He'd had so many women before her. She'd be no match for him. If Maxwell thought she was sexually retarded, Troy would too. After this, every time they saw each other, he'd look at her with disappointment. Remembering her as the one who didn't measure up. The grandest let down.

"Never cover up, Camryn."

Sobs wracked her chest, and she couldn't even have the decency to hide it. Add basket case who cried during sex to the mortification list.

Before a tear could fall, he let go of her wrists and cupped her face. He stared down at her. "It's just you and me, Cam. No one else. Get him out of your head."

Erratically, she nodded her head, sobs subsiding. "I'm sorry."

"Don't you dare. Don't you dare apologize to me." He took one of her hands and pressed it to his chest. Below her palm, his heart thumped violently. "That's for you. That's what you do to me."

He looked at her a second more, and lowered his head, kissing her with the same force but with more passion. More...everything.

Her chest eased, releasing the panic. She let go, wrapping her hands around his back, lower still to the elastic of his pajamas. As she tugged them down, she broke their kiss to place her mouth over the pulse on his throat. Bringing her leg up, she slid his pants down the rest of the way with her foot.

He rolled them to his side of the bed and fished inside his bag on the floor, drawing out a condom, then rolled them back so he covered her once more. His forehead dropped to hers. Their gazes locked as he brushed his knuckles over her belly, to her hips, and inside her boxers.

Every hair on her body stood erect, anticipating more. Fearing more.

Her boxers and panties skimmed off, down her thighs, across the room. He positioned himself between her thighs, the weight of him demanding, the feel of him so new. There was nothing between them now. Without separating so much as a centimeter, he donned the condom. His forearms pressed her hips in the act, causing an unraveling effect to every sensory nerve.

They were doing this.

Staring down at her, so intense she held her breath, he flicked a finger across her swollen wetness.

She gasped, closed her eyes, and arched off the bed to meet him. One of his hands slipped under her head, cradling her as his mouth closed over her throat. His other hand snaked behind her back, drawing them closer. She didn't think they could get any closer, and yet it wasn't close enough. She'd never felt such demand in her life.

When he entered her, stretching and filling her absolutely, there wasn't a trace of emptiness left inside. He groaned against her skin, part whimper, and all male. Her ache became tremors, the tremors became shudders, until her entire body tensed and erupted.

Her head flew back, a cry ready in her throat. His hand closed over her mouth, containing the noise, riding out the crest with her.

As her quaking ceased, he removed his hand and replaced it with his mouth. Fevered, frantic kisses that had her insides churning again. *Again.* She could feel the long, hard length of him, still pulsing, still wanting.

"Troy..."

"Not done," he murmured against her mouth.

Right. He wasn't done.

He broke away and looked down at her. "You're not done. I'm not done with you."

"Oh," she said, heart pounding, throat closing. *Oh.*

While watching her, he cupped her breast, brushed the pad of his thumb over her nipple. A stifled hum escaped her throat, and he moved inside her. His hand slid down, over her side, and locked on her hip. The other hand did the same, and her pelvis rose from the bed, thrusting him deeper.

So, so much deeper.

Her skin lit like fire, her bones liquefying. His mouth fell over her breast, biting, sucking, until the only thing she could do was hold on. She fisted her hands in his hair, dug her heels in his backside.

He cried out, the sound muffled by her breast, and as he pounded inside her, she came undone a second time. His arms slid between the mattress and her back, enfolding them together, closer yet. The rhythm he set was tormenting. Maddening. Without warning, she came a third time, and by then all she could do was whine.

He tensed, paused, and drove twice more before shuddering against her.

She laid there, jolted, exhausted, and humming with satisfaction, wondering how in the heck she'd gone this long without feeling like this. Troy didn't loosen his hold, didn't move one iota. She looked down at the top of his head, his cheek resting between her breasts.

"You're going to have to give me a minute, Cam."

"Um, all right." What was wrong with him? That was sheer amazement on her end. Was he let down? Was she *that* bad?

After pulling out, he disposed of the condom in the trash next to the bed, and rolled them so she was on top. "You surprise me. I don't surprise easily."

She rested her head on his chest, unable rationalize what happened. Everything just changed. Everything. He grabbed a fistful of her hair and lifted her head to look her in the eye. Feeling exposed, she swallowed and looked down.

"Don't do it, Cam. Don't shut down on me."

She shook her head as the room closed in. He may do this everyday, but she didn't. She wasn't used to someone holding her, giving her multiple orgasms. Being nice. She made a move to climb off, but he abruptly sat up, snaked an arm behind her back, and closed his mouth over hers.

Oh, his mouth. So much talent in his kiss.

Hating herself for being weak, she melted. He made her weak. No one had ever broken her down like that, made her feel bare and fragile. She was not fragile, darn it.

Returning his kiss, she held the solid mass of muscles bunching his shoulders. Arms that held her like she meant something to him. Like she meant more to him than sex. This kiss wasn't hot, frantic. It was slow, sweet. He was being sweet.

For how long? Until the next blonde came along? Until he got tired of testing the waters of ordinary?

She edged back and pressed her lips together so he couldn't kiss her again. "I'm just going to wash up. I'll...be right back."

He looked wounded, shocked. But to his credit, he dropped his hands to the mattress and nodded.

Troy watched Cam's retreating back, and then the bathroom door as it closed, wondering what in the hell just happened. He understood the great sex part, but immediately after, Camryn closed herself off. She all but had a panic attack.

Hearing the shower turn on, his gut sank. She was trying to wash him away.

He looked around the room, seeing her shirt by the balcony doors, her shorts near the closet, the condom wrapper on her nightstand. Standing, he disposed of the wrapper and picked up her clothes, bunching them in his hands.

He looked at the bathroom door in front of him, her clothes, the door again.

He braced his arms on the door frame and leaned into them. If he allowed himself to believe it, this entire trip had been building to this moment. To what he'd do, how he handled it.

And he'd finally met his match in Cam, 'cause he didn't know what in the hell to do with her, himself, or the feelings rising between them.

Closing his eyes, he knocked lightly on the door. "Cam?" She didn't answer, so he knocked again.

"I'll be out in a sec," she said. Back to calm, normal Camryn.

To hell with this. He was anything but calm. And she should be anything but. He opened the door, stepped inside, and dropped her clothes on the vanity. He yanked the shower curtain aside and stared at her as she fumbled to cover herself.

He made an exaggerated point to look down the length of her before speaking. "I've seen you naked. And I told you to never cover up."

"I said I'd be out in a sec. What are you doing?"

Since he didn't know, he asked her a question instead. "What was that in there?" He pointed toward the bedroom as if it were an antagonist. It was beginning to feel that way.

She had the gall to look confused. "Sex?"

His teeth gnashed. "After the sex."

"I..."

He sucked in a deep breath. "I, what, Cam?"

She looked away, swallowed, and stared at the water circling the drain. It dawned on him right there and then how vulnerable she looked. She wasn't calm at all. Dripping wet, yes. Exposed, yes. And...scared. Of him?

He stepped in the shower and closed the curtain behind him. Her eyes flew wide. Taking her hands in his, he laced their fingers and looked her in the eye. He leaned in to kiss her, and she backed away.

"Stop it, Troy."

"Stop what?"

She released his hands and covered herself again, all anger now. "Stop being so damn nice to me. You checked off another item on your list, so I don't need pillow talk and..."

"Did you just say...?" His teeth ground a second time as he grabbed her hands again. "I can't believe you. What happened in there was not on my list. I didn't just have sex with you because of a list..."

"Then why did you?" she asked, her tone pure anger but her eyes all grief.

She was serious. Completely serious.

"Because I wanted to. And so did you." She crossed her arms in another attempt to cover herself. Taking her wrists, he pinned them behind her and pressed her back to the tile. "Stop covering yourself. You're... Hell, you're beautiful, Cam."

A distressed sound rose from within her as she shook her head. "Let me go," she whispered. "Please, Troy, just let me go."

Hell no. He had a feeling people had been letting her go her whole life. He wouldn't be one of them. "What did this Maxwell guy do to you to make you like this?"

Her eyes glazed as she stared over his shoulder. "Nothing."

"Who then? Who made you like this? Where you can't trust even me?"

Her eyes drifted closed, tears flowing from them and onto her cheeks. Seeing her like this was humbling. And painful. This wasn't on his list, wasn't in his plan, but her crying had to be a good sign that she was letting him in. Letting someone in.

Kelly Moran

Finally.

"No one did this to me. I am what I am. Now, please, let me go."

He looked at her a second more and shook his head in defeat. He released her and stepped back, wanting to help her like she'd done for him all those years ago. He didn't want the help then, and she didn't want it now. Thankfully, she hadn't listened to him as a kid. She was there when he needed her, even if he didn't realize it at the time. He'd repay the favor.

But at some point, she had to let him. She had to give in. And she wasn't there yet. So he stepped out of the shower, dried off and left her alone.

Like every other worthless jerk had done.

Cam tiptoed downstairs, hoping not to wake the house. She was going to find a pint of ice cream if she had to make it herself. She didn't care if she fit into the bridesmaid dress or not. She didn't care if she gained a hundred pounds and had to use the handicap seat on the flight home, then waddle her way through life like a duck.

She was having ice cream. Middle-of-the-night ice cream. Pathetic.

Walking around the corner, she stepped into the kitchen and found Heather sitting at the island, eating ice cream.

"You better have saved me some. I'll kill without it."

Heather held out the carton. "I'll share. What are you doing awake?" Her question ended in a horrified gasp lasting ten seconds long. Her eyes bulged as she pointed an accusatory finger. "You slept with him!"

Darn sister of hers. "Troy? Of course. We're sharing a room. Sleeping together is required."

Heather's eyes narrowed, not amused in the least by her

156

sarcasm. "You know what I mean, Camryn!"

"Do you have sexdar or something?"

"You did. You slept with him!"

Camryn whipped a glance to the hallway and back again. "Would you keep it down? You'll wake up the house." She grabbed the cookie dough ice cream from her sister and sat down across from her, spooning a heapful into her mouth.

Mm, cookie dough.

"What does this mean? Are you dating for real?"

"Don't be ridiculous, Heather."

"Why is that ridiculous?"

Camryn raised her eyebrows in response, trying for Mom's I'm-not-too-old-to-spank-you look.

"How did it happen?"

"When a man and woman love each other..." She stopped short on her jab, realizing what she just said. There was no love involved between her and Troy. Not in the romantic sense. There never would be.

Heather didn't seem to notice. "Knock it off. Was he good? I'll bet he was good. He has a body like Thor."

Camryn passed her the ice cream, not having the heart to tell her Troy's body trumped Thor. And Green Lantern's. "Yeah, he was good." Not the correct adjective for what just went down upstairs, but it would do for this time of night.

"Then what are you doing down here eating ice cream? You only eat midnight ice cream if something's wrong." When she didn't answer, Heather bombarded her again like a fanatical reporter. "You freaked out, didn't you?"

"I did not freak out."

Heather passed the carton back to her. "You did too. You freaked out. Or you two had a fight. Make-up sex is the best. You should go upstairs and..."

Camryn had enough. She whipped a spoonful of cookie

dough ice cream at Heather. It landed dead center on her forehead, then plopped to the granite countertop.

Heather's jaw dropped. "Did you just throw ice cream at me?"

"Yes. I'm not sorry, either. You should shut up once in a while."

"I'm going to ignore that," she said, pretending to be dignified despite appearances otherwise.

Of course she'd ignore her. Everyone did. Heather wiped the ice cream off her face with a nearby napkin and stared at her long enough for Camryn to know another brilliant insight was forthcoming.

"You're different," Heather said in awe, as if talking to a psychic reading her palm.

"I am not."

"Yes, you are. You smile more. You joke around."

Camryn dropped her spoon in the carton and passed it back, losing her appetite for even her safety net. "Sarcasm is not joking. Sarcasm is a response to stupid."

"I think Troy is good for you."

"So are carrots, but you don't see me eating them." She needed a topic change, not that Heather would allow one. "What are *you* doing down here? You're not getting nervous about the wedding, are you?"

Heather shook her head. "Not nervous, just excited. And don't change the subject."

Camryn dropped her forehead to the counter. *Bang head here.* Raising her head, she stood. "I'm going back to bed."

"Cam, he's bringing out the best in you. Why not try with him?"

She sighed. "Heather, Troy and I have absolutely nothing in common. We're complete opposites."

"And where did dating someone you had things in common

with get you?" Suddenly her sister was Yoda. Heather stood and threw the carton away. "Besides, opposites attract."

"So do magnets until you flip them over."

Chapter Thirteen

Life Lessons According to Camryn:
Reputations are nothing more than history in rumor form.

Camryn finished rubbing sunscreen on Emily and capped the bottle. "Remember, no swimming alone. Someone has to be in the pool before you get in."

Emily nodded and bounded off. Camryn sat back in her lounge chair and closed her eyes, lifting her face to the sun. They were taking it easy today. The extended family and Heather's friends were due to fly in tomorrow. The Hortons had booked an entire floor at a hotel through the weekend.

Two more days and this would all be over. She just had to get through the rehearsal dinner, bachelorette party and the wedding.

"Camryn Covic," her mother shouted from across the pool. "Do you have sunscreen on?"

As if she hadn't lived in this skin for thirty years to know how easily it burned. "Yes, Mother. I let Emily put it on. I figured tiny white handprints in sunburn would go nicely with the lavender bridesmaid dress."

Troy laughed from his chair next to her.

"Is she trying to be funny?" her mother asked to no one in particular, her voice as shrill as an air raid siren.

"Trying, being the operative word," Fisher said.

"You better put more on," Mom insisted.

She wondered if they made SPF 3000 sunscreen, then she

could take a trip to the sun and away from here. She should email Coppertone to suggest it.

Before she could explain to her mother that she just applied SPF 50 ten minutes ago, Troy mumbled, "Here, I'll do it. It'll shut her up."

It was the first thing he'd said to her since the shower last night. Taking the bottle from between them, he straddled the chair behind her and rubbed the lotion over her shoulders and back. From behind her sunglasses, she closed her eyes and ordered herself not to respond to his touch. She'd responded enough last night.

When finished, he leaned forward. "We're having a talk tonight, Cam. Like it or not." Standing abruptly, he walked the few feet to the pool and dove in.

She swallowed, not liking the sound of that. Wishing on stars, dancing in the rain, and scaring the crap out of her with clowns was one thing, but talking was another. She couldn't hide from him, so whatever he wanted to discuss would most assuredly leave her vulnerable and bleeding. She didn't do talking. Not well anyway.

Emily walked to the edge of the pool and held her arms out for Troy. Grinning, he told her to jump. Scared, Emily shook her head. Troy assured her niece that he'd catch her, reminding Camryn of his experiment in the woods the other night. In response, Emily sat on the edge of the pool and slipped in. As promised, Troy caught her. Camryn watched them with a smile as Troy glided Emily through the water.

From the chair next to her, his cell chimed. "Troy, you have a text."

He deposited Emily in the shallow end and swam to her side of the pool, crossing his arms over the side. "Go ahead and check it."

She reached for the cell and touched the screen.

From Lindsay: Missing you in my bed. Can we get together

later?

Her stomach recoiled as she stared at the blatant reminder of why they could never be a couple. One of many reasons. She'd never even heard him mention Lindsay's name. He probably didn't even remember her.

"Who is it?" he asked.

She touched the screen to save the message for him. He'd want it once they were back in Milwaukee. And that shouldn't hurt this much.

"Spam."

He nodded, heading back to retrieve Emily and swishing her through the water.

"You know, Camryn," Tetaka Myrtle said, "you're going to get a tan line from the swimming suit straps."

And they weren't done discussing sunburns. Hooray. She looked down at her plain, white one-piece. She'd only been outside fifteen minutes, for crying out loud.

"You could borrow one of my suits," Heather suggested, just to make peace.

She was getting a little tired of that. Why did her sister always have to be the peacemaker? Why did there need to be a peacemaker? They were supposed to be a family. Families weren't supposed to be this neurotic.

"I have another suit without ties," she went on to say.

If Heather's strapless bikinis looked like kite string on her, they definitely wouldn't fit Camryn. "I'm fine, thank you."

"That's not a bad idea. Maybe you should," Kuma Viola said.

Troy lifted Emily out of the pool, and got out himself, standing next to Camryn while he dried off. "You're getting mad," he said for her ears only.

She shaded her eyes. "I'm around the loony bin escapees. I'm always mad. You just never noticed."

"Camryn, listen to them," her mother shouted.

"Stand up for yourself," he whispered.

"What are you talking about? I'm not starting a fight..."

"I didn't say fight. I said stand up for yourself." He crossed his arms, water dripping off his man candy body.

What did it matter if she stood up for herself or not? They'd never listen, and she'd just wind up with laryngitis.

Probably another thing on his list. Why would he care if she yelled back? If she did spontaneous things? Wished on stupid effing stars? What the crap was his idiotic list about anyway?

"Are you ignoring me?" her mother asked, voice as ear-piercing as ever.

Troy raised his brows, waiting on her. She peered around him to address her mother. "I'm trying to ignore you, but you're making that difficult."

Troy leaned over and braced his hands on her armrests. "Stand. Up. For. Yourself," he whispered. "And while you're at it, curse."

She glared at him. "I've had it with you and your list, Troy."

"Prove it," he challenged. "In all the years I've known you, I've never heard you curse. You probably censor the thoughts in your pretty little head too."

Pretty little... She ground her teeth. "Shut up, Troy."

"Or what?"

Emily climbed in her lap, soaking her dry suit. "Daddy's gonna wash your mouth out with soap for talking back. He tells me that all the time, but he never does." After this announcement, she got up and bounded back to Anna.

Her mother wasn't finished. "Camryn Covic, don't get sassy with me. We're trying to help..."

Troy spoke over her mother. "Curse, Cam. Stand up for yourself and..."

Camryn flew off her chair. "Enough!" she shouted, quieting the peanut gallery from hell. "I'm not a damn child. You needn't worry that I'll ruin Heather's wedding. No one will be looking at me, anyway. It doesn't matter if I have sunburn, or tan lines, or my hair shaved from stitches. No one ever sees me with her in the room." She glared at Troy, hands fisted. "Are you *fucking* happy now?"

Justin's dad exited the patio doors. "I'm ready to put the steaks on. How does everyone like theirs cooked?"

Camryn looked at him, the poor, poor man. "Better make mine a chicken breast, Tim. I'm already too fat for my dress. Mustn't rip the seams for Heather's big day."

Bending over, she whipped her beach towel from her chair and stalked into the house.

Troy dropped his towel to the cement, shaking his head and wanting to laugh. Cam had cursed. And fought back against her family's constant nagging. Check and check. Now they were getting somewhere.

He looked at Tim, standing near the grill with a pan of uncooked steak, wearing a man apron and looking shell-shocked. Troy picked up his cell and sat in the chair. "I like my steak medium-rare, Tim. And Camryn likes hers well-done."

"Troy Lansky," her mother said. "Why are you grinning?"

"Hey, just because Cam got mad and left doesn't mean you can harass me in her wake."

Heather looked at the other shocked faces. "I thought she was happy for us. I thought she wanted to be my maid of honor. Why is she so mad?"

Troy sighed. The family still didn't get it. "She is happy for you, she just doesn't understand why your wedding has become about her."

"I've never heard her swear before," Anna said. "It was like The Twilight Zone. I'm going to have nightmares."

Troy grinned, but Mom wasn't done. "I don't see why asking her to put sunscreen on upset her. She could get skin cancer."

Bernice, ever quiet until now, dropped her hand from her chest. "Perhaps asking her instead of telling her would be better received. If she had known you were worried about skin cancer and not what she looked like in her dress, maybe she wouldn't have gotten angry."

Well said, Bernice. She deserved a huge pat on the back for that one. Plus, it shut up Cam's mom. Not an easy task.

Troy tossed Dad the bottle of sunscreen, as his bald head was turning pink. Dad stared at it before saying, "What was this fat business?"

Troy wanted to know the answer to that too. Camryn had a beautiful body. After last night, he could attest to that firsthand. Hell, he'd never forget that body as long as he lived. All curves and lean muscle. She wasn't an anorexic model, but she was far from fat. She was normal, healthy...

He flashed back to their meals, and couldn't remember her finishing a plate of food. She'd eaten, but not as much as normal. Or was that normal for her? He'd never paid attention. Even on their Paris day, she'd only eaten one crepe, one croissant.

At the sound of voices, Troy looked up. Apparently over Cam's outburst, the family moved on to relaying to Tim how they wanted their steaks cooked, and arguing whether Nana could eat steak with dentures.

Troy touched his cell screen to pull up some music and tune them out when he saw he had a saved text. Wondering why Cam saved a spam note, he opened it.

Shit. Lindsay. He'd dated her two years ago for all of a week. Every once and awhile she'd booty text him when she was lonely or desperate. As always before, he sent her a message to decline.

Out of town. Also happily with someone else now. Best to

you.

Cam had seen this. He wondered how she felt about another woman, in the picture or not. After last night, he couldn't tell what she wanted. He thought she wanted him like he wanted her, disastrous as that may be.

She'd had no reaction as far as he could tell when she opened the text.

Either way, he warned her. They were going to talk. He would get some of his answers tonight.

They were all cowards, the lot of them. They'd sent Emily to her bedroom to fetch her for dinner. Only her family would use an innocent three-year-old as a buffer.

So there they were, sitting around the tables outside, eating dinner in silence. It was the craziest, most wonderful thing Cam had ever experienced. Silence from her family. Who knew? Troy had riled her to the point she'd lost it, defending herself, as he called it, *and* cursing. It wasn't something she planned on doing often, if ever again, but perhaps there was some merit to this list of his. Anything that could shut up the Covics couldn't be all bad.

What she'd really like to know was what Troy's motives were.

Camryn cut another bite of her perfectly cooked, well-done steak and slid it into her mouth.

"What's fucking mean?" Emily asked.

Nana spit out the baked potato she'd been chewing. Heather pounded her on the back as she coughed. Mom and Dad exchanged horrified looks. Bernice's jaw dropped to the picnic table. And Troy...laughed.

"Emily Covic," Fisher chastised, setting down his corn on the cob. "We do not use that language!"

Emily glanced around the table. "But Auntie Cam did! I want to know what it means!"

"Well," Anna said calmly, "when you get older I'll explain it."

"But I'm older than I was this morning!"

"Still not old enough," Tetaka Myrtle mumbled under her breath.

"I am too. I'm free years old," Emily argued, not helping her cause. "I'm not a baby."

"You'll always be our baby," Mom said, not helping the situation in the least.

Emily crossed her arms over her chest, huffing like Puff, the Magic Dragon on steroids. "It's not fair."

Fisher nodded. "Life's not fair. And we're done talking about this. Eat your dinner."

"I don't want to. I want to know what..."

"Eh hem," Cam interrupted, causing the collective whole to look at her. If it was one thing she learned from her niece, it was kids never forgot. They had a one-track mind. Emily would not let this go until she got an answer, no matter what the answer may be.

Cam finished chewing and said, "Fucking is a noun formed from a verb by adding the 'ing' suffix after it. A suffix of nouns formed from verbs expresses the action of the verb or its result, product and material. And your dad is right, it's a naughty word. So, I can trust you'll never say it again. Just like shit, hell and damn."

Nana's silverware clattered to her plate. The rest of the family stared at her in stunned silence, forks suspended in midair. They kind of resembled a paused movie. It was quite entertaining, actually.

Camryn took another bite of her steak and chewed. "The steak is very good, Tim."

"Um, thank you."

Emily looked at Fisher. "Why didn't you just say that?"

Justin laughed. "I'm not sure your dad even knows what Auntie Cam just said. I know I don't."

Cam looked at Troy out of the corner of her eye. He put a hand to his chest. "Camryn, that was the sexiest thing I've ever witnessed."

She thought he was joking until she fully looked at him. His dark eyes were three times the size of normal, and his mouth hung agape. Huh. He was as insane as the rest of them.

Yjaka Mitch grimaced. "Troy, come on..."

"No, seriously," he insisted. "*The* sexiest."

"It *was* kinda sexy," Justin mumbled, which received an honorary slap from Heather. "What? It was."

"What's sexist mean?"

Fisher rubbed his forehead. "Great, Troy. Thanks a lot."

"Not sexist," Heather corrected, "sex*iest*."

"Heather!" Fisher shouted.

Emily slammed her hands on the table. "*Well*, what does it mean?"

They all turned their heads to Camryn. "Cam, please tell her," Troy pleaded. "I can't wait to hear this one."

"Me either," Justin agreed, receiving yet another slap from Heather.

"We don't hit people, Auntie Heather! Use your words." Emily looked at Camryn again. "Tell me."

They'd always made fun of her in the past for having an intellectual brain. For being a plethora for useless knowledge. Now they were interested?

"Uh," she mumbled. "Sexy is defined as generally appealing and attractive. By adding the suffix 'est' it implies the most appealing or attractive of all."

Troy nodded. "Exactly."

"Is it a naughty word?" Emily asked.

Fisher pointed at Camryn with raised brows. "You be careful how you answer that, dear sister."

Camryn rolled her eyes. "No, Emily. It's not a naughty word, but it is a very adult word, so you should only use it when you're much older, and in the correct context."

Anna shook her head. "I'm so calling you when it's time to discuss the birds and bees."

"Why would you call Auntie Cam about birds and bees?"

"She means puberty, sweetie," Kuma Viola supplied.

"Damn it!" Fisher howled, causing Troy and Justin to laugh like drunk hyenas. "Would you all shut up? You're going to get her kicked out of preschool if she repeats this."

Emily stoically looked at her father, seeming much older than her years. "Auntie Cam said damn is a bad word. So don't say damn anymore. Right, Auntie Cam?"

Cam smiled. "Right, honey. Damn is a damn bad word. No more damning. Now, you should eat your damn dinner that Tim spent a damn hour grilling before it gets damn cold."

Fisher threw his head back and stared at the darkening sky as if praying to a higher power. Troy and Justin all but fell off their seats laughing. Justin was turning the same ugly shade of fuchsia as the shirt Heather bought her. Even Bernice was laughing from behind her napkin.

Emily and Camryn commenced to eating while everyone but Fisher giggled into hysteria. Eventually they calmed down and finished their meal as the waning light descended behind the mountains.

"What's puberty mean?"

Chapter Fourteen

Life Lessons According to Camryn:
Good conversation can be as rousing as espresso,
and just as hard to sleep after.

Troy trailed Camryn into their bedroom and kicked the door shut. Before she could take another step deeper into the room, he grabbed her arm, swung her around, and pinned her back to the wall. Cupping her cheeks, he stared into her widening eyes.

"Did you see what happened at dinner?" he asked. "You had them all laughing. You were hilarious."

"Yes, I saw them," she said, placing her hands over his. He thought she was going to remove them, but instead she interlaced their fingers and dropped them to her side. "All but Fisher, who will kill me later." She paused. "Thank you," she whispered.

A rigid thump pounded inside his chest as he looked at her. Cam thanking him was a huge leap, and not an easy one for her to make. "You're welcome. I meant the other thing I said too. How you diffused Emily and her questions was damn hot."

A doubtful look crossed her face. "Uh huh. Reciting definitions and basic grammar lessons gets me all hot and bothered too."

He leaned into her and grabbed her hips. "Joke all you want, but I'm serious. No one else could've done that. All that knowledge locked in your head is fascinating. You never forget anything."

Her head tilted as she eyed him. "You're increasing insanity is alarming."

See, right there. Even the way she talked had him hard. "Define insanity."

"Excuse me?"

His gaze dropped to her mouth and he moaned. She still smelled like lemongrass. He wondered if it was her shampoo or some kind of body wash. It wasn't fruity or girly, just clean. Fresh. "What is the definition of insanity?"

She stared at him a second more before answering. "By definition, insanity is a derangement of the mind. But Einstein said, 'Insanity is doing the same thing over and over again and expecting different results.'"

Air seeped from his lungs. It physically hurt how bad he wanted her. "Then I am insane, Cam, because I want you. Now. Over and over again. Without the shut down like last night."

Without the inevitable way this is going to end.

Her lips parted as she breathed, her gaze taking in every aspect of his face before looking into his eyes. "I make it a rule not to sleep with crazy men."

His mouth quirked into a half-smile. "Make an exception, just this once."

He dropped his hands and walked to his bag by the bed, pulling out a condom, and then walked back to her.

She looked at the condom, then up at him. "Here?"

Oh God, yes. Against the wall. Upside down. In a tree. He didn't give a damn, just so long as he had her. "Yes, here."

"There's a perfectly good bed right there."

Flattening both palms on the wall, he smiled and pressed his body to hers. "And there's a perfectly good wall right here."

He leaned in to kiss her, stopping just before touching her mouth so he could watch her eyes haze with passion. Before last night, he didn't think Camryn had that much passion inside her. Oh, how wrong he was. It only proved to solidify his desire to show her everything she locked away. Everything she thought she wasn't.

"I love that look on your face. You know that?" Her eyes cleared as she stared at him, confused. Surprised. "The look you have when you forget to breathe."

To get the look back, he slid his fingers up her thigh, under her dress, and inside the waistband of her panties. Almost...there. Tugging her panties down, he watched her eyes widen. Such big damn beautiful eyes. He unzipped and dropped his jeans. He left them around his ankles until he helped her step out of her underwear, and then he kicked his aside. Purposely being methodical, he grinned as she watched. For once, she didn't seem ashamed.

He rolled the condom on, keeping his eyes locked on hers. Almost...there. She pressed her hands to the wall behind her as if bracing herself, holding herself upright. He tugged off his shirt and threw it aside. She stared at his chest through lowered lids, as he watched her pulse beat hard against her throat.

He stepped closer, brushing his skin with the fabric of her dress. Her nipples pebbled in response. She sucked in a breath and held it, arching toward him. He touched a strand of her hair, sliding it through his fingers and inhaling lemongrass before letting it fall to her cheek.

It was the shampoo. He'd never smell anything like it again without thinking of her, right now, like this.

This throbbing for her had begun with that first kiss in the yard, and it hadn't stopped after last night. For unknown reasons, burying himself deep inside her, watching her come over and over, hadn't satiated this desire for a woman he shouldn't want. Tonight wouldn't stop it either, yet he was doing it anyway.

And she wasn't stopping him.

Almost there. His hands dove under her dress, cupped her backside, and spread her thighs. She gasped, wrapping her legs around his waist. Her hands held his shoulders, kneading the muscles with tense fingers. She'd done that every time he kissed her, and again last night during sex. One of many things she did that shoved him over the edge.

He paused near her opening, watching her eyes, wanting. His mouth hovered over hers, waiting...

There.

"That look right there, Cam. Just beautiful," he whispered, closing his mouth over hers and thrusting inside.

She cried out, the sound contained by his kiss. *So hot.* Her fingers squeezed his shoulders before fisting in his hair. *Oh, so hot.* Then her heels dug into his back, drawing him as deep inside her as humanly possible, and damn...

He absolutely lost it. Gone.

There was no finesse now, only raw animal instincts. He braced one forearm on the wall and drove into her with everything he had, until her body tensed and he felt her clench and tighten around him.

He'd been with a lot of women, but none of them came like Camryn. Fast, fevered, and with all the emotion she tried to bottle. Cam made him *want* to wait, teetering on that brink between torment and release. To pleasure her over and over just to watch the mystery of her.

He tore his mouth away from her kiss to suck in air, only to bury his face in the soft skin behind her ear. Clutching the back of her neck, he listened to her squeak out a moan, and felt her shuddering, rocking against him before he emptied completely.

Swallowing, he wrapped his arms around her, utterly shaken. He stood holding her longer than it took for them to do the deed.

"Dear God, Cam," he said, unable to speak more. She made

a noncommittal sound of agreement.

Before his legs could give out, he carried her to the bed and sat her in his lap. He disposed of the condom and unzipped her dress, wanting her skin against his. Her arms came up without question, allowing him to pull the dress over her head.

She shivered, so he reached behind her and wrapped a blanket around them. Keeping her straddled on his lap, he leaned against the headboard as she dropped her cheek to his chest. This was so much better than chasing her into the shower. Though maybe later...

"This takes getting used to," she said.

He looked down at the top of her head. "What does?"

"This cuddling stuff."

"You don't usually cuddle after sex?" She didn't answer. "I told you we were going to talk tonight, Cam."

She lifted her head. "Is that why we had sex? So you could loosen my tongue to check off your list?"

He bit down until his molars ground. "I said it before, and I'm only saying this one more time. Sex with you isn't an agenda, Camryn. I do it because I want to."

Or because somewhere inside I have to.

She looked at him, probably considering if the information was worth storing in her brain. He wondered how many more times they had to have sex before she believed him.

He sighed. "We'll play twenty questions. My rules. Twenty questions, and you have to answer all of them honestly."

She dropped her chin to his chest. "What part of this is on your list?"

He kept it simple. "To spill your guts."

"Spill my guts," she repeated dully. "Fine. I'll play your game if I get to ask you questions also. No limit."

He didn't like the sound of that. No doubt she'd outsmart him, but fair was fair. Depending on what she asked, maybe his openness would encourage her.

He nodded. "I'll go first. Answer my question from before. You never cuddle after sex?"

Her eyes lost their edge. "No."

He waited for her to elaborate, but she didn't. He realized it wasn't her who didn't want to have the intimacy, but the men she was with. Over the years she'd grown accustomed to sex as more an act than joy.

"You've never been held after sex?" She shook her head. "Is that the reason you shut down last night?"

She shrugged, but nodded her head. He knew that wasn't the entire story, but he let it slide for now.

"Don't do that," she whispered. "Please don't feel sorry for me, okay? Not everyone is as emotionally open as you."

"Trust me, it's not pity I'm feeling."

"You asked three questions. It's my turn."

Nice try. "Asking for elaboration on an answer isn't an additional question."

Her eyes narrowed. "That wasn't stipulated in the rules."

He smiled. "It is now. Ask your question."

"Who's Lindsay?" Not even a hesitation.

Interesting first question, and that another woman would be in her head. Was she jealous? He didn't think Cam capable of such a raw emotion. "A woman I dated briefly a year ago."

Her eyebrows lifted. "And you're still sleeping with her?"

"No. Why did Emily call you ugly?"

Her gaze darted down, then back to his. A battle waged over her face until she reluctantly answered. "She overheard me say it."

Troy's suspicion all along, though he'd hoped otherwise. He had mistaken her insecurity as confidence. "Explain."

She stared at his chest. "I was trying on the revolting

garments Heather bought for me in the boutique. This was after they made me highlight and cut my hair. I mumbled, 'you can't fix ugly,' to myself. Emily heard."

"You don't think…"

"My turn," she said, cutting him off. "How many women have you been with?"

What was with all the questions on his dating life? "A lot. Not as many as you'd think, however."

"You never wanted to marry any of them? Do you even remember their names?"

That sounded like an insult wrapped in a question. "No, I never wanted to marry any of them. And yes, I remember all of their names. Karen was the first, in the backseat of her car after Homecoming. There's no sense in going through them all, but I do remember each of them. They were all special, but not right for me in the long term."

She looked at him with genuine surprise. "You cared about them, didn't you?"

"Yes. You don't seriously think you're ugly, do you?"

She sighed. "Ugly is a strong word…"

He pushed off the headboard, sitting upright, and looked into her eyes. "Answer the question, Cam. Do you think you're ugly?"

She grabbed the sheet from next them and climbed off his lap. With way too much focus, she wrapped herself in the sheet and lay back. It was as much of an answer than if she'd outright said…

"Yes. Well, no. Not ugly, but not beautiful either. I'm average. One of those people that others pass by and hardly notice. I used to like it that way."

His gaze whipped to her, studied her, but she wouldn't look in return. He'd notice her in a room full of women, even if they'd never met. She stood out that much. Somewhere along the way she got used to hiding. This gave him several ideas for his list.

"You're not, Cam. You're *not* ugly. Whoever told you...?"

"What happened that day?" she asked, cutting him off yet again to take the focus off of her. Her tone softened when she clarified. "The day they took your dad away for good?"

His jaw dropped, but he snapped it shut before she looked at him with her huge eyes. His hand flew to his stomach, not expecting her to go there. Her gaze dropped to his hand and back to his eyes.

"Jesus, Cam..."

She sprang to a sitting position. "I'm sorry. I...I always wanted to know. The caseworker just said he was getting locked away for a long time. You were eighteen, but she came to our house anyway, and asked if we'd take you in until you finished high school."

He ran a hand over his face, but the images wouldn't disappear. He was expecting honesty from her, she deserved his. Maybe talking about his past would take the pain away. Or much, much worse, show her just how bad it still hurt.

He swallowed, praying he wouldn't cry and make an ass of himself. "Remember my birthday that year? You and Heather came by the house with a gift. A new shirt and a cake." She didn't answer, so he looked at her, seeing the only person he'd dare to tell this to. "I don't even remember what kind of cake..."

"Strawberry shortcake," she said. "I remembered it was your favorite, so Heather and I made one."

"It was my first and only birthday cake."

Her eyes bulged. "Excuse me?"

"Dad wasn't domestic." He shrugged it off, like everything else. "His memory wasn't great either, especially on Christmas and birthdays."

"But we celebrate your birthday every year at home."

"Without a cake. My request of your mother."

She looked around the room, not seeing anything, but

trying to remember. He could tell just by watching her that the gears were turning. While she was distracted, he blurted out the rest.

"He shot the cake with a hunting rifle and blew a hole clean through the new blue shirt before raising the gun on me. A neighbor heard the shots and called the police."

Her hands fisted in the sheets. "I almost got you killed?"

Leave it to her to conclude that by this conversation. "No, *he* almost killed me. You played no part in his drunken tirades. The whole year had been building to that point. He'd been drinking more than ever. I had enough sense to run to my bedroom, but he followed. It was the stupidest thing I could've done. He saw the things your family had given me through the years. I tried to save them instead of myself."

She clutched the sheet to her chest, tears spilling onto her pale cheeks. "What things did you try and save? What was more important than running away, Troy?"

She'd never understand, no one would, yet he told her anyway. "Fisher's old tackle box from the first time we went fishing. The Christmas ornaments from Heather. A book Nana gave me." *A little blue Matchbox truck from you, which I still, to this day, carry in the glove compartment of my car.*

Slowly, her head shook. "You don't think we would've been mad, do you? You're more important than some stupid stuff."

"They weren't stupid. Not to me."

As her tears dried, recognition dawned. He should've known Cam would understand. Never underestimate her, never. Perhaps this was why he never talked about it, so she didn't feel that kind of fear and emptiness too. She stared at him so long he felt like he was ten again and trying to be strong in front of her. When he looked down, her hands were shaking.

"Because they were the only nice things someone did for you, so you tried to save them," she said, her voice flat. "It was bad, wasn't it? Worse than I ever thought. What did he do,

Troy? I want to know."

This game was getting out of control. "No, you don't."

Her beautiful cherubic face transformed into a hardened, sad version he wanted erased. To never see on her again. "Tell me."

He rubbed the back of his neck, trying to find a way to tell her without reliving it. "It started with food. He'd hold it over me for control. Not feed me as punishment. Stupid things like not wearing a hat to school or leaving toothpaste in the sink. When I got old enough, he'd punch or hit instead, often with whatever was available. There was usually no reason for those outbursts. Sometimes it would only be a few hits, sometimes I couldn't stand after. If I yelled, it was worse. He was smart enough not to leave bruises where anyone would see, that's how he got away with it for so long. One day, he went too far and broke my arm. Social Services stepped in, and I was dropped off on your doorstep."

When silence filled the room, he finally looked at her, expecting pity or contempt. Instead, he found tears again. Hers and...his. He swiped a hand over his face.

"I should've done more," she whispered.

The tremor in her voice had him stumbling to stop his tears. "No."

She looked him straight in the eye and must've seen something in his expression. She tried to subdue a sob, but couldn't. As her tears pooled and fell, his chest cracked watching her. "I should've done more, Troy."

"You did everything," he said, grabbing her arms and shaking her. "Don't you get it? I was damn lucky compared to most. It's rare to be placed with the same foster family. In the end, I think I spent more time at your place than mine. Your parents took me in, gave me a home. Your brother was the first friend I ever had. Heather drove me crazy, finally having a little sister around to bug me and help me forget. She made me feel normal. And you..."

Oh, Camryn. She didn't even know how much she meant to him. There were no words.

"Me?"

Yes, her. "You got my ass out of bed and made me go to school. You helped me with homework. You made me sandwiches and...and never told anyone the things you saw or heard. You told me I could do things, made me think I was somebody."

That was the damndest part. Camryn made him feel like a somebody, when inside he was just no one. The only time in his life he felt worthy of anything was when she was around. He'd spent the better part of his life in pursuit of that feeling, only to realize now she was the reason for it. He let go of her arms and sat back.

He never should've touched her in the first place.

"That's what this list is about, isn't it, Troy? Payback for being nice to you? Some twisted form of thanks?"

Yes. No. Partly. It may have started out that way, but it wasn't why he was doing it now. "No. And don't you pity me now."

"Troy..."

She swallowed, reaching out and cupping his cheeks, her hands so warm compared to how cold he'd become. The pads of her thumbs swiped the remnants of tears, reminding him of just how weak his father could still make him feel. Leaning over, she kissed each cheek, and as her lashes fluttered across his face, he had the sickening thought that this was as good as it would get for him. A temporary someone like Cam who could cry for him freely, but was ashamed to for herself. Who thought only of him and not herself.

Someone who took the cold away.

No one had ever cried for him before. "Cam, stop crying. Please."

Her fingers clutched his biceps as she pressed a kiss to his chest, right over his heart. He closed his eyes and slid his fingers into her hair.

"I don't pity you," she said. "I'm killing your bastard father in my head."

The painful knot in his gut began to loosen, his throat not so tight. "What?"

She looked at him, the pillar of poise he was used to seeing from her before this trip. "It's what I do."

"You kill people in your head?"

She smiled, and the knot disappeared. "No. When situations get overwhelming, I envision things in my head so I can't overreact."

Now that explained a lot. "Give me an example."

She stared at his chest. "When Maxwell broke up with me, I wanted to cry, but instead I pictured him with horns and hooves. It always works." She looked at him. "Except with you."

Huh. "Why not with me?"

She shrugged. "Your stupid list, I guess. Or you..."

He wondered if it worked before the list, but even he wasn't sure he was ready for the answer. "Or what?"

"Or you just bother to look deeper. See past my defense," she said.

"For the record, Maxwell was wrong about what he said to you."

She shook her head, closed her eyes. "Whose turn is it?"

"Mine," he said, wanting to turn this back on her. "Where did you get this image of yourself? Why the walls and pretending to be composed?"

She shrugged. "I don't know. Maybe watching Heather cry her way out of everything as a child. Or disgust for these women who refuse to stand on their own, spending more time worrying about eye shadow and fall colors than the six o'clock news."

"I get your independence and intelligence, Cam. In fact, I respect it. But why the walls?"

Looking down, she shrugged again. "I grew up hearing nothing but how beautiful Heather was. How handsome Fisher was. When your friends come over just to drool over your brother, and your prom date spends the night hitting on your sister, then leaving with someone else, it does things to a girl's head."

How did he not know this? Right under his face and still no clue.

"Where's your mother?" she asked.

He almost got whiplash. "Um, she went to prison when I was two. For prostitution. She died of an overdose there."

"Do you remember her?"

"No." And perhaps that's why he had no feelings on the subject. "How many men have you been with?"

Troy had no idea where the question came from, or why he asked, but suddenly he had to know if every guy treated her like Maxwell had. If any of them bothered to show her love, or whether they just walked out like her damn high school prom date.

"Two."

"Two," he repeated, the concept foreign. "Two including me?" Oh God, could it be he was only the second person she'd been with?

"Three, including you."

With the sheet around her, she got up and walked across the room, grabbing her panties off the floor. After slipping them on, she went in search of pajamas. She only bothered with the shirt, leaving the boxers on her bag. While he watched, she hung her dress in the closet, and climbed back in bed to lie on her side, facing him.

"Did you love either of them?" he asked, laying down and facing her. He propped his head on his hand.

"Both. I don't have sex unless..." She stopped short and slapped a hand over her mouth. "Well, I guess I do have sex without love. Or just this time. I mean, I don't love you. You know, not like that."

If he wasn't so amused at her babbling he might've been insulted. And hurt. "Not like what?"

"Not like car shopping and sharing a bank account kind of love."

He stared at her. This list was either teaching her nothing, or she was lying. "Don't you mean happily ever after and two point five kids?"

"How do you have point five kids?"

"Is that your next question?" he asked, smiling. He liked this side of her, just before she fell asleep, when her voice was lulling, her eyes heavy, and she smiled without thought. She was so lovely it hurt.

"No. Did you love any of the women you slept with?"

Before he could answer, her eyes drifted closed. In seconds she was asleep. He watched her, a thousand thoughts swimming through his head, none of them appropriate or sound where he and Cam were concerned.

Facts were facts, and feelings were feelings. He'd gone and fallen in love with her. He'd probably been in love with her all along.

He wasn't most men. The thought didn't scare him into a blind panic. But it did make him want this list to work. Needed this list to work. Because otherwise, Cam would continue down her same sensible path of life she always had before, and marry someone who didn't love her an eighth of how much he did. She wouldn't know how precious a gift love truly was.

And he'd go back to dating woman after woman, hoping one of them might make him feel a semblance of how she made him feel. She'd wind up becoming the one who got away, the one he never got over. Like some Hemmingway poem.

He'd waited almost thirty years to finally feel like this, knowing it existed and wanting nothing more than to get there. And he fell for Camryn.

Here he was, a nobody pretending to be a somebody, and her, a someone pretending to be a no one. He lived his life day by day because that's all he could handle, and she planned everything down to what color underwear to wear on Thursday.

Glancing down, he smiled. Purple underwear today. Very nice.

Slowly, to not wake her, he lifted the sheet and draped it over her, then did the same with a blanket, tucking it under her chin. He brushed a strand of hair away from her cheek, letting his fingertips linger when it didn't disturb her.

Closing his eyes, he shook his head. "I only loved one of them."

Chapter Fifteen

Life Lessons According to Camryn:
Other people's opinions should matter, just not to you.

Camryn pulled a batch of blueberry muffins from the oven and set another in to bake. After a few hours of fitful sleep, she gave up trying at three and came downstairs.

The conversation with Troy last night still had her hands shaking, her heart hurting. Troy's childhood had been far worse than she ever thought. Through the years, she tried not to think about what he must have gone through. He seemed fine now. But as she watched him last night, trying to hide the obvious tears, she knew it wasn't over for him. Not by a long shot. No wonder he didn't take life seriously, why he moved from one woman to the next.

She wondered what number she was on his very long list of lovers. Wondered how she rated compared to them.

She'd never had sex like that, not that she had much to compare to. Troy made her forget everything but him and her. She'd never been able to shut down like with him. Just feel. The world fell away, and they were just two people, enjoying each other. He made her believe, for just a little while, that he meant the things he said. Like she was actually beautiful and funny instead of ordinary. She closed her eyes. He even had *her* believing the illusion.

In the early morning hour, before sunrise, she allowed herself the fantasy of them. Still together once home in Milwaukee, maybe living together, doing everyday things like arguing about whose turn it was to do the dishes. Sharing their day over dinner, and then making love half the night. Slow dancing nude in a silent room, pretending to hear music lofting in from an open window. He'd say something silly, and she'd laugh until the breath was gone from her lungs.

She opened her eyes to reality. Troy and his list were cruel. Making her think these things were real, possible. Life wasn't like that.

Reality was her relationship with Maxwell. Having sex in the same position, sex that could be timed by the reliability in his movements. Him leaving right afterward without so much as a kiss on the top of her head or a good-bye. Dinner conversations about whether a condo would be more commonsensical than a yardless two-bedroom ranch. About the strategy for their next meeting. No whispered endearments late at night. No laughing under the stars. No kind words.

"Whatcha doing?"

Camryn jumped and pressed a hand to her pounding heart as she looked down at Emily. "Shh, everyone is still asleep. I'm making muffins. Do you want to help?"

Muffins weren't a birthday cake, or a mend for his past, but maybe he'd smile.

"Yeah," Emily said, climbing onto a stool by the island.

Camryn set a bowl in front of Emily and handed her a whisk. After adding the dry and wet ingredients for a new batch, she said, "Okay, stir that together now."

Emily stuck the whisk in the bowl and tried to stir. Apple cinnamon muffin mix went flying onto the counter. "Oops."

At least this batch didn't have blueberries. Camryn smiled, placing her hand over Emily's and demonstrating how to stir. "Like that, honey."

She moved over to the coffee maker to start a pot while keeping an eye on her niece. Once brewing, she checked Emily's progress. "Good job. I'm going to run upstairs for a second. Stay away from the oven, okay?"

Though Emily nodded her consent, Camryn set the self-cleaning latch to lock the oven in case her niece got any wild ideas. She scribbled a note on a piece of scrap paper, then carried a muffin and the note upstairs.

She turned the knob to their bedroom and tiptoed to the nightstand. She set the note and muffin down and peeked at a sleeping Troy. On his stomach, his arms and legs were sprawled over the bed like he'd been practicing skydiving in his sleep. Shaking her head and smiling, she quietly closed the door on the way out.

Emily was still hard at work stirring when she returned to the kitchen. "It looks good. It's missing something, though."

Emily thought that over. "Chocolate?"

Tempting. "Hmm. No, not chocolate. I know! It's not the batter missing something, it's you."

Emily looked down at herself as if she forgot to get dressed. "What?"

"This," she said, lifting the whisk and drizzling a tiny bit of batter on her head.

Emily smashed her hands on her head, smearing the batter into her curls. She then proceeded to wipe her hands on the front of her pajamas. "*Oooh.* Daddy is going to be so mad. I'm telling on you."

Camryn bent over and kissed her cheek. "Go ahead. I'm older than him, I can take it."

Emily eyed her through speculative eyes. Cautiously, she dipped her finger in the bowl, and then dabbed it on the end of Camryn's nose. She paused, waiting to get yelled at.

"You're doing it all wrong." Camryn stuck her hand in the bowl and smeared the mix over her cheeks. At least she'd smell good today. She wiped the remainder of the batter from her hand into her own hair. "See, like that."

Emily giggled and pointed. "You look ridoc...redunk..."

"Ridiculous," she corrected. "You do too."

187

Her niece stopped laughing and tilted her head, staring Camryn down. After a long examination, Emily asked, "Did you remember where you lost your smile?"

"I don't know what you mean, honey."

"Uncle Troy said the reason you don't smile is because you just lost it for a little while. Did you find it? He said you would."

Troy said that? "Yeah, I guess I did." She grinned for effect, and for once, the expression didn't feel foreign on her face.

"Oh, my goodness," Anna said, coming into the kitchen. "Would you look at you two!"

"Auntie Cam did it, honest!"

Anna looked doubtful, so Cam saved her niece. "It's true. All me. Sorry."

Anna started looking at her with the same speculative glare as her daughter, so Camryn turned and filled the last muffin tray for the oven, then began placing the finished muffins in a bowl. After setting them on the table, she poured herself a cup of coffee and turned to Anna, who was wiping batter off Emily's face while grinning.

"Anna, would you mind taking that last batch out when the timer goes off? I'm going to sit out on the patio for awhile."

"Sure," she said, looking at her as if addressing a stranger. "You okay, Cam? Perhaps a shower or...more sleep?"

Camryn shrugged. "Later maybe."

Jackie, one of the Hortons' staff, came in the back door and set her keys down on the counter. She glanced around the kitchen, then paid particularly close attention to Camryn. "You made breakfast?"

"Emily and I did, yes. Do you mind? I couldn't sleep."

She smiled, waving her hand. "Of course not. I'll just...clean up, then." She looked around the kitchen as if expecting a clan of cockroaches to waltz by.

Camryn loved to cook, and she usually wasn't this messy

about it. Even though it looked like she got caught in a Duncan Hines explosion, the kitchen was pretty clean. "There's only the muffin pans and the mixing bowl to wash." Camryn smiled at Emily. "Everything else got on us." She looked back at Jackie. "Would you like help?"

"Oh no. Thank you." The look on her face pleaded, *please don't.*

Anna tossed the washcloth in the sink. "I'll take Emily upstairs for a bath."

Jackie got to work on the pans, so Camryn slid the patio door on its rail and stepped outside with her coffee. Watching a pink sunrise over the horizon, she sat down and took a deep breath. Another first for her.

A quiet mind.

The house was so far back from the main road that there wasn't a car to be heard. A woodpecker tapped in the distance. A whippoorwill called out, the sound oddly relaxing. She was used to noise. Car horns. Irate morning commuters. At the very least, church bells from down the street when in Milwaukee. She didn't know whether to find the quiet peaceful or disturbing.

Her dad came outside twenty minutes later. He halted before reaching a nearby chair, staring at the caked batter in her hair and on her face.

She shrugged. "I ran out of soap."

His mouth hung open. Then he laughed and sat down next to her. He took a cautious sip of coffee and glanced at the mountains. "What are you doing out here without a book or a laptop?"

"Just sitting."

"Did you have a fight with Troy?"

"No."

"Nana? What did she say now?"

Camryn smiled, looking at his bald head and narrow face. "Nothing, Dad. I'm just sitting."

"Never known you to just sit."

She drank the last of her coffee, pretending not to notice him staring at her.

"You know, Camryn, one Easter Sunday, you must have been nine or ten, your mother dressed you in one of those fluffy pink dresses for church. Everyone said how beautiful you looked. They gushed over you. You stomped your foot and screamed. You claimed you didn't want to be beautiful, you wanted to be smart."

She didn't remember this at all. Furthermore, she was wondering what this had to do with just sitting outside. "And?"

When her dad looked at her, she had to catch her breath. He looked lost. Ashamed. "And I didn't understand how to tell you that you could be both. Smart *and* beautiful. You were so adamant, so insulted, that we never dared bring it up again. Every once in a while we'd say you looked nice, but you'd get this look on your face like we'd hurt you. Before long, we just stopped saying it."

Her fingers had gone numb, her heart rate slower than molasses in winter. "What are you getting at, Dad?"

His gaze met hers. "I never should've stopped saying it. I think you misunderstood our intentions. You *were* beautiful. And smart. You still are, always were. But now, you don't know that anymore, do you?" He shook his head. "I'm very sorry."

Her mouth trembled open, his face blurring before her eyes as tears formed. "Dad?"

Rising, he looked around, patted his pockets, and then settled his gaze back on her. "That's all I wanted to say. I wanted you to know." He checked his watch. "Do you know if the Brewers won?"

She laughed, wiping the tears away. "I don't know."

Nodding, he went to head inside. Before hitting the door, he paused, but didn't turn. "I've never seen you look more beautiful than right now, covered in baking...whatnot and wearing pajamas. A smile looks good on you." He turned fully to face her. "Do we have Troy to thank for that?"

No words formed, so she just stared at him as he saluted her with a coffee cup and went in.

Blowing out a breath, she sat back in her chair. She'd told Troy that people don't change. It was something she firmly believed in. So why was she having long, deep midnight conversations and painting herself with muffin batter? Why was her family making a big deal of how she was behaving? It wasn't so different from her usual self, was it?

Troy was making her do things, say things, feel things she normally wouldn't. No man had her smiling first thing in the morning, looking forward to bed at night just to see what evil, funny idea he had in store next. She was finding herself thinking about him when he wasn't around, wanting his opinion on things.

As far back as she could remember, she'd always cared about Troy. But now she wanted to hold his hand and kiss away the pain. Make love every waking second. She'd told him things last night she wasn't even sure she was aware of. She was positive he never talked about his father with anyone. What had changed? Where was this coming from?

Troy still hadn't told her what this list was about, but it was shifting things, not just between them, but inside her. He was making her... happy.

Swiftly, she stood and headed inside before she allowed herself to dream. Dreams and wishes were dangerous. They allowed a person illusions, uprooting facts and replacing them with empty, unrealistic desires. Dreams weren't any more real than the idea she and Troy could be more.

When she opened the door, the family froze, staring at her as she entered the kitchen. Okay, she was a big mess. In more ways than one. "I'll go shower," she mumbled.

"Hold on," Fisher said, closing the fridge. He set his glass of orange juice down on the counter. "What's going on with you and Troy?"

She looked around at the faces in the room, frozen solid as her skin prickled like tiny ice shards. Did they know this was all a lie, and if so, how? *Oh, please. No, no.* They only had two more days to get through. Just two and everything would be back to normal. Bleak, boring and normal. She looked at Heather, but her sister only shrugged.

"What do you mean?" Camryn asked, hoping the tremor wasn't obvious to everyone.

"Troy came downstairs this morning claiming he wasn't hungry and just wanted to go for a run."

Camryn looked at her brother in shock. Did her gesture with the note and muffin upset Troy? She wanted him to wake up smiling, like she had. Wanted to do something nice to say...

"A run?" she repeated, not understanding the information.

"That's what *I* said," Nana claimed. "People should only run if they're being chased."

"A run," Fisher confirmed.

Her mother set down her muffin in front of her at the table. "I don't see what the big deal is. Does he usually go jogging in the morning?"

"I..." Well, she wasn't sure. It wasn't as if they were really dating. "I don't know."

"You don't know?" Tetaka Myrtle asked. "Aren't you his girlfriend, Camryn?"

They looked at her, accusing, questioning. This whole thing was going to blow up in their faces. The family would spend the rest of the weekend screaming and belittling her for not only lying, but for hurting Troy. She was hoping to be back in Milwaukee when this "breakup" was to occur. That was the plan.

"They don't live together," Heather said. Loudly. "I mean,

she's been in Chicago and he's in Milwaukee. She wouldn't know if he jogs. Right, Cam?" Heather's eyes bulged, forcing Camryn to agree.

"Yes, right."

Fisher was looking angrier and angrier by the second. "The only time I remember him running is to blow off steam. That I'm aware of, he hasn't done it in years. So what did you do, Camryn?"

What did *she* do? Why is it always something *she* did wrong? Troy couldn't be this upset over a note and a muffin. Or maybe he was. If he only went jogging when angry, and he was sleeping when she last checked, it had to be about her. God, the last thing she wanted to do was hurt him.

"I didn't do anything. I'm going to shower."

"Don't you want some breakfast?" Kuma Viola asked.

"I'm not hungry," she said, rounding the corner and climbing the stairs before her stomach could revolt.

Troy's feet pounded the gravel in a steady pace alongside the road. Sweat dripped from his face and onto his soaked tee. His legs had started burning over a mile back, but he didn't stop. He was too out of shape for this. The last time he went running was his father's birthday last year. Memories had crept up, and the only thing he could do to expel them was to run.

It had worked then. It wasn't working now.

Camryn had been doing these little things for him half his life. Buying him peanut butter, framing a family photo, giving him a toy truck. Things to remind him of better days, to keep looking forward. That she cared. But what she did this morning was different. So very different.

Leaving a muffin with a birthday candle in it on his nightstand. It wasn't even his birthday, just something nice to replace the bad memories. A memory only she knew, the only person whom he told. He didn't even let himself remember.

How did she do this? Time and time again, saving him from his past and making him believe he was worth it. *Why* did she? Part of him wanted to believe she was coming around, changing the way she saw life. Part of him hoped it was because she loved him back. If this list was working, that is, and she believed in love.

If the damn muffin was just one more nice gesture, he was in for an agonizing awakening. If she couldn't love him back, he'd never be able to look at her the same. Look at her at all. Because in those huge hazel eyes was something he'd never get from another. The yielding pink mouth he'd kissed compared to no one. Her hands, soft and healing, touched more than his skin.

She was everything. No other woman would press a kiss to his chest, over his heart, to fix the break. Could feel his pain, understand it, and ease it away. Would wipe away tears too long in coming as if to silently say the past was over now.

No one ever cared enough to leave a note on his nightstand that said, "You are someone."

He turned and headed back in the direction of the house, picking up his pace to relieve the burn inside. Each step resounding her words. *You. Are. Someone.*

Was he someone? If only to her? Because he could live with that. Be a son to the Covics, a friend to Fisher, a brother to Heather. And the world to Camryn. If she was the only one who really knew him, understood him, he would die happy.

First, he needed to ask her out. Date her. For real this time and not a lie to save her from the family. Find out if she returned these feelings at all, or if this was just great sex on her end. Most women confused sex with love. Cam wouldn't. And before now, she didn't believe in true love. He needed to know if that was still the case.

Each step hammering the gravel was closer to her. Each

labored breath a metaphor for how she stole his breath. Troy believed in hope, but it had been hard to come by in his life. Once, he'd hoped for a family who loved him. Hoped for a friend to play and share things with. A home of his own that no one could take away or pollute. He'd stopped hoping after obtaining those things, thinking life was complete. His life wasn't complete, though.

Now he hoped for her.

Slowing his pace to a walk, he made his way up the driveway. Hearing the family out back by the pool, he snuck inside the garage door to not be seen. He jogged up the stairs and into their room to shower before going in search of her.

The bathroom door was cracked open, steam billowing out from her shower. He walked to the bathroom door and dropped his hand to the knob, but she spoke before he could knock.

"Yes, I got your text. I thought you sent it by mistake."

She was on the phone. Removing his hand, he stepped back to give her privacy and wait.

"What was I supposed to think, Maxwell? You slept with someone else. You broke up with me, remember?"

Troy froze, eyeing the door.

"Excuse me? What about Alicia? You said you were so good together. You called me a robot, among other cruel things. I obviously wasn't good enough..." She sighed. "No, Maxwell. I'm in Colorado for the wedding. I can't have dinner..."

Troy's gut knotted as hope depleted. Her ex wanted her back. He was no match for an ad executive who could give her financial stability. A big house in the 'burbs. Two point five kids.

"Yes, I brought someone... No, a family friend... Yes, I have friends... That's none of your business."

And hope flew out the window along with all the air in his lungs. He was just a friend. A friend she could have sex with, but nothing more. There was his answer, and he didn't even have to humiliate himself by asking her.

"Fine, Maxwell. I'll call when we get back. I don't know… Yes, I still have the key. Okay, Monday."

Troy backed to the bedroom door to leave, but the bathroom door flew open first. She stood wrapped in a towel, hair damp. Her eyes widened.

"You're back."

He swallowed. "Yes."

She looked behind him to the nightstand and back to him again. He fumbled for something, anything to say. But overhearing her conversation with Maxwell shot comprehension to hell.

She walked around him and tossed the muffin, complete with candle, plus the note in the trash.

"What are you doing?" He walked over and pulled the note out, setting it back on the nightstand.

"Look, I'm sorry. I didn't mean for the note or muffin to upset you. I just thought…"

Jesus, he was an ass. "I'm not upset."

"You look upset."

Expelling a huge breath, he walked over to her. She may want this Maxwell guy over him, but she was still Cam. She was still the considerate, cool-headed woman she always was. She deserved an explanation, because in her eyes, nothing had changed. Pulling her to him, he held the back of her head as she pressed her face to his chest.

"I'm not upset, Cam. What you did…it was very thoughtful. Thank you."

"Are you sure?"

He closed his eyes. "Yes."

"Why did you go out running then?"

As his eyes opened, so did his mouth, ready to tell her how he felt about her. Then he remembered hope was quashed. "I just needed some air. It had nothing to do with you. Honestly, thank you again for the note. It, um..."

Stepping back, she looked up at him. "I see," she said.

In the blink of an eye her expression regressed to old Cam. Her gaze darted away seconds before she did. Across the room. Away from him. As he watched her dress with angered, jerking movements, he felt like the lowest life form. After sliding her feet into flip-flops, she made her way to the door.

He needed to tell her how much her gesture meant to him, or else this would be another thing in her beautiful head that she thought she messed up.

"You're the only person on Earth, Camryn, who ever made me feel like a somebody."

From the corner of his eye, he saw her turn. "You *are* a somebody."

Damn her.

Pivoting, he made his way to the bathroom before he could open his mouth and lose everything.

Chapter Sixteen

Life Lessons According to Camryn:
Real women don't cry, they wine.

"The plane landed an hour early," Heather said, setting her phone on the kitchen table and drying her wet swimming suit with a towel. "The airport shuttle can't get them for two more hours."

Heather's two best girlfriends, Shana and Katie, were supposed to fly in early in time for the rehearsal, along with Justin's friends, John and Cade. Though they weren't in the wedding party, they had an active role as ushers and doing readings. The extended family was coming in later tonight and going right to the hotel.

The family was out back by the pool, thinking they had a few more hours until they needed to get ready or pick up their friends. Troy was still upstairs, taking the longest shower in recorded history.

"I can go get them," Camryn said. "You need time to get ready. I'll do it."

After Maxwell's phone call and Troy's sudden distance, she could use some alone time to drive. Katie, most assuredly, would be a distraction. Heather's oldest friend was one of those women that every man wanted and every woman wanted to be. Despite that, Camryn liked her a lot.

"Do what?" Troy asked, walking into the kitchen. Wearing a pair of khakis and a fitted black crew, he looked so handsome in casual dress clothes. His dark blond hair was still wet from his shower, brushing his collar and ears. Fire churned in her stomach, lighting her nerves.

She'd never had such a physical response to a man like with Troy. Looking at him made her think of all the wicked things they could do. Things only he could teach her. Things she'd only do with him.

Wicked was not in her vocabulary.

Heather looked between the two of them. "What's going on?"

"Nothing," Troy said, shoving his hands in his pockets.

Heather looked doubtful, but didn't pry further. "Our friends' plane came in early. Cam's going to pick them up."

Troy nodded, darting a glance at Camryn, and swiftly away. "I'll go with her."

"That's not necessary," Camryn said, but he glared at her, shutting out all protest.

"I said I'll go," he barked. His hands propelled to his hips. "I'll get the keys from Bernice." He turned and left the room before Camryn even had time to react.

"Wow," Heather said. "Lovers quarrel?"

Camryn didn't do fighting, so she had no idea what to do with Troy like this. She didn't even know why he was so upset. The abuse from his past obviously still hurt him deeply. She thought by leaving him the note he would understand how she saw him, that he wasn't just a someone, but a someone to her. Maybe by her doing that he realized what a mistake they were making, and he changed his mind about them. Or seen as an act of nastiness, it just brought back all the painful memories he tried to block out.

Camryn rubbed her chest. "Tell Troy I'll meet him in the garage."

She walked through the laundry room and into the garage. Opening the back door to the Hortons' SUV, she grabbed the lever to extend the third row seat, but she couldn't maneuver both the seat and handle to pull it out.

A large hand slid over hers, stopping her movement. From behind, Troy's body pressed against her back, adjusting the seat and flipping it into position. Without delay, he stepped away and climbed in the passenger seat.

"Thanks," she mumbled, standing with the open rear door between them. Tremors coursed through her body, making the heat outside feel like a bitter Wisconsin winter.

He extended his hand out the passenger window, the keys dangling from one finger. She closed the door and took the keys, then rounded the car and got in. Her hands were shaking too much to start the car on the first attempt.

His glance darted her way. "Want me to drive?"

She stared at the steering wheel. A heavy weight pressed down on her chest, tears clogging her throat. The only man who ever seemed to want her now couldn't even look at her. All those nice words and items on his list that had been changing her, making her happy, were now another harsh slap and regret. Just like everything else. How stupid she was to think things could be different. That they could be different. *She* could be anything other than what she always was.

"What pictures are in your head now, Cam? What are you imagining this time so you can stay ever calm, not feeling a damn thing?"

She jerked. The cruelty of what he said, throwing her honesty and secret in her face, had her fighting a waging battle to stay in control, to not to die of embarrassment and shame. Nothing had ever hurt this bad. Like being ripped apart. No shred of hope or promise left. There were no visions or imagination that would ever erase this.

She sucked in a breath, swallowed, and turned the key.

Drive. Just drive.

He said nothing more, the car eerily quiet until the GPS dinged, instructing her to turn right. To kill the silence, she hit the radio power button, and classical music softly played. He reached over and hit a preset, blaring hard rock through the speakers. She turned it down two notches and kept her eyes focused ahead.

Heather's friends were waiting outside of baggage claim when they pulled up. Troy and Camryn exited the car as Katie jumped up off a bench. Her blonde curls bounced almost as emphatically as her breasts. Camryn glanced at Troy. Katie was the type of woman Troy usually dated, except Katie had more brain cells.

"Oh wow, look at you!" Katie gushed, hugging Camryn until suffocation loomed. "I've never seen you in turquoise before." Camryn looked down at one of Heather's purchases she wore, not by choice. "It looks nice on you. Makes your eyes stand out. And your hair! So cute."

"Thank you."

"Where's Heather and Justin?"

Troy grabbed the suitcases and hauled them to the rear hatch.

"Back at the house, getting ready," she answered, holding the door open.

Shana, Cade and John climbed in before Katie. John—an average-looking man of five-seven and neatly combed black hair—was more Camryn's speed than the others. Having been Justin's old roommate at UWM, he seemed to have nothing in common with the rest of their group. Camryn went out of her way to talk with him whenever they got together. He always seemed out of place. Like her.

She smiled at him. "How are you, John? It's been a while."

Troy brushed past her to get to the passenger door. "Get in the car, Cam," he muttered.

She could feel the smile fall from her face. John looked at her. "Doing great, thanks. How's Chicago?"

She shrugged. "I'm moving back to Milwaukee soon," she

said, shutting the door. She rounded the SUV and climbed in. Checking her rearview, she pulled out of the lane before security could think she was packing mass weapons by parking so long.

"Are you all ready for a rockin' bachelorette and bachelor party?" Katie asked from the seat behind Troy.

Cade spoke first. "Justin and Heather made it quite clear there was to be no parties. You know that."

Camryn smiled. Heather and Justin didn't want the traditional extravaganza the bridal party typically tortured a couple with the night before their wedding. They just wanted a small get-together at the house with drinks and music. They thought it more fun to stay together and share the night with friends.

Katie sighed dramatically. "I know. I think it sucks. Not even a stripper! What about you, Troy? Wanna be our stripper?"

Camryn accidently veered over the yellow, dotted line before righting the car.

"Your lane is over here," Troy said, sarcasm dripping.

Sarcasm was her angle, not his. "I know that!"

"Holy crap," Katie said. "It's true. I didn't believe Justin, but it's true. You two *are* a couple! You even fight like a couple."

"When's *your* wedding?" Shana joked.

Camryn didn't veer the car this time, but she thought about it.

"I didn't know you two were dating," John said. "When did this happen?"

"A year ago," Troy said, voice harsher than necessary. "Yes, it's true, no it's not a joke, and we're not fighting."

The car grew silent. Stayed silent. *Insert crickets here.*

Camryn sighed, not wanting Heather's friends to feel bad. "It's been a long week. We're just...tired. Do you want to check into the hotel first, or go right to the house?"

"House," they all agreed.

"I think Cam should walk down the aisle with Troy," Heather said, addressing the group.

Camryn crossed her arms and glared at the grass. They'd been going at this rehearsal thing in the yard for an hour now, and still had yet to actually rehearse anything. This was, of course, after a half hour debate on why Heather and Justin weren't having an Orthodox ceremony.

Bernice had showed the family where the aisle, chairs and altar were to be placed in the yard, an area on the east side of the house. The reception and dinner were on the west side of the house. The company they hired to bring in equipment was setting up early tomorrow morning, so they were going off of imagination for rehearsal.

Her family had no imagination.

Camryn looked at Troy. He seemed to have no opinion on how or with whom he walked down the aisle. He hadn't said anything since the car. If one could call what he said talking. More like bitching. What was his problem anyway? He was starting to piss her off.

"I mean, Cam's the maid of honor, and Fisher the best man," Heather went on to say when nobody spoke up. "They were supposed to walk down together, but why not just keep the couples together?"

"Heather, whatever you want," Camryn said, having enough. "Let's just get on with rehearsal."

Her mother's hands flew to her hips. "Camryn Covic, just because you're having some snit with Troy doesn't mean you take it out on your sister!"

Snit? "I only meant that the caterer will have dinner ready to go in twenty minutes. We need to get on with it. And Troy and I are not doing anything, especially snitting."

"We most definitely are snitting," Troy said. His mouth firmed into a thin line.

"You're not helping, Troy."

He looked at her from behind his sunglasses. She couldn't see his eyes, but she was sure steel was in them.

"I knew they wouldn't last," Nana said.

Camryn closed her eyes before she said something she'd regret. When she opened them, Nana was twirling a flaming baton and kicking her legs like a Rockette. Just before her sequined outfit caught fire...

"Okay," Heather said, raising her hands. "Cade and John, you walk the parents down the aisle." Heather went on to place them in position as if they were Ken dolls. "Once they are seated, then Anna and Fisher walk down." Anna and Fisher did as asked, then stepped off to the side of the altar. "Good. Troy and Cam."

Cam looped her arm through Troy's and did as asked.

"No, no," Nana argued. "Slower. This isn't a twelve-yard dash."

Wanna bet? Nevertheless, both slowed down and separated at the altar.

"Now, Emily," Heather said, "your turn. You'll have a basket with flower petals. Just drop them as you walk down. When you get by Mommy and Daddy, stop. Okay?"

Emily nodded, acting the most adult in the group, and calmly walked down to stand in front of Anna.

Heather held Dad's forearm and walked down to meet Justin, who was grinning like an idiot. No cold feet for that guy. It must be nice, Camryn thought. To have someone that confident in your future together by your side. Someone looking forward to the next forty years and whatever surprises life brings.

She looked at Troy, arms crossed and head down, wondering if he'd ever find someone he loved that much.

Wondering if she'd have the courage to stand up here and pretend she was happy for him if the time came.

Father Wieland, the Hortons' three hundred pound Irish priest, cleared his throat. He proceeded to summarize the ceremony, then directed Katie and Shana where to stand for their readings. Emily sat down by Cam's feet, having had her fill of rehearsal.

She couldn't blame her. By the time all was said and done, Camryn was ready to hop a plane back to Milwaukee. Alone.

"Wait? What?" Katie asked, holding the back door open and staring at Heather. "Oh no. You can't sleep in the same room. That's bad luck!"

"I don't believe in bad luck."

Of course Heather didn't. The only thing in her life that could constitute bad luck was a broken fingernail.

"Heather, the groom can't see the bride before the wedding," Katie insisted, following the others into the house.

Heather smiled. "We're staying in the same house. How do you propose a way around that?"

Troy placed his sunglasses on top of his head as they entered the dining room. "I'll bunk in Justin's room. Heather can sleep with Cam in ours."

Camryn stared at Troy. She wanted to talk to him alone tonight, find out what was going on. That wouldn't be possible if he slept in the other room. He stared at the china in front of him, refusing to look at her.

Everyone sat at the table. Nana pointed at Camryn. "He doesn't even want to sleep with you now. You lost a good one here. Hope you're happy, missy."

Camryn dropped her head in her hands. "Everything's fine, Nana."

Nana huffed in disbelief. Kuma Viola wouldn't let her off so easy. "Then why are you fighting? You two broke up, didn't you? Way to ruin the wedding, guys."

Justin kept staring between Camryn and Troy. "Look, Troy's helping us out by sleeping in our room, okay. Tradition is tradition, like Katie said. All couples fight. It's obvious Troy loves her..."

From next to her, Troy placed his palms on the table and stood. "Camryn, a word in private, please."

"Now?"

He took her arm and tugged her out of the chair. "Yes, now." He wove them around the dining room table, through the kitchen, and into the library. He kicked the door shut.

"I can't do this," he muttered, for the most part, seemingly to himself. He ran a hand over his hair, dislodging his sunglasses. He stared at them in his hand, then pocketed them.

"Can't do what?"

"This," he shouted, pointing between the two of them.

Yeah, even her fake boyfriend couldn't stand her after a few days. She'd definitely cry over that later. "I'm sorry, Troy. I never should've asked you to do this. I didn't think things would..."

"That's not what I meant." Impatience waned. "Look, this morning..."

"Troy, you have to stop this. I'm sorry for what I did. I really am. And though this has to be about more than my note, we can discuss that later. You have to pretend...*we* just have to get through the next two days, and you can be free of me..."

"What if I don't want to be free of you?"

Her gaze shot to his. He didn't look mad, frustrated maybe, but not mad. She watched his Adam's apple bob, his gaze focused at her feet. She'd never known Troy not to look someone in the eye.

"What does that mean?"

Frustration drained to a blank, unreadable expression. Her heart thumped, then died, waiting for him to explain. Because that sounded an awful lot like...

"Never mind. Forget it." He glanced around the room, then back to her feet. "I'll try harder. Let's go back in by the others."

If he felt anything for her, he shouldn't have to try.

He made his way to the door, but she stepped in front of him. "I would never do anything to hurt you. You know that, don't you? Tell me you do. If nothing else, Troy, we're friends. What I did this morning was my way of saying that." His eyes slammed closed, so she cupped his cheeks, forcing him to look at her. "And I won't ever tell a soul the things you told me. What happened to you wasn't your fault..."

Jerking away, he paced the room. "Now isn't the time for this."

"Yes, it is," she argued, because he wasn't staying in her room tonight, and his defenses were back up. Once home, they wouldn't ever have an opportunity like this for her to say these things. They'd go back to their lives as if this week never happened. "What your father did wasn't your fault. And no matter how mad you get at me, no matter how hard you push because I know the truth, I'll always be here."

He turned his back on her to stare out the window. He was shutting her out, like he did everything else that resembled importance. He had his moments taking things seriously, but Troy had his limit. Apparently, he'd reached it. She wished, and not for the first time, that she'd done more for him growing up. Maybe he wouldn't hate the world. Maybe he'd live and thrive, instead of putting on a damn good show for everyone else's benefit. Maybe if she had, he'd know how special he was.

Riddled with guilt, she waited a full minute before reaching for the doorknob.

"Don't," he said before she could walk out.

She turned, and from across the room, he looked like that ten-year-old boy who got dumped on their doorstep. Scared, hopeful and ashamed. The years hadn't changed him after all.

He stepped closer. "I'm not angry with you, I'm angry at myself. The things I said to you in the car..."

"Forget it, Troy."

"No," he ground out, marching right up to her and grabbing her wrists. "There was no excuse for that. You deserve better. Someone will do better with you than I can. Just...promise me you'll let him love you the right way, Cam. With candlelight and roses and..."

"The list again," she growled, tugging her wrists free, her heart shattering with every damn syllable uttered from his lips. How dare he? Trying to tell her how to love someone else. As if he knew how. As if she could ever feel about some other man the way she felt about him.

Her jaw dropped. *Oh no.*

"That's right, Cam. I have a couple more things on the list for you, then the last item you must do yourself at home." He paused, looking seemingly through her, not at her. "You have to fall in love. True, real, crazy love that you can't live without."

She almost laughed at the irony. He did all this to show her what his version of love was, just so she would fall in love with some man she may or may not have met yet. When all along it was him she'd fallen for.

They were both idiots.

"Whatever you say, Troy."

Before he could mutter anything else to kill her slowly, she turned the knob and walked out. He waited a few seconds and followed. When they neared the dining room, he grabbed her hand and squeezed.

The family was halfway through their salad when they sat down to join them.

"Aw, good," her mother said. "You made up."

"They don't look made up to me," Yjaka Mitch said.

Exhaling heavily, Troy looked at her. "Forgive me," he

mumbled for her ears only.

He cupped the back of her head and pulled her to him. As his mouth fell over hers, she gripped his arm, holding on for dear life. His lips moved against hers, his tongue darting inside. How could he kiss someone like this, in front of a room full of people, then want her to fall for someone else? God, no one kissed like Troy. No one.

By the time he pulled away, she was nearly laying in Yjaka Harold's lap in the next chair.

Troy glanced at the other faces. "See, all made up. Does anyone else need a kiss to make it better?"

Jaws dropped. All but two. Shana and Katie raised their hands. Kuma Viola looked like she wanted to raise hers. As the room laughed, Camryn picked up her fork, pretending everything was normal, and pushed salad around her plate.

Heather tapped her wine glass with a fork. "Justin and I wanted to thank everyone for being here. Bernice and Tim, you couldn't have made this more special. We're just very grateful to have all of you with us."

Wine glasses raised and clinked.

"I'm grateful for wine," Katie said. "Now, what are we up to tonight?"

"Karaoke," Justin said, inserting a huge bite of salad into his mouth and winking at Troy.

Camryn dropped her fork and glared at Troy. This had to be his damn idea. A thing on his damn list. And now she was damning in her head!

"Oh, how fun," Shana said.

Troy leaned over and whispered, "We're almost through the list, Cam. Tonight, you make a fool of yourself."

Her eyes narrowed. Good thing she'd dropped her fork or it'd be in his eye. "Not doing it."

He smiled, the conniving jerk. "Yes, you are. And you're

going to have fun doing it. For you. For me."

"Like hell."

His gaze dropped to her mouth and up again. "We already checked cursing off the list. Shame on you."

The caterers removed their salad plates and replaced them with a heaping bowl of pasta. Cam stared down at her plate, wondering where all this food was supposed to go. Troy's lap would be a great place...

"Oh," Troy said to the family. "There's a rule about karaoke tonight. Someone else picks the song you sing. Everyone pulls names to see who picked whom."

Son of a...

"This is going to be *sooo* fun!" Katie shouted with way more enthusiasm than Camryn could muster on a good day. "We do have hard alcohol, right?"

Chapter Seventeen

Life Lessons According to Camryn:
Every day of my life I have a most embarrassing moment.

Troy was up next. He glanced through the title list Justin had printed out of the songs programmed for the karaoke machine, wondering who picked his name and what song they chose.

Camryn's dad was doing his best rendition of "Blue Suede Shoes", making Troy's ears bleed in the process. Nana was laughing so hard he was sure a heart attack was in the near future.

From his table in the back, he glanced around the media room. Justin and Heather's friends were sitting up front on the floor, well on their way to a drunken coma and urging Dad to pop his hips like Elvis while he sang. The aunts and uncles, along with Justin's parents, were winding down on the sectional, half-mast smiles christening their faces. Heather and Justin flanked Troy, rupturing his eardrums, encouraging Dad along as if front row at a Bon Jovi concert.

Camryn was in the far corner at another table, talking to John, Anna and Fisher. Emily was nodding off in Cam's lap. As Cam laughed at something John said, her hand fell on Emily's head, stroking the little girl's hair. Troy wondered if, when the time came, her kids would have hair like hers, the exact shade of a cinnamon stick swirling in a cup of tea. Or her smile, subtle. Endearing. Or her eyes, huge and hazel.

Before this week, those eyes were listless and distant. Now, Cam had life back. His list was opening her, and closing him.

He used to get anxious alone, rarely making it a night or two without calling some woman to fill the silence or popping into one of his favorite bars. Now all he wanted was him and her. Alone.

But that wasn't the best of ideas even on a bad day. Pretending to date and actually having romantic feelings were two separate things. When this all came down, the family would desert him. They may love him, but Camryn was their real family. He was just some guy they helped out once upon a time. He should have stopped this thing between them after the first kiss in the yard on day one. Fisher may not have meant what he said back in Milwaukee, but he was right just the same.

Troy wasn't good enough for her.

She deserved more than a construction worker whose only family resided in jail. More than his genetics for her future kids. She needed someone with a five-year plan, who wanted the same things from life. Someone who made her smile like she was now. He turned the key with this list, she opened the door. Now, whoever she chose to spend her life with would wait across the threshold, and she'd be able to love him openly.

Maxwell wanted her back. The thought tore his insides to pieces. Troy wondered if she'd go back to him, and if she did, if she'd regress back to old Cam. Or maybe she'd date someone like Justin's friend, John. The guy'd had a crush on Cam from the second Heather introduced them a few years back. John looked at her the way Fisher looked at Anna.

Heather whooped next to him as Dad finished his song with a painful flourish. "Your turn, Troy."

Anna stood. "Hold on, I have to put Em to bed."

Emily's eyes widened. "I don't want to go to bed."

"It's late," Anna said, "and we have a big day tomorrow."

"But you promised I could sing a song with Auntie Cam!"

"Let her go ahead," Troy said. "I'll take my turn after."

Cam carried Emily to the front of the room and pushed

some buttons on the karaoke machine. She set Emily on her feet in front of her and gave her the microphone. Her hands were shaking. Good. Nervousness was a sure sign this was embarrassing the hell out of her. Cam pretended she didn't give a damn what others thought of her. But she did. Her adult life had been spent in camouflage, hoping no one would notice her. She needed to make a fool of herself. Needed to feel awkward.

The music for "Somewhere, Out There" began to play as Cam kneeled behind Emily. She adjusted the monitor, and as the lyrics came on the screen, she pointed to them and sang along with Emily. Only Cam could turn karaoke into a teaching lesson for Emily, showing her what the words looked like as they sang them to start recognizing how to read.

Emily's voice overpowered Cam's, but from what he could hear, her singing voice sounded just like her speaking voice. Soft. Lilting. She wasn't half bad. From across the room she looked at him and smiled.

Yeah, definitely wanted her alone. Now.

Heather grabbed his arm in a vice grip. "Ow. What's wrong with you?"

Heather's eyes bulged from her sockets. "You're in love with her!" she said in a loud whisper.

Troy glanced around, but no one was paying attention. When he looked back at Heather, he thought about denying her accusation, but what was the point? He'd almost lost control with Cam earlier today and told her he loved her. "So what if I am?"

Heather looked at Camryn, then back to him. "You have to tell her how you feel."

Now that was even funnier than watching Nana sing "I Love Rock and Roll". Plus, he didn't need Heather's advice. "I know how to handle a woman, thank you very much."

"She's not a woman, she's Cam." Heather bit down on her lip, examining him, acting like she wanted to say something but couldn't. After a long pause, she finally said, "God, Troy. Please don't break her heart."

Okay, now he was starting to get a little pissed off. "Everyone's so worried about *her* heart. What about *me*? What about *my* heart? I do have one! What if she breaks *my heart*?"

The room erupted into claps and cheers as Emily and Cam finished. Troy tore his gaze from Heather to look at Camryn. Hell, she'd already broken his heart. A couple times now. His point with Heather was moot.

Camryn made her way to the back of the room once more while he concentrated on breathing. It wasn't until she was seated that Troy realized the item on his list wasn't checked off.

"Uh uh," he argued. "Singing a song with Emily doesn't count, Cam. Get back up there. Who picked Cam's song?"

John stood. "I did."

He walked to the front of the room while Camryn shot Troy little ice daggers through her glare. Heck of a superpower, that. Resigned, she stood and returned to the front of the room. John punched some buttons on the machine and sat down. As her song started to play, she beamed a grin at John so immense that Troy's chest constricted in jealousy.

Great. He'd never been jealous of anything a day in his life. Not even when he should have. It left a sour, frightening taste in his mouth.

And then recognition dawned over the song John picked. "This is cheating," Troy insisted. "This song has no words!"

"Sure it does," Cam said into the microphone, smile never faltering. "Tequila!" she sang.

Katie, Shana, Cade and Heather joined her, dancing around the front of the room. Troy didn't have the heart to argue. One look at her and he knew she was having fun. It may not constitute fully making a fool of herself, but it was damn near close enough.

Sitting back, he swiped a hand down his face.

"I picked your song," Justin said.

Troy's eyes narrowed as he looked at the wicked, wicked grin on Justin's face. "Dare I ask?"

Anna left the room to put Emily to bed.

Camryn shouted out the last "Tequila!" She fell against Katie, laughing.

He swallowed, wanting to look away and couldn't. If he never saw beauty again, the image of her like this would tide him over.

"Come on, Troy," Justin urged.

Troy's glance darted to the front of the room where Justin was waiting on him. Troy hadn't even noticed Justin get up. Slowly, he rose, ready to take his own punishment. He took the microphone from Justin.

"Be happy I didn't pick the *Titanic* song," Justin whispered. "That was my first choice."

Troy grimaced. Justin's choice had to be a step up from Celine Dion, right? Katie whooped at him, shaking her chest like a Brazilian native. Well, at least he wasn't the stripper like she'd suggested in the car earlier.

And then the music started.

Troy whipped Justin a deathcon stare. Camryn and John laughed so hard she fell off her chair, then scrambled to get back on. This wasn't the first time his list backfired on him, but by God it would be the last.

Deciding to make the best of it, and figuring more than half the room was too drunk to remember this tomorrow, he started to unbutton his shirt. Why not? He'd always been the life of the party before.

Camryn stopped laughing. Katie whooped again. And as he started to sing "Total Eclipse of the Heart", the entire room sang along with him. Poorly.

Troy slid his shirt down his arms, raised his hand, and

swung it over his head like a propeller. Heather jumped up and rooted him on. Bernice covered her eyes and shook her head. Dad let out a groan loud enough to uproot the weeping willow on the front lawn. Camryn remained frozen, pretty pink mouth hung open in shock.

Checkmate.

While singing the second verse, he strutted over her way and sat in her lap, gyrating his hips for good measure. She turned six shades of red. For a girl who hated color, she sure looked good in red. *Now* she was embarrassed. Ha.

Standing, he moved behind her and leaned forward, singing in her ear, walking his fingers over her collarbone in a public seduction even a drag queen would be proud of. She covered her face with her hands. He grabbed her hands and held them down.

Knowing the song was near complete, he strutted back to the front of the room, belted out the last chords, and unbuttoned the fly of his pants.

The song ended before anything else came off. Intentionally so. The family clapped like circus monkeys. Katie and Shana looked disappointed. And he was pretty sure Miller Lite was taking his man card.

Grinning, he shook his head while donning his shirt. The older crowd excused themselves to bed. Fisher and Anna joined them. Katie was barely standing, Cade flopped on the couch near comatose, and Shana was still giggling from Troy's mediocre striptease.

"We should get you guys back to the hotel," he said.

Katie pouted. "So early? How 'bout one more drink?"

He looked over at Cam as she walked toward them. John slammed his drink back and joined them, more than a little tipsy himself. "One drink, Katie dear, then we leave."

Justin moved behind the small corner bar and set out a row of shot glasses. He poured tequila and passed them out to the others. He raised his shot. "To family, friends and Cam reminding us of tequila!"

They took their shots, all but Cam and Troy, and set the glasses face down on the bar. Before the tequila could kick in, Troy ushered them to the garage as Heather and Justin headed to bed. Cade was already passed out when Troy hauled his dead weight into the passenger seat.

Cam looked at them and shook her head. "We should just let you guys crash here."

Shana hiccupped. "Can't. Justin took all our stuff to the hotel."

Cam looked at Troy. "Can you carry him once we get there?"

Troy nodded and passed her the keys. She'd only had one glass of wine, which was hours ago, but he'd had a few. Not enough to be drunk, but he wasn't taking the chance. The girls climbed in back, while John and Troy took the middle seat. Cam pulled the SUV out of the drive and headed for the highway.

"Keep 'em awake," Cam said, looking at him in the rearview.

"Oh, we're awake," Katie shouted, then laughed. "Cam, I didn't know you were this much fun. Seriously, I always thought you were a tight ass. A nice tight ass, but a tight ass."

From his vantage point, Troy could see Cam smiling. "She is fun, isn't she?" Her glance darted to his, then back to the road.

"I mean," Katie went on as if Troy hadn't spoken, "seriously fun. Seriously. Did anyone else know she was this fun? And Troy, man, you need to take *all* those clothes off next time. Your body is seriously hot! Hey, John, why didn't you strip? I always wanted to see you naked. Seriously naked."

John rubbed his forehead. Troy clamped his mouth shut. Heather's friends were *seriously* close to breaking the friend boundary here. Alcohol made tactless truth-tellers of even the best people.

"Have you thought about your speech for the wedding dinner, Cam?" Troy asked, changing the subject.

"Uh, no. Not really. I thought I'd just say the same thing I did at Fisher and Anna's wedding, just inserting different names."

"Oh no," Katie argued. "A wedding toast must be funny and sweet. And funny..."

In the rearview, Camryn's glance darted to the backseat, and then to the road. "I'm not really the funny type, Katie."

"Coulda fooled me after tonight," Katie muttered, then laughed as if that were the most hilarious thing she'd said in a decade. "Heather and Justin are in love," she sighed. "That's so sweet. I want to be in love, don't you, John?"

Cam pulled into the circular drive at the hotel entrance and cut the engine just in time to save John from answering. "Anyone have the room key?" she asked.

"Oh, I do!" Katie said. She dumped out the contents of her purse into her lap. Here's my house key!" she shouted, as if this were the greatest discovery to mankind.

"The *hotel* key, not your house key," Shana corrected. "You cannot handle your alcohol, babe." Shana's eyes rolled back in her head, two seconds from passing out herself.

"Everyone out!" Troy yelled to wake them before he had to carry them all inside. They jumped, on full alert.

Troy grabbed the keycard from Katie's lap and shoved the rest of the scattered contents inside her purse. He handed the card to Cam and hauled Cade over his shoulder. Katie leaned heavily into Cam, while John and Shana stumbled behind them through the lobby.

"Where's the key for the guys' room?" Cam asked near the front desk.

They all shrugged and swooned. She sighed and turned to

the attendant. "We need a replacement card for room..."

"Two-fifty," the desk clerk said, eyeing Cade over Troy's shoulder. "Is he dead?"

"No, bachelor party." That should explain everything.

"Can we speed this along?" Troy urged. "He's not as light as he looks."

The clerk smiled. "That keycard opens both rooms. They have an adjoined, shared room, as requested."

"Lovely," Cam said, cinching Katie closer to her side when she slumped. "Let's go."

Once in the elevator, Katie's eyes drifted closed. "I love you, Cam. Seriously love you. We have to hang out again..."

"Crap," she muttered, tapping Katie's cheeks as the door dinged open. "A few more steps, Katie. Come on. Stay awake."

Cam slid the keycard into the lock and kicked the door open. Dragging Katie to the bed, she fell when Katie didn't release her hold, sprawling on top of her.

Troy's back couldn't take much more. He opened the adjoining room door and dropped Cade unceremoniously face down on the bed. When he came back in the room, Cam was trying to get Shana out of the chair. John was passed out in the other chair.

"I'll get her," he said.

"Hold on," Cam said, straightening, looking between John and Katie. "I have an idea."

"What kind of idea?" he asked, just wanting bed. It was near one a.m. and he was shot.

"Did you see the way Katie was looking at John tonight?"

Troy glanced at both parties, then at her. "No."

"I think she likes him."

Troy mustered the energy to laugh.

"I know, it's as preposterous as you and I, but I think she

likes him."

Troy sobered. "What are you getting at, Cam?"

She looked around the small room. "What if they woke up together tomorrow? Fully clothed, nothing devious. Maybe she'd make a move. Maybe he'd look at her differently."

Troy stared at Camryn, his heart swelling inside his chest. It was working. The list was working. She believed in love, in happily-ever-afters and seeing past what was in front of her to...magic. She was actually trying to set up John and Katie to give them the opportunity to act on something they may not have before. He rubbed the back of his neck, wanting to touch her. To weep for how much he wanted her.

"I'm sorry. Bad idea. Never mind..."

In response, Troy bent down and slung John's arm over his shoulders, carting him to the bed Katie lay in. Then he walked into the other room and moved Cade to the couch. Last, he carried Shana into the bed Cade vacated. He propped the adjoining room door open with a book and straightened to look at Camryn.

She swallowed, staring at him from across the room with the very expression she had a week ago in the Hortons' yard. Shock. Want. Sentiment.

He wanted the smell of lemongrass out of his memory as badly as he wanted to take her. Now. For always. Somehow break the laws of physics and alter what they were to make this crazy thing between them work. Too soon, the pain of reality reared, knocking him off-balance.

"Let's head back," he said.

Slowly, she nodded and preceded him out.

Once in the lobby, she stopped at the front desk. "Room two-fifty and two-fifty-two need an eight thirty wake up call. Could you please keep calling until you get an answer?"

"Yes, ma'am."

They drove back in silence, and he couldn't help but

wonder what she was thinking. What she did tonight proved she was changing. Would she want Maxwell after they got home? Would she strive for real love, for better? Because she deserved so much better than what she'd settled for in the past.

"Cam, I know I asked this before, but I have to ask again. Did you love Maxwell?"

Her grip tightened and slackened on the steering wheel. "I don't know," she said quietly. "I thought I did, but now..."

"Now what?"

She shrugged. "I don't think I did. No."

"Did he love you?"

"I doubt it. If so, he had a funny way of showing it." She sighed. "That was my fault, though. In a way, he was right. I didn't give him everything, so he got it from someone else. I can't even be angry anymore. Who would blame him?"

Troy could. Troy could blame him with a fist to Maxwell's face just fine.

She pulled into the garage and cut the engine. When he made no move to exit, she looked at him.

"We are friends, Cam. And as your friend, I'm asking a favor. Please, for me, don't go back to him. Find someone else."

"Where is this coming from, Troy?"

His gaze shot to the door, his fingers gripped the handle. "My heart."

Without further explanation, he exited the car, leaving her in the garage still behind the wheel. He strode through the house and hiked up the steps. He turned toward their bedroom before remembering to go to Justin's room instead.

As he opened the door, he found Justin on the bed, typing away on his laptop. "Why are you still up?" he asked, tossing his wallet on the dresser.

Justin shrugged. "Couldn't sleep. Thought I'd check my email."

Troy pulled his shirt over his head and threw on a tee from his bag. "Not getting nervous, are you?" he quipped, dropping his pants.

"Nope. Proposing to Heather was the smartest thing I ever did." He closed the laptop and set it on the floor, then stretched out under the blankets. "You know, I'd suggest you do the same with Cam, but this was all a lie."

Troy paused by the bed, staring at Justin. "I thought Heather was the only one who knew."

"Wrong. It wasn't that hard to figure out."

Troy climbed in bed, wondering who else had drawn the same conclusion. He'd done this for Cam, who'd done this for Heather to not ruin the wedding.

"Don't worry," Justin assured, "no one else knows. In fact, I'm not even sure *you* know."

"What's that supposed to mean?"

"You tell me, man." His eyebrows rose.

Justin stared, waiting for a response from him. Troy wasn't going to give him one. Justin may have figured out the lie, but that didn't mean Troy had to spill the truth.

A corner of Justin's mouth quirked. "Looks like you fell for the lie too."

Troy exhaled and ran a hand down his face. "I don't know what to say, Justin, other than Cam and I will never work. So, just let it go."

Justin leaned over and turned off the bedside lamp. "If you let her go, the joke will be on you."

"This wasn't a joke."

"Nope, sure wasn't." Justin paused, looking at him in the dark. "Sure isn't funny either, is it?" Justin rolled away.

Troy stared at Justin's back, hating how right he was. After a few minutes, when he thought Justin had fallen asleep, he laid down and flopped an arm over his face.

"Oh, and Troy?"

Troy frowned. "Yeah?"

"Stay on your side of the bed. Tempting as I may be, I'm getting married tomorrow."

Troy laughed and rolled over.

Chapter Eighteen

Life Lessons According to Camryn:
Bad decisions make for good stories.

The men were restricted to the media room, and the women to the library. Katie was taking this *don't see the bride* thing very seriously. Poor Bernice was stuck handling the setup crew by herself. The only time they'd seen her was when she walked in to announce a weather report, claiming seventy-five degrees and sunshine.

Camryn peeled an orange while chewing the last bite of her toast. She wasn't the bride. The manicurists and hairdressers weren't coming for another hour. She could leave to help Bernice for a bit.

"I'll be back in an hour," Camryn said, rising.

"Can I come too?" Emily asked, jumping up from the table.

Making a three-year-old stay in one room until three thirty was cruel too, even if she did have an endless supply of coloring books and movies. Camryn held out her hand to take her along.

They found Bernice outside on the east side of the house, watching a crew of twenty set up white folding chairs on either side of a white runner. The way Bernice planned it, the bridal party would exit the house from the back and loop around.

"I think you missed your calling," Camryn said, holding out the orange slices for Bernice. "You should have been a wedding planner."

Bernice smiled, then startled. "No!" she called out to the crew. "The arch goes on the platform for the couple to stand under during the vows." She turned to Camryn. "Would it sound silly if I said I always wanted to have a wedding here?"

"I don't think so. And thank you for this. My family is not an organized group. If Anna's family hadn't taken over their wedding, we'd have been in trouble."

Bernice grinned and turned to Emily. "Are you excited?"

Emily nodded emphatically. "I get to wear a pretty dress and get my hair done like Auntie Heather."

"Can we do anything to help?" Camryn asked, glancing around. The crew had a lot done already.

Bernice bit into an orange slice. "No, but thank you. I'm mostly just supervising. I have to go check on the others."

They followed her around to the west side of the house where another crew was setting up a makeshift dance floor, a bar and round tables for dinner. A cable cord dropped from a tree past the stage.

Emily looked confused. "What are they doing in the trees?"

Bernice smiled, tilting her head while watching the men. "They're inserting strands of white lights through the branches so it looks romantic."

"What's romantic mean?"

Flustered, Bernice turned to Emily. "Um, well..."

Camryn saved her. "When people are in love, they do things that are romantic to show their love. Like flowers." *Or dancing in the rain.* Camryn closed her eyes and shook her head. That wasn't love, it was Troy checking off a list.

Emily wasn't convinced. "But Christmas lights aren't love."

Camryn looked out over the yard, picturing what it would look like tonight after dinner. "When it gets dark, and the music starts to play, people will dance right over there, holding hands and spinning like in a fairy tale. On the tables there will be beautiful flowers and soft-lit candles. But up in the trees, that's where the real romance is. All you'll see are thousands of little white lights, twinkling like stars watching down on Auntie Heather and Uncle Justin. Won't that be pretty?"

When she looked away from Emily and over at Bernice, tears were clinging to the woman's lashes. "Well said, Camryn. That's exactly what I was going for. Looks like I'm not the only romantic one around here."

Strange thing was, Camryn had never been romantic. Until recently, she had always been about logic and necessity. Romance was silly. An illusion created to cater unrealistic versions of true love. The explanation she'd just given Emily was so out of character she almost gasped.

Swallowing, she looked at Emily. "Why don't you go run around for a little bit? Once you get your hair done and get dressed, you won't be able to play for a while."

Emily nodded and took off toward the trees, arms wide open like an airplane. Making a hard right, she piloted herself behind the stage and spun in circles.

"Did I say something wrong?" Bernice asked.

To soothe Bernice, Camryn smiled. Her stomach felt like an avalanche. "No. I'm just not acting like myself this week, that's all. I think I'm out of my element here."

Bernice nodded, watching Emily play. "You know, acting differently from your usual behavior doesn't mean you're still not you, Camryn. It just means you're letting out a different side. Everyone has another side. To restrict that would restrict your full potential."

Camryn looked at Bernice, chest suddenly tight. No one had ever talked like this to her before, had explained something so simple in a way even Camryn couldn't feel guilty or abnormal. Perhaps Bernice was right. Maybe she just didn't allow herself to think or act on this side of her personality, having always been the grounded member of her family.

Her family needed grounding.

"I think," Bernice went on to say, "you and Troy make a

lovely couple." She turned fully to face her, a smile in her eyes that didn't reach her mouth. "Not just lovely outside, but inside too. You balance each other, bring out the best qualities in the other. I believe those are the couples who last, the ones who don't have everything in common. It keeps the relationship from growing stale, don't you think?"

Camryn opened her mouth, but shut it again. Could this be why she felt so differently about Troy than she had any other man? Not just because they had a connection through friendship, through childhood, but because together they completed each other?

Another romantic idiocy. But one that almost made sense. Except Bernice didn't know this was all a lie, and if she did, then she wouldn't be saying this now. Truth be told, whatever this thing was between her and Troy, it wasn't love. It could never be love. He'd grow tired of her and want someone fun. She'd grow frustrated with him and want someone stable.

Poor Bernice was just trying to be nice, so Camryn bit back the tears and smiled. "Thank you. That was nice of you to say."

Several cars pulled in the driveway. Camryn watched as Gregory, the man who'd highlighted and cut her hair in the boutique, emerged from the first car. She sighed and looked for Emily, finding her near one of the tables.

"Emily, we have to go in now." Without argument her niece bounded over and clasped her hand. "If you need help, Bernice, just ask. I don't need to be in there all day."

Camryn walked Emily to the library and opened the door. Before she could step inside, Katie rushed out.

"I need to talk to you!"

"Okay," she said, worried there was something wrong with the wedding. She directed Emily inside the library, waiting back as the hairdressers and manicurists filed in, then closed the door.

Katie pulled her to the hallway outside the room. "I got

drunk last night. *Really* drunk."

Understatement of the century. Camryn smiled. "Yes, you did."

"I don't remember a lot." Katie's eyes widened. "This morning..."

Camryn was wondering if anything had happened between Katie and John after she and Troy set them up. "What about this morning?" she prompted.

Katie ran her hands through her blonde curls, disrupting them into chaos. "Look, for a couple months now I've been having feelings for John. More like a crush. You know, just wondering and all. But this morning we woke up together. In the same bed."

"I see," Camryn said, using every reserve she had not to laugh. "What happened?"

"That's just it! I don't know. I thought maybe you could help. You drove us to the hotel. That's the last thing I remember."

This wasn't what Camryn had in mind. Her stomach started to churn with guilt. "We dropped you off and came back here."

Katie sighed. "We were dressed. So nothing happened, I guess. Except when we woke up..."

Hmm. "And?"

Katie's glance shifted from her feet to Camryn's eyes. Her lip quivered. "I never thought he'd see me that way, as more than a friend. I always thought he liked you. You two are both..."

"Tight-asses."

Her eyes widened again. "No, that's not what I meant. You're just very reserved, very..."

"Tight-assed. That's the word you used for me last night."

"Oh, God! I didn't, did I? Cam, I'm sorry..."

Camryn shook her head and laughed. "No worries, Katie. I *am* a tight-ass. Now, what's got you so upset?"

Katie's gaze fixated on the wall behind Camryn. "When I woke up, there he was. Lying next to me on the bed, staring at me. Before I could even wonder how we got there, he leaned over and kissed me."

So her plan had worked, and she'd been right about Katie liking John. Her guilt eased. So what was the problem?

Katie's eyes filled with tears. "It was earth shattering, Cam. I'm in deep. I mean, real bad. This could kill our friendship."

Camryn knew the feeling. But advice on love and relationships was not her expertise. "You should talk to Heather about this. I'm not the right person..."

"You know how I feel. You and Troy, it's the same thing. What do I do?"

Camryn swallowed. "Katie, I just don't know. I don't know what I'm doing either." Katie's face deflated, so Camryn struggled to find a way to help. "How does John feel?"

Katie shrugged. "When he pulled away after the kiss, he apologized and went to shower."

"I see." Camryn glanced down the hall toward the direction of the media room. She'd go check on the guys and see if she could find anything out. This was her fault. She should've known better than to meddle with romance. Camryn was more the stepsister than Cinderella. "Okay, stay calm. You'll have a chance to talk to him after the ceremony. Nothing will get solved until then. It'll be okay."

Katie nodded and wiped her eyes. "Is it worth it?" she whispered. "Taking the chance with a friend? Even if you know it's all wrong but it feels right."

She wasn't in love with Troy any more than he was in love with her. What they had was a whirlwind brought on by circumstance and the moment. He did make her feel different. Special. And she did care for him so much it was starting to hurt. In the long run, love or not, this fling between her and Troy would pulverize her. But was it worth it? After all was said and done? She wanted to say no. All the pain that would come later was not worth the few moments of bliss. But that would be a lie.

"Yes, it's worth it." Camryn sucked in a breath. "Head back inside. I'll be back in a couple minutes."

"Where are you going?"

Camryn turned. "To play Fairy Godmother."

She walked down the hall, through the kitchen and to the opposite side of the house. She knocked once on the media room door and entered. Justin and Fisher were sitting in recliners, pounding their thumbs against a video game controller in a racecar battle. The others were cheering them on from behind. In the far corner, John was staring at the TV alone, looking like he wasn't seeing anything at all.

As she walked over to him, he glanced up. "Something wrong?"

She smiled, shaking her head. Nothing wrong at all. Poor John was just as freaked out as Katie. Had the same despondent expression. *Guess sometimes things are meant to be.*

She leaned over, taking his hand and whispered in his ear. "She feels the same way about you. Ask her to dance later. Tell her how you feel."

His hand fisted in hers. "Are you sure?"

"Yes." After kissing his cheek, she straightened.

She turned to leave. Troy was watching her from across the room. She smiled and nodded, hoping he understood that together they did something good last night.

Troy fiddled with the bowtie for his tux, trying to figure out what in the hell Cam meant by that look on her face earlier. Had she taken his advice and asked John out? Because that's not exactly what he meant when he said fall in love. In the optimistic, stupid part of his brain, he'd hoped she chose him. Hoped she'd fallen in love with him.

Growling, he stripped the tie from his collar.

John walked over and took it from him. Without a word, he fixed the tie and nodded.

Troy looked in the mirror. "Thanks." John grinned and sobered, then grinned again. Whatever he and Cam talked about had the man happy. "Why are you grinning like an idiot?"

Okay, not exactly smooth, Troy.

John shook his head. "Let's just say I'm saving a dance for your woman if this all works out tonight."

Troy turned. "What did she do?"

"I thought I made a huge mistake." John looked at him and realized Troy wasn't following along. "Katie and I woke up in bed together this morning. I kissed her." He laughed. "I don't know what came over me. I just... I thought I wrecked everything. But then Camryn told me I hadn't. She told me to ask Katie to dance later and tell her how I feel."

"Camryn said that? *My Cam?*" Well, damn.

Justin came over and smacked his shoulder. "Time to go, man."

Troy nodded, following the guys out of the room and through the front door. They veered around the house and into the side yard.

There were at least two hundred people sitting in chairs on either side of the aisle. The priest waited on the platform, wiping his face with a handkerchief. A truckload of white roses decorated the area around him and the arch above.

At least he didn't have to stand through a two hour Orthodox wedding like Fisher and Anna's.

"Last chance," Fisher warned Justin. "No one will blame you if you take off."

Justin laughed. "Not on your life."

When the eight-chair orchestra began to play "Canon in D", John and Cade lined up to escort Nana, Mom and Justin's parents down the aisle to the first row. Justin followed to stand next to the priest without so much as a tremor.

Troy looked over his shoulder, seeing Anna with Emily, followed by Cam, coming out the patio doors. His heart stopped mid-beat.

The lavender dress fit her like a glove, the perfect color against the cream of her skin. Her hair was wrapped in curls behind her head, exposing her cherubic face and huge eyes. She'd done her makeup differently. Something to make her eyes even bigger, her mouth a cherry red.

"Wow."

She looked down at herself. "Thanks, I think."

"Thinking is overrated. And, God, Cam... You look beautiful."

For once, for one splendid second, she didn't question the compliment. She just smiled and said, "Thanks."

She handed Anna her bouquet of purple foxglove and white lilies and squatted to address Emily. "Remember, wait for me and Uncle Troy to get down the aisle before you start. Drop the flower petals as you walk down."

The music changed to "Clair de lune", Fisher and Anna's cue to start. Once they were at the altar, Troy led Camryn, counting in his head slowly so Nana couldn't yell at him later for rushing. At the altar, they turned and took their places, watching Emily. She took two steps and dropped the basket of petals, then proceeded to walk toward them.

The guests laughed, causing Emily to stop and look around. Camryn looked at Anna, who shook her head and walked to Emily.

"But Auntie Cam said to drop the petals!"

The guests laughed again. Anna took Emily's hand and straightened, her smile embarrassed. She picked up the basket and sprinkled the petals with Emily until they finally reached the altar.

And then Heather walked out with her dad. The guests stood and gasped at her beauty, her dress, the mounds of white roses in her bouquet. A picture flawless enough for a magazine cover. Justin looked like he wanted to weep.

But after a fleeting glance, all Troy saw was Camryn. The sunlight through her cinnamon hair, the late-day sun across her skin, the smile which never left her face in happiness for Heather. He wished she could see herself the way he did.

She glanced at him once after Katie did the first reading, doing a double take when she saw him watching her. Her eyes darted to the couple, silently telling him to pay attention. He didn't need to. He'd rather watch her. Subtly, he shook his head. Her lips pursed, eyes narrowing, before she tuned back into the ceremony.

He watched her when they said the vows, when Fisher handed over the rings, and right up until Justin and Heather kissed to seal the deal.

He watched her, knowing this was their last night together. Watched her, wondering if things could be different.

They posed for the photographer and stood in the greeting line. By the time they were seated at the head table for dinner, Troy was ready to haul Cam inside and lock their bedroom door. Lock out what should be for what could be.

Justin stood and tapped his crystal water glass. The crowd hushed to listen. "If I were to die today, I would go out as the happiest man. When I first saw Heather, I knew immediately that she was the one for me." The guests cooed and gushed. "Heather and I want to thank all of you for coming, some of you from very far, to celebrate with us."

Glasses clinked. Fisher and Anna stood and gave their speech together, leaving Troy wondering if he and Cam should have done the same.

Too late now. Troy rose and took the microphone.

"Heather, can you put your hand down on the table?" She did as asked. "Good. Now, Justin, place your hand over hers." Justin, still grinning, did as directed. "Take a good, long look. Justin, this is the last time you'll have the upper hand." The guests roared with laugher. Troy lifted his champagne flute to toast. "To giving up manhood for love. Worth it, in my opinion."

When he sat down and Cam rose, he wished he had let her go ahead of him. Cam would probably use her recycled speech from Anna and Fisher's wedding. Not dull, but not from the heart either. Had he gone last, no one would remember her speech, and she wouldn't feel like she'd done one more thing wrong in a long line of wrongs.

She took the mic and cleared her throat. "Fairy tales are just words in a book. Stories of love and conquering all to achieve that beloved, seemingly unreachable feeling," she said.

Troy glanced around at the dropped faces, knowing this wasn't a carbon-copy speech, and hoping it wasn't her view of real love either. Damn, they should have done a speech together. This was going to be ugly. As he was about to stand and save her, she continued.

"But as someone recently taught me..." she paused to smile down at him, stealing his breath, "...it's not whether or not they're real that matters, but rather if we believe they're real." She looked back at the guests, and then to Heather and Justin. "May this day be your once upon a time."

As everyone cheered and clapped, toasting Camryn's speech and the couple, Troy stared at the woman he'd known more than half his life, but not at all. And in that moment, he made the decision to fight. He would fight for her, for them. He would not give her up to anyone, whatever the consequences, however it panned out. It didn't matter that he was a simple construction worker, that his father was a drunk. He'd never touch another drop. He'd give her all the kids she wanted. Do everything in his power to make her happy.

If she wanted him.

Camryn sat down next to him. Before she could scoot her chair in, he gripped the back of her neck and kissed her. Right in front of everyone, letting them know she was his.

Pulling back, he dropped his forehead to hers. "That was beautiful, Cam."

"Thank you." She leaned back, allowing the waiters to set their plates down. She lifted her fork to cut the salmon. "You're rubbing off on me. I'm turning into a gushy female. You know I actually intervened for Katie and John earlier. *Me.*"

She laughed. He swallowed.

"Camryn..."

She looked at him, and he couldn't find the words to express everything he felt. There weren't enough words in the English language that could remotely explain this feeling. Like drowning. In her.

A worried look crossed her face. "Are you okay?" He shook his head. She turned in her seat. "Have you eaten today?" He shook his head. "You look pale, Troy. Eat something."

"Food won't fix this."

"Then what's wrong?"

Staring into her hazel eyes, he tried to blink. Tried to spit out three simple damn words and couldn't. Now was not the time. Here not the place. He needed her alone. Just him and her.

"Nothing," he said. "Never mind. Let's eat before it gets cold." She looked doubtful, so he took a bite of wild rice to prove he was fine.

By the time cake was served and cleared, dusk had fallen. Lights flickered on in the trees, casting a white glow through the leaves. Justin led Heather to the open space in the center of the arranged tables and onto the platform. The DJ cued their song for the first dance.

Camryn dropped her chin in her palm and watched, looking like a starry-eyed little girl imagining her big day. She was different. Everything about her was different.

She was still Cam—quiet and too smart for her own good. But she didn't have all the weight on her, all the reservations which tied her down.

Perhaps he'd done that. Perhaps this whole charade was leading them here, where they were meant to be.

Emily bounded over and climbed in Cam's lap. "The lights do look pretty," she whispered to Cam. "Is everyone going to fall in love now? 'Cause of the romantic."

"Romance, you mean?" Camryn grinned at her niece, and Troy's pulse beat hard. He hadn't seen her smile like that ever. Before now, there was always a pause before she smiled, as if needing to tell herself to do the act.

"Maybe," she answered Emily. "If they're lucky enough to fall in love."

Holy shit. He did it. He had her believing in magic and love and ever afters. Had her grinning carefree, and laughing out loud. Making a fool of herself, doing something spontaneous, getting angry...all of it had worked. Watching her now, he knew. She believed.

But did she want him in return?

Fisher came by and swooped Emily off Cam's lap. "The next dance goes to you, Em."

A small crowd of guests had filled the dance floor. Fisher made his way there with Emily. Once he was out of earshot, Troy looked at Camryn. "If I ask you to dance with me, will you let me lead?"

She laughed. "That depends. Can you dance?"

"No, but I can fake it."

He took her hand and walked to the edge of the floor. He tugged her against his chest and danced. She let him lead. Closing his eyes, he smiled into her hair.

Lemongrass.

"Would you look at that?" she said.

With great regret, he pulled away. His gaze followed hers over to Katie and John, dancing and smiling. "Looks like you did it after all, Cam. And you said you didn't believe."

Her cheek brushed his when she turned back toward him. She felt too right, too real in his arms. He only had one task on the list left. One more night with her. After that, after tomorrow, he was supposed to let her go.

But his heart wouldn't stop pounding.

"Camryn, tell me something. Did these other men you were with before me make your heart pound? Your stomach flutter? Your laugh giddy?"

She stopped and leaned back to look at him. A thousand emotions dissolved together until he couldn't even breathe waiting for her answer.

"No," she said, looking away, setting them in motion again.

"Do I?"

Again, she froze, this time not looking at him. Her fingers tightened in his. Her breath fanned his neck. "Did the women before me do that for you?"

Crazy thing, he almost said there were no women before her. "No."

"Do I?" She was using his tactic against him. Clever girl.

"Answer my question, Cam."

John tapped her shoulder. She whirled.

"Let me borrow Camryn for a moment," John said. "I just need a quick word. I'll give her right back."

Troy looked at her, her eyes cast down, shoulders tight.

He'd waited this long for her, he could hold out a few more minutes. Troy nodded.

"I'll wait for you by the table. We'll finish this conversation."

Chapter Nineteen

Life Lessons According to Camryn:
Sometimes the beholders of beauty need glasses.

Camryn watched Troy walk away and breathed for the first time in what felt like minutes. John took her hand and began to dance. Her head spinning with Troy's question, she nearly jumped when John started talking.

"I took your advice."

She forced herself to concentrate and smiled at him. "By the looks of it, things turned out okay."

"They did." He paused, staring at her. "I never thought of Katie as anything more than a friend. When I woke up this morning and saw her, something inside me shifted. Strange, you know? She was right in front of me."

"I understand." Too well, she understood. At least it would turn out well for John and Katie.

"I'm glad I came to the wedding, got to know you a little better. You're not who I expected you to be."

Her eyebrows shot up. "Who were you expecting?"

His shoulder lifted and dropped. "Honestly, I always thought of you as aloof. An untouchable woman. Guess I was wrong. You seem happy."

She nodded, the truth cutting her in half. "I hope you two are happy also."

The DJ played an up-tempo song when the other ended, one of Heather's favorites from a hair band Camryn hated.

"That's my cue to sit down."

He held her a second more. "Thank you, Camryn."

"You're very welcome."

An arm grabbed her from behind, dragging her deeper onto the dance floor. When she turned, Heather was grinning.

"Dance," her sister ordered.

Camryn crossed her arms. "I'm sitting this one out, Heather."

Katie wrapped an arm around Camryn and Heather, tugging them together. Before Camryn knew it, she was jumping and dancing through two sets. Though it couldn't have resembled dancing, she had fun.

Justin's friend, Jessie, caught the bouquet, and Cade caught the garter. Camryn frowned. Now there was a pair. Several of the guests started heading back home or to the hotel after that.

"My feet are killing me," she said to Katie. "I'm going to sit for a minute."

But her father had other plans. The music shifted to a slow song and he took her hand before she could even get to the grass.

"You look very nice tonight."

"Thanks, Dad. So do you."

He smiled down at her. "Two of my three kids are married off. When's it going to be your turn?"

Camryn laughed. Her dad's eyebrows rose.

Backpedaling, she shook her head. "Um, when I'm ready?"

"You've been dating Troy for more than a year."

It never dawned on her until now just how heartbroken her parents might be with the breakup. Troy was like one of their own. Seeing Troy and Camryn together probably made them happy. After the shock wore off anyway.

"Dad, don't be upset if this doesn't work out, okay?"

"What do you mean by that?" His gaze was worrisome, not fierce, which had Camryn's stomach flopping.

"Nothing. Well..."

"Is there something I don't know?"

Yeah, everything.

Fisher tapped her shoulder at the song change, taking her father's place. Her dad stood back and watched, the disappointment evident in the turn of his mouth. She knew this was coming. Troy and she were breaking up tomorrow once they got back to Milwaukee. But seeing that look on her dad's face made her wish for a better outcome. Made her wish she could conform to their ideal version of a daughter.

Her dad turned and walked away.

"What did you do to upset Dad?"

Camryn looked at Fisher and shrugged. "He wants another wedding."

"And?" She didn't answer. "You don't want to marry Troy?"

Oh man, she kind of did. Scratch that, really did. "I'm trying to be realistic."

"I don't get it."

She didn't either. For the remainder of the song, Camryn danced with her brother, avoiding eye contact and hoping he wouldn't talk anymore. When the music ended and another fast one began, Camryn took off toward the bar before anyone else could stop her.

She ordered a white wine and turned her back to the guests. Smiling at the bartender, she took the glass he offered and sipped.

"I've been waiting at the table half the night, Cam."

After briefly closing her eyes, she opened them and turned. "Sorry, Troy. I got caught up."

He'd taken off his jacket and tie. The first two buttons of

his shirt were undone. She wanted to undo the rest. Spread the shirt open...

He took her glass and set it on the bar. Gripping her elbow, he steered her away from the noise and around the corner of the house.

"Explain to me how this breakup is supposed to go. Are you going to dump me in front of the whole family at the gift opening? On the plane? Perhaps you'll be kind and wait until we get home. Let's just get it over with. We can have a huge fight right now. I'll take the DJ's microphone and stop the music."

His nostrils flared, his mouth firmed. Her mouth dropped open, wondering where this sudden burst of temper came from. Her gaze roamed over his face, settling on his eyes. Though narrowed to slits, there wasn't anger behind his eyes, or behind this outburst.

She swallowed. "I'm not leaving you, Troy. None of us are. The end of this...relationship is not the end of..."

"To hell with this, Cam." He grabbed her arm and pulled her to him. "Do you feel anything for me?"

"Yes, of course I do."

He growled. "I don't mean as your friend. Do you have feelings for me?" He drew out each word as if talking to a small child.

Why did he care? Troy didn't do committed relationships. He may say he wanted love and marriage, but his actions proved otherwise. Except in his eyes was something she'd never seen from him, from any man. The way he was looking at her...

No air. The breath ripped from her lungs.

He dropped her arm, his face softening until the edges were no longer harsh. "I need to know, Cam. Please. Is there any room inside there for anything besides friendship?" His finger traced the outline of her dress, over her heart.

She gasped, closed her eyes. To admit the truth would

leave her raw. But she couldn't lie to him. Not tonight. Not after all he'd done.

Her eyes opened. "Yes."

He stared at her, a cross between relief and pain. Slowly, his Adam's apple bobbed. He lifted a hand to touch her, but jerked it back. After a few seconds, he tried again, this time cupping her cheek.

"Come upstairs with me. I have to show you something."

Unable to deny him, she nodded.

Taking her hand, he led her around to the front and inside the garage door of the house. They made their way through the formal living room and up the stairs in silence. Inside their bedroom, he shut the door and locked it. He walked to the patio doors and closed the drapes. He unbuttoned his shirt, removed it, and tossed it aside.

From across the darkened room, she watched his back, waiting for whatever he had to show her. He was so beautiful. So handsome. What in the hell was he doing with someone like her? Even if only for pretend, they had crossed the line, gone too far to take it back now. She wanted to know why he did. After a long pause, his head dropped and his hands fell to his hips.

"Come here, Cam," he whispered, showing her his profile.

She undid the straps of her heels and slid them off, bumps skating over her skin. He'd never been like this. She'd never come to him. In their lovemaking, he'd always been the initiator.

She walked across the floor, taking his hand in hers. "What do you want to show me?"

"You. I want to show you yourself."

Gently, he tugged her to the bathroom. Except instead of stepping inside, he closed the door, leaving them standing outside and looking into a floor-length mirror.

He came behind her, dropping his hands on her shoulders.

243

"Look in the mirror, Cam."

She did as asked, watching their reflection and feeling more exposed than if she'd been naked.

His hands lifted to her hair, pulling the pins out one by one. "Your hair is the color of cinnamon, so different from your Serbian heritage. It smells like lemongrass. I'll never smell anything close to it again and not think of you."

Her hair fell to her shoulders as he ran his hands through it. She shivered at his gentleness, wondering where he was going with this mirror thing.

His eyes watched her in the mirror, but his mouth hovered over her ear. "No one has eyes like yours. They show your every emotion, no matter how hard you try to hide them. Your mouth is small, pink, but when you smile it expands your entire face. I can't stop staring at you when you smile."

His lips skimmed over her neck, to her shoulders. She closed her eyes. "Open your eyes and watch." She obeyed, swallowing as the zipper of her dress skated down. "Your skin is soft. I absolutely love the little freckles on your shoulders."

The dress fell to the floor. She tried to cover her bare breasts, but he took her hands and dropped them. "You have curves, like a woman should." His finger traced over one breast, down her side, and to her hip, scorching a trail across her skin. "Your breasts fit in my hands," he said, and proved his theory by cupping them.

She arched back, wanting more. Wanting everything. But he wasn't done.

Sliding his fingers into the waistband of her panties, he went around her and tugged them down, over her hips, her thighs, and to her ankles. He followed the path down, kneeling in front of her. She stepped out of her dress and panties, shaking when he didn't rise after.

"Your legs are long and perfectly shaped. When you have them wrapped around me, I lose my mind." His finger trailed up her inner calf, to her thigh. "What's between those legs drives me mad."

Without warning, he closed his mouth over her heat. She gasped, her legs buckling. In one fluid move he rose and caught her. "That's the best part, Cam," he said, breathless. "Watching you like this. Knowing only I get to see you like this." His breath fanned her cheek. "Look in the mirror."

Her heart pounded against her ribs, constricting and convulsing to a rapid-timed beat. Her throat closed. Opening her eyes, she looked at them. His back to the reflection, arms around her. His taut muscles, her soft curves. His tanned skin to her light. Together.

"This is how I see you, Cam. You're beautiful."

Her eyes slammed closed to contain the tears.

"Open them," he demanded. "Look at yourself. Say it. Say, 'I'm beautiful'."

A muffled whimper rose from her throat, and if she hadn't felt it escape, she wouldn't have believed it came from her.

She was right. He would leave her raw. Stripped down to the bare, basic impulses and needs. The very thing she sheltered herself from. No other man would compare to him. No one else would make her feel like this. She'd spend the rest of her life empty, waiting in vain for this feeling to come again.

He stepped back, unbuttoned his pants, and dropped them to the floor. "Say it, Cam."

"You're beautiful," she whispered, staring at him.

One corner of his mouth quirked. "Camryn..."

"I'm beautiful."

His smile came easily, disengaging in its charm. "Now believe it."

Her gaze darted up, away. Tears fell over her cheeks. "Your list, Troy?"

"Yes, this is on my list. The last item. It doesn't make what

I said any less true. I meant it. Do you want to know why I created the list, Cam?" He swiped one of her tears away with his thumb.

She looked at him, realizing she didn't want to know. A few days ago maybe, but not now. Whatever his motives, they were his. The reasons didn't matter, only the result. She'd rather have the illusion.

"No."

She looked away again. He touched her chin and drew her back.

"Say it and mean it this time, Cam. Believe it, 'cause it's true."

Her father's words came back to her as she stared at Troy. All the things her dad said about why she hid from beauty, how she got this image of herself. Then Troy's words began to sink in.

"I'm beautiful," she said, looking him straight in the eye and wanting to do more than repeating his words as a thank you.

She reached out, splaying her fingers over his chest. When he leaned in to kiss her, she held him off. Troy's insecurities about his past held him back as much as hers did. If he could have a list, she could too. So then maybe he would meet the right woman someday and love her, just like he wanted her to do with someone else.

She turned him around to face the mirror, keeping her back to the reflection.

"Camryn..."

"Shh. You listen now." She touched his forehead with her fingertips. "In your head are all the bad things your father did and said, making you second-guess your relationships. Those around you don't have a motive. We're here because we want to be."

He grabbed her arms, ground out her name. "You are not

turning this on me."

She tugged her arms free. "In here," she said, touching his chest, "is a good heart. A guy who would never hurt another person because he knows how bad it feels. Because he's stronger than his dad ever was. You have a conscience. A good soul."

His arms fell to his sides. His jaw ground, bunching the muscles for her to see. When her gaze drifted to his eyes, he closed them.

"Open your eyes," she directed, just like he demanded of her. "See the truth, Troy."

Slowly, his eyes opened and he glanced at her. He expelled a shaky breath and looked away. "Enough, Cam. You made your point."

"That mouth of yours," she said, ignoring him, "is quick to crack a joke or kiss me senseless. No one's ever kissed me senseless. But the real talent there is your disarming smile." She grinned, remembering. "Your eyes are wicked and dark, like you seek out mischief."

Her fingers drifted down over his shoulders, his arms, while he stood erect, trying not to respond. "I could go on and on about your fabulous body, about all the things we've done together, but you know all that."

She leaned back and took his hands, weaving their fingers together. She waited until he looked at her before she finished. "Your hands are your best feature. Proof that you work hard, that you refuse to fall victim to your past. Despite how rough and calloused they are, your touch is gentle."

She pressed her body to his, skin to skin, heart to heart, and wrapped her arms around him. It took him several seconds, but his arms came up and held her back.

He shuddered out a breath. "Why did you do that? This was supposed to be about you. Are you trying to disarm me? 'Cause it worked, Cam..."

"I thought you should see my truth, the way you showed me yours."

"What does all this mean? You and me. I need to know. You need to spell it out for me."

They were back to this already. Not even a chance to make love one last time. Reality and tomorrow looming.

Swallowing, she backed away and bent down for her dress. She walked to the closet, and hung the dress before closing the door. As she reached for her bag on the bed, his hand clamped down on hers. He tossed the bag out of her reach.

"Would you stop avoiding my questions? Just this once?" he asked, his voice dangerously low, obviously on the brink of losing it. "You and me, Cam. Spell it out for me."

Sadness turned to anger in a flash. She knew it was a defense, but she didn't give a damn. "Fine, Troy. We had a great week together. Is that what you want to hear? You broke me down, we had a few good heart to hearts, and some great sex." She pushed him away when he stepped closer. "Tomorrow, we leave. All goes back to normal. Is that clear enough?"

His eyes bulged. His mouth curled. Anger radiated off him in waves so strong she felt herself shaking.

"Is that all this was?" he barked. Her chin raised. He strode the few steps to her, pinning her back to the bedpost and her wrists above her head. "Answer me!"

"I believe I did."

Breath heaving, he stared her down. Nose to nose. His gaze was vicious, and she could tell he was holding onto a thin shred of control. And damn, she wanted him out of control. His erection pressed against her abdomen, and she fought the urge to lean into him. Holding onto her own anger was easier. Safer.

"The hell you did," he ground out, slamming his mouth over hers.

Chapter Twenty

Life Lessons According to Camryn:
Flying into a rage only forces a bad landing.

She couldn't have been any clearer. Come tomorrow, this was over.

His body didn't get the memo. Neither did his heart, but he'd worry about that later. For now, for tonight, he had her.

And his anger.

His temper hadn't subsided one iota. He'd tried to breathe. He'd tried to walk away. Instead, all he got was a raging erection.

His hands dove into her hair, his kiss swallowing her whole.

Not enough.

"You frustrate the hell out of me, Cam."

One long leg wrapped around his waist. "Good. We're even."

Without finesse, he lined himself up and drove inside her. So tight. So hot. She ground against him, crying out, and he almost didn't get his hand over her mouth in time. He wanted to make love to her at home, in his bed, if for no other reason than to hear her come without restraint.

Shoving his hand away, she crushed her mouth to his, wrung tighter than a drum. His hands fisted the bedpost above her head as he pounded into her. She came again, sliding down the post as the tremors quaked.

Hell no. They weren't done yet. Not even close.

He grabbed her ass, swung her around, and landed on the bed with her on top. She didn't miss a beat. She clutched the headboard above his head, propelling her breasts into his face. Her head flew back, thrusting him so deep he saw Heaven.

"Camryn..."

"Shut up, Troy."

"Okay."

He came off the mattress, wrapping his arms around her and pumping. A mangled whimper rose from her chest, vibrating her breasts crushed to his chest. Her face pushed against his neck, her hands fisted in his hair, driving him to insanity and back again when they both came.

Hard. Fast. Without an ounce of restraint.

She shook against him, panting. His hold around her tightened, an ineffective way to calm himself. To pretend she wasn't leaving him. He couldn't tell if it was her heart or his hammering. Probably both. Only his was broken.

"We forgot the condom," she said.

He froze. No matter how attractive the woman, no matter how good the sex, he never forgot a condom. Never. Cam had him so riled, so freaking turned on that it wasn't even a thought in his head.

"It's not the right time in my cycle. We should be fine." She pulled back to look at him, seemingly calm as ever. "Are you safe?"

His teeth ground. "I wouldn't have touched you in the first place if I wasn't safe. Give me some damn credit."

"You're the one who's slept with half the population of Milwaukee. It was an honest question." She rose and walked to the bathroom.

He flew off the bed. "What in the hell does that mean?"

She tried to shut the door. He palmed it open.

"Connect the dots, Troy. It was a no-brainer."

"Jesus. And we're not done fighting yet."

She laughed bitterly. "You're the one who wanted me angry. 'Get angry, Cam,' you said. For my list. You're not good enough the way you are. Do these things and you'll be a woman instead of a robot."

Her mocking him had his control gone again. He grabbed her arms and hauled her into the shower. "I never called you a robot. I never said those things. And you are good enough!"

She looked down at his hold on her, then into his eyes. When her eyebrows rose, he looked down too. Her feet were a good six inches off the ground. He released her at once, letting her feet drop to the tile.

He wrenched the water on, the hot spray pouring over them. In seconds steam filled the room as they stared at each other.

"Want to hit me?" she asked, as if not fazed at all that he just manhandled her like a barbarian. As if they were discussing what type of syrup to have with their pancakes.

Her question sank in. "What? No!"

"Yet you're mad at me?"

What in the hell was she up to? "Beyond any measure of vocalizing."

"So, now you see. You're not your dad."

Now he considered hitting something. Like his fist right through the tile. "You got me pissed off on purpose to prove a point?"

"No. That was mere circumstance, but my point is proven. Now you can stop wondering if you're able to control your temper. I, on the other hand, am still angry. Let me out of the shower."

"Three orgasms didn't do it for you?"

"No."

He grinned. "I'm getting to you."

"Yes, like a parasitic insect. Move, Troy."

His erection sprang anew. Camryn was sexy as hell when angry. He could do this all night. In fact, they probably would. She had a lot of aggression buried way in there, and he'd love nothing more than to help her release it.

He crossed his arms, blocking her way. "No."

Her eyes narrowed. "Move, Troy."

"I love it when you say my name."

"Troy..." she growled, and he nearly came right there in the shower.

God, the way she said his name. Like a curse. He'd never been so hard in his life. He slowly backed her to the tile. Taking one wrist, he pinned it above her head. Thump. He took the other, doing the same. Thump.

She fought. He grew harder until the erection was more pain than pleasure.

No one made Camryn Covic lose control. He was getting to her, she just wouldn't admit it. That's what all this anger was about. All this hot, livid sex. She'd rather be mad than admit any feelings for him, than admit his list proved her theory of love wrong.

He pressed so tightly against her that there wasn't room for even the water. He leaned in to kiss her, but hovered over her cheek instead. She started shaking again.

"What do you want, Cam? Tell me."

"Let me go."

"Uh huh. What do you really want?" His tongue darted over the wet skin on her cheek, down her neck. He moved to the other side, licking every drop. "Tell me, Cam. What do you want?" When she refused to answer still, he slid his knee between her legs, and she moaned. Deep, long.

He could feel the moment her anger drained.

"You. I want you."

Oh God. *Yes.*

He drew back, let her wrists go, and stared into her eyes. "You have me."

Camryn opened her eyes and stared into the dark room while Troy snored quietly in the bed next to her. In fact, he had been snoring for the past four hours. Right after they had sex in the shower. And in the bed. Again.

You have me.

She didn't dare ask what that meant. Didn't dare hope. His version of a relationship and hers were very different. His future goals and hers not even close to being in sync. So why had he fought so damn hard earlier? He could've just let her go. Why ask questions as if he planned to take this further?

Because he felt sorry for her. That's what his list and everything this week was about. It had to be. Her boyfriend said mean things and dumped her. Troy took pity and agreed to step in. He glimpsed her version of life, how pathetic he thought she was, and gave her tasks to do to make herself better. More presentable. Less boring.

So maybe the next guy who dumped her won't say anything on the way out.

She was nice to Troy as a kid. Helped him out a time or two. He all but admitted this thing between them was to pay her back for her kindness. He should've just said thank you. That would've hurt less than this.

Grr! Her brain wouldn't shut off. Of all the times in her life she really needed solace, and she couldn't quell the feelings, the images of the past week.

Sighing, she glanced at the bedside clock. Everyone would be up in a few hours. The gift opening was this morning. Afterward, while Justin and Heather flew to Cancun for their honeymoon, the rest of the family would fly back to Milwaukee.

Quietly, she rolled out of bed and tiptoed to the closet, picking out a plain, white dress. The only garment Heather hadn't stolen days earlier. Lord, had it only been days? Exiting the closet, she peeked at Troy, finding him still asleep. She went into the bathroom to wash and dress. After applying her makeup she stepped out and opened her bag.

The mundane task of packing to go home grounded her, gave her the composure she needed. It was time to return to reality. Time for her to get back to normal.

After folding the last of her shirts neatly in the bag, she packed her cosmetics. She paused, looking at Troy's toothbrush on the counter. The intimacy of seeing it lying there next to hers made her hands shake. Maxwell never left his toothbrush at her apartment. Maxwell never left anything but a hollow gap where a boyfriend should be. Troy was different. They weren't even a real couple, with the commitment and boundaries an actual relationship should have, but yet he gave her his all. Mind. Body.

He'd been here with her all week. Not just a stand-in, but a presence. How could she ever go back to her old life after this?

Shaking her head, she packed Troy's clothes too, leaving his toiletries in the bathroom for when he woke. She set his bag on the dresser.

Bag in hand, she stood by the door feeling oddly sentimental. She told herself she was just checking the room to make sure nothing was left behind. She would not come back up here again. She'd bank down these emotions, get through the gift opening, and go home.

But just one last look wouldn't hurt.

Her gaze fell on Troy as he slept. She'd leave him and what they'd done together in here too. Where it belonged. As a memory. A dream.

As the only good thing to ever happen to her.

Swallowing, she mentally told him good-bye so she could

move on. To make this moment final. It shouldn't hurt this bad. From day one they knew this wasn't true. They never existed. If anyone understood the reality of this past week, it was her. Her life reality.

Never let them see you hurt. Never let them see you cry. Never let them in.

Troy, damn him, had gotten in.

Closing the door behind her, she stared at it, resisting the urge to rush back inside. *Look away. Go!*

She turned, walked downstairs, and headed for the kitchen. After starting a pot of coffee, she set out the bakery items Bernice had purchased for breakfast. She whipped up a quick fruit salad with what was in the fridge and set that on the table too.

The others would be awake soon. For the first time in memory, she couldn't wait for the family. The sooner they woke, the sooner this day would be over. She glanced out the window when lightening flashed. Rain beat against the glass and cascaded down.

After pouring herself a cup of coffee, she walked out the patio door and under the awning to watch the rain. The sound reminded her of that night on their balcony when Troy made her dance. Smiling, she sipped her coffee.

The crew the Hortons had hired had cleared away all remnants of the wedding. All that lay out over the yard now was the rain-soaked grass. She'd miss this place once she got back home. Miss the quiet, the clean mountain air. Miss Troy.

Thunder boomed overhead as the first of the family straggled into the kitchen. She turned, seeing Fisher pulling orange juice out of the fridge and Emily watching her from the doorway. She held her hand out for Emily to join her.

"I hate rain," her niece declared, emerging from the doorway, a pout forming her bottom lip.

"I love rain. It smells clean. The sound is relaxing."

Emily looked at her. "You can't play in the rain. It sucks."

Camryn grinned. "Don't say *sucks*. Your dad will get mad. And you *can* play in the rain. It's quite fun actually."

"Dad says I can't. I'll get all wet."

"Well, not today then. Some other time."

Her niece looked doubtful. "You'll take me?"

The rest of the house was awake by the sound of it. She looked at Emily. "Sure. Sometime soon, okay? Let's go inside before Tetaka Myrtle eats all the chocolate donuts."

Emily laughed and bolted inside. Camryn glanced out over the mountains one last time and followed her niece.

At the second crack of thunder that morning, Troy groaned, barely able to fight the urge to burrow deeper under the covers. Changing his mind, he reached out for Camryn to tug her under with him.

The bed was empty.

He opened his eyes to confirm. Sitting up, he looked around the room, not finding her, or any trace she was there in the first place. He got up and headed for the bathroom. Her cosmetics were gone.

He walked out of the bathroom and eyed the closet. The closet was empty too.

His gaze landed on the dresser as he raked a hand through his hair. She'd packed his bag for him. Well, at least she wasn't subtle.

He sighed, a heavy weight settling in his gut. She was done.

But he wasn't. If he were to tell her how he felt, would she love him back? Last night she'd said she wanted him. His hands dropped to his hips, wondering if that was a physical want or an emotional one.

He didn't think Camryn was the one-night-stand type. Or

in their case, one-week stand. Even after everything, all the checks on his list, she didn't know true love when it was standing right in front of her. Too scared to think someone could love her that much. Too scared to give in and let herself love.

Maybe she didn't know how emotionally invested he was. Maybe she didn't know if she herself was capable. If he took this gamble, if he laid out every raw emotion she invoked inside him, would it change her mind?

Hell, what other choice was there?

He bolted back inside the bathroom. He shaved, brushed his teeth, and dressed. Shoving the items in his bag, he ran out the door and down the stairs, hoping to catch her before the family...

Was sitting at the table eating breakfast. *Great.*

He dropped his bag inside the doorway. "Morning, everyone."

A few mutters greeted him in return. He poured himself some coffee and sat across the table from Camryn. She was decisively pushing the fruit around her plate, gaze cast down, not joining in on the conversation around her. She wouldn't even look at him.

"What does hung over mean?" Emily asked, looking like Groucho Marx with her chocolate donut mustache.

Fisher rubbed his forehead, sighing. "Thank you very much, everyone."

Heather rolled her eyes. "Relax. It's not a curse, for crying out loud."

Mom grinned. "Hung over is what your daddy used to be every Sunday before you were born."

"Mother!"

Exasperated, Emily turned to Camryn. "What's it mean, Auntie Cam?"

Camryn's head shot up. "What?"

Yjaka Harold laughed. "Looks like Cam's hung over too."

"I am not."

"Then what's wrong with you?" her mother insisted.

"Nothing." Oh, she was a terrible liar. Always was. She looked at Emily. "What did you ask me, honey?"

"What does hung over mean?" The three-year-old drew out every word as if talking to an idiot. Hilarious, because Camryn was the only non-idiot present.

Camryn wiped the chocolate off her niece's face with a napkin. "When adults drink too much alcohol they get sick the next day. They call it hung over."

"Hung over what?"

"A slang term for a sickness that carries to the next day."

She had yet to look at him. He felt like a piece of meat tossed to the side. At least he could blame his mood on alcohol or sleep deprivation if anyone asked. Technically he was still her boyfriend, so pretenses needed to be made. But the second they were alone...

Bernice stood. "If you guys want to make your flight, we should get going on the gift opening."

The family rose from the table like a swarm. Troy stayed where he was until the room emptied except for Cam and Bernice. Cam helped Justin's mom clear away the plates and clean up the kitchen.

"I'm so sad you're leaving today. You'll have to come back and visit us again."

Camryn placed a hand on Bernice's arm. "I would love to. Thank you again for everything. Your home is beautiful, and you made Heather's day lovely."

Bernice nodded and left for the living room, where a shouting match had already ensued over whether to open the cards or presents first. Camryn dropped her elbows on the counter and rubbed her forehead.

Now or never. Tell her he loved her or watch her run. Fight for happiness or live in regret. There was no option really. Panic set in just the same.

"I have a sure-fire cure for a headache."

Her head whipped up. "I didn't know you were still in here."

"Obviously. We need to talk."

She straightened. "Not now, Troy."

"Yes, now."

Shaking her head, she pivoted and headed toward the hallway. *Do not let her run. Do not let her get away.* He was off his chair and across the room before she could even hit the doorway. He closed his hand over the doorframe, blocking her exit.

"Troy, let me go."

Laughable statement. "I can't." Frustrated, he ran his free hand through his hair. "See, that's a huge problem. I can't seem to let you go, Cam."

"Camryn!" her mother shouted from the other room. "Get in here."

She turned to go, he grabbed her arm.

"Listen to me. The list started out with me wanting to show you how to live, how to love. I wanted you to believe in those things too. You're too smart a woman, Cam, to not believe love exists. I wanted to show you that the things your ex said weren't true." He knew he was talking too fast, knew he sounded like a rambling moron, but she had to see the whole picture. "Things changed, though, after I kissed you. Then it wasn't about you believing in love. It was about you falling in love with me."

She gasped, looking doubtful and innocent as her eyes rounded. Had no one told her they loved her before?

"Did it work, Cam? Did you fall in love with me?"

"Camryn!" This time the order came from Nana.

God, could they shut up for once? Just once? "She'll be there in a damn minute," he yelled, scrubbing his hands down his face.

"Troy?" she squeaked out. Disbelieving. Traumatized.

Damn it. He sucked at this. She sucked at this. "What if this wasn't for pretend?"

She stared at him, her beautiful hazel eyes pleading for him to stop. Her mouth trembled open to probably tell him no.

He cut her off. "Go out with me."

She blinked. "Excuse me?"

"Go out with me. On a date. Not just here, but for real."

She swallowed. A fleeting look of hope registered on her face. "You're insane."

His hands dropped to his hips. "Yes, but for a week, so were you. We were in this together. This is crazy. *We're* crazy. But it feels right. I want you, Cam. Not just pretending for a week, but for more. Make this real and..."

"I can't believe this!" They turned and saw Fisher standing in the other doorway.

"Are you kidding me?" Fisher barked, the question obviously rhetorical. "You lied? This was all a damn lie!"

"What's going on in there?"

Before Troy could even open his mouth, or punch his best friend in the face, the entire clan had invaded the kitchen.

"What's all the yelling about?" her mother demanded.

"They lied," Fisher screamed. "They're not dating. They made the whole effing thing up."

In unison, the collective whole turned to stare at them.

"Is that true, Camryn?" Dad asked.

Camryn's eyes closed. He watched her fight for control, wanting that superpower. And as his gut knotted, he recognized the shame on her face.

"Answer him!" Fisher demanded. "Tell them how this was all a joke. Did you think this was funny?"

Troy stepped forward, to do what, he didn't know, but Camryn interrupted him mid-stride.

"No," she said softly. With finality. She directed her gaze at him, as if answering his declaration from before. He couldn't tell what she referred to. No to Fisher's question, or no to him. All he did know was his blood stopped circulating, and the cold he'd fought so hard to banish returned.

Clearing her throat, she raised her voice. "It wasn't meant to be a joke. But it is true. We lied. *I* lied," she corrected. "Troy was nice enough to go along with it. We're not dating. We never were." She looked around the kitchen at her family, one by one. "I asked him to do this because..." She trailed off, her gaze growing distant. "It doesn't matter why now. I'm sorry. Don't blame him. This is all my fault. Like everything else."

The room fell silent for all of five seconds before Nana laughed.

"I told you so! I told you he'd never date her!"

Pause. Shock. Then the kitchen commenced to chaos. Everyone shouting, arms flailing, their true Serbian temper erupting through the air like a Carolina heat wave.

I don't believe it!

But they were kissing!

Where's the real boyfriend?

She probably lied about that too!

Troy looked at Camryn for a reaction. Her glazed eyes focused on the counter in front of her. Her hands clutched the granite with such force that her knuckles were white. Like being trapped in the eye of a storm, they stood there while everything around them swirled and flew to Kingdom Come.

She told the family it was a lie. She never responded when

he told her how he felt. Everything he ever hoped for ripped away. His whole life, all he ever wanted was love. Someone to love him because no one ever had.

Perhaps she was right after all. True love didn't exist. It was just some fruitless dream he created to survive.

Tears welled in her eyes, fell down her cheeks. "This was a mistake," she whispered through the anarchy, probably for her ears only.

But he heard. Loud and clear.

Chapter Twenty-One

Life Lessons According to Camryn:
No one's born smart, but one does have to work
awfully hard to stay stupid.

The fasten seatbelt light chimed off as her mother continued her babbling about not understanding why Camryn had lied. Troy was sitting with her dad a few rows up. He looked every bit as miserable. At least he was miserable in silence. Mom didn't know when to shut up.

Camryn directed her gaze out the window, trying to tune out the noise. Her seat was right on the left wing, reminding her of an old *Twilight Zone* episode. A gremlin appeared on the wing with a grin straight out of hell. The ugly little creature pointed to the exhaust propeller, silently questioning whether to mangle it in her honor. She almost smiled and nodded, imagining the plane going down in a smoldering pile of ash. John Lithgow replaced her mother in the next seat, violently shaking his head.

A hand closed over hers, drawing her back.

"Camryn," she pleaded. "Please, just tell me why you did this."

If her family wasn't so damn adamant about her finding a man and marrying in the first place, none of this would've happened.

"Maybe I just got sick and tired of not being good enough. Maybe I just got sick of being the butt of every family joke. Sick to death of having marriage rammed down my throat. I thought if I showed up with someone, you'd leave me alone."

Tears formed in her mother's eyes. "Oh, Cam. We just want you happy."

"I was perfectly happy before this trip."

"You think you were happy? Happy was watching you and Troy together. That was the first time I've seen you happy in years." Her mother gripped her hands in hers. "Maybe it wasn't all a lie. Maybe you could work it out..."

She pulled her hands back. "There you go again. I don't need to be with someone to be happy. I'm not like the rest of you, depending on others for contentment. It was a lie, and it's over."

A lie that felt awfully true. The pain in her chest confirmed. And she was happy with Troy. She may not have realized it at the time, but she did now. She wished she never knew the feeling, lived the rest of her life in ignorant bliss.

Her mother wiped her eyes. "I pushed you too hard. I didn't mean to. We never worried about you like we did for Fisher and Heather. Except when it came to love. It's not that you're not good enough, Cam. You're so successful in your career. You have a stable life. But that's not happiness." She sighed, staring at her hands in her lap. "I just wanted you to love someone, like I love your father. To know what that feels like." Swallowing, she looked back at her. "Love isn't giving up your identity and independence, it's sharing your life with them. Having someone to wake up next to and go to bed with at night."

Sighing, Camryn felt her anger drain. Perhaps she'd misunderstood all along, just like the beautiful thing with her father. How wrong she'd been about so many things. But not where Troy was concerned. "I appreciate your intentions, Mother. But Troy and I never were anything but an illusion. Now, drop it, please. I'm tired. Okay?"

Disappointment distorted her mom's face before she nodded and reluctantly turned away. Camryn glanced out the window, but the gremlin was gone.

What a shame.

After a few minutes, Emily climbed over Mom's lap to sit in Camryn's.

"Mommy says maybe I should stay with you tonight. 'Cause you're lonely."

Camryn slowly closed her eyes and opened them. She had a job interview in Milwaukee tomorrow. Afterward, she planned on going apartment hunting before meeting with Maxwell in Chicago. Having Emily with her tonight would combat the loneliness she refused to acknowledge aloud.

"Sounds like a plan. We'll watch a movie."

"With cockporn?"

Instead of correcting her niece, she smiled. "Sure. With cockporn."

After Camryn dropped off Emily at her parents' house, she battled the late-morning traffic toward downtown Milwaukee. She was rethinking her apartment hunt in the western suburbs to forgo the rush hour commute. Then again, Milwaukee traffic couldn't hold a candle to Chicago's. Finally seeing her exit, she blew out a relieved breath.

She'd left in plenty of time, but as she pushed the elevator button and checked her watch, she was only five minutes early. She was hoping to make a better impression than this. Of the three interviews lined up, this was the job she wanted. If she didn't get any of them, she may be forced to stay at her parents for a while.

Shuddering at the thought, she exited the elevator and checked in at the front desk. Before she could sit in the waiting area as directed, a man poked his head around the corner and called her name. He looked like he'd just woken up from a frat house drinking bender.

"I'm Trevor. If you could follow me back, we'll get started."

She did as asked, noting his dark mass of hair was arranged in a seemingly purposeful bed head look. His jeans were frayed at the hem. He had on a blue polo—untucked.

Dear God. Please be the IT guy and not my possible new boss.

She followed him back to a spacious office with a great view of Lake Michigan. Sailboats dotted the water in the far distance. Action figures lined the shelves behind his desk. Spiderman. Captain Kirk. Yoda. A Ryan Braun bobble head. Creepy, those bobble head things. She sat in a chair across from him, watching all the eyes staring back at her.

"So," he started. "Tell me a bit about yourself."

Her gaze darted back to the boy-child. Why did they always ask this question in interviews? How was she supposed to answer this?

"I'm from Milwaukee, but I've been working in marketing in Chicago since I graduated. I'm very organized..."

He waved his hand to cut her off. "No, no. I know all that. I have your resume. Tell me about *you.*"

Her life in Chicago flashed through her memory. The secretaries calling her *The Ice Queen.* Spending weeknights, and most weekends, alone. Working crazy long hours to fill in the void. Eating lunch alone at her desk because everyone was too scared to talk to her. The only office Christmas card she got was from her secretary, who was probably too threatened not to send one.

As she looked at the man in front of her, she made a decision. She would get this job. She would make friends here. She would not be a stiff flagpole who censored everything she said. She would be personable and friendly and...

"I'm from a large, crazy Serbian family, and most of the time I think I'm adopted. I'm single, but I'd like to get married someday. I swear I'm not obsessive about that, though. No bridal magazines stashed away. I like to read, watch very little TV, and hate long walks on the beach."

He stared back at her long enough for Camryn to know she blew it. What was wrong with her? She'd never said things like this, especially in an interview. It was so unprofessional. Any chance of employment now was...

Trevor threw his head back and laughed. Her jaw dropped.

"I like you. You're funny."

No one ever called her funny before. At least, not in a favorable way.

He leaned forward. "I started this company three years ago from my apartment. Last year, I had to expand I had so many clients. We do mostly Web design and maintenance, but lately we've had questions about marketing and long-term layouts. That's where you would come in. I need someone to do projections. Get some bigger clients in. Research the industries for the sites we manage. Occasionally you'd meet with clients, possibly travel, but that's minimal. You'd also be responsible for our advertising, such as social media sites, handling commercial shoots, that kind of thing."

These duties were the more pleasurable aspects of her old job. This was too good to be true. She waited for the punch line.

He stood and gestured for her to follow him out of the office. He pointed out several offices lining the south wall. Two young women and a man her age occupied each.

"These are our graphic designers, Ashley and Susan, and our techie, Ben." They waved. She waved back.

She followed him across the suite to the north wall. "This is our conference room, and over here's the break room."

The conference room was a cheery yellow, and had a large, black oval table. A projector and an iPad station were set up in the corner next to a fifty-inch flat screen TV. The break room was a spring green. Two cafe tables adorned a corner. On the counter were a cappuccino machine, a coffee maker, a microwave and a toaster. A fridge plastered with Post-it notes stood next to the sink.

Impressed, and jealous, she nodded, following him back to his area on the east wall. Instead of going in his office, they entered another office close to the size of his.

"A lot of this job is also human resources. I've been doing that until now. I hate it. We have an accountant, but he's part time and really only handles the books. You'd have to do payroll when he's on vacation. This would be your office."

Her jaw dropped for the second time. A corner office? Overlooking Lake Michigan? Floor-to-ceiling maple shelves lined the entire area behind a matching desk. There was a closet. The room was painted a cornflower blue. A navy leather loveseat was positioned in the corner under the window. Her old office barely had room for her computer chair, and she nearly ran the department.

"Does this all sound reasonable to you?"

She looked at him and cleared her throat. "Yes, of course."

They walked back to his office and sat down. "This is a very laid-back environment. Instead of casual Fridays, we have casual Mondays. Mondays stink, it makes the day better. Otherwise we have informal business dress, except when meeting clients."

That explained the jeans. And the hair.

He picked up her resume and glanced over it. "It looks like you're familiar with all the responsibilities. I already checked your references. You come highly recommended. Salary-wise, I can match what you're making now. I can't really offer more until we get more clients, which I can't do without filling the position." He leaned back in his chair, folding his hands behind his head. "So, you want the job?"

She felt her eyebrows shoot to her hairline. Was he serious? "When do I start?"

"First, I have to tell you something. Something very

serious."

She knew it. It was too good to be true. Though she had thoroughly researched the company before coming in, having seen a solid rise in business and good judgment, she wondered what the catch was. "And what's that?"

He frowned. "I'm Croatian. It could be a conflict with you being Serbian." A slow, easy grin spread over his face.

A laugh bubbled out before she could hold back. "As long as you don't tell my mother, we should be fine."

"Good," he said, rising. "You can start next Monday. See the secretary on the way out. She'll get your papers in order."

Grinning, she shook his hand and walked to the doorway. Yet a nagging doubt resounded through her head. She turned.

"This may sound dense, but can I ask why me? You must have had several interviews for the position."

He crossed his arms and shrugged. "You're a mature presence with experience. You're also the first person who didn't give me a carbon-copy answer when I requested to know more about you. I need a personality."

He thought she had personality?

She stared at him, feeling a lump in her throat. A week ago, she would have been dismissed for the job. A week ago, she'd been a statue. A robot like Maxwell said. Troy changed all that. Opened her. Showed her who she was underneath and allowed her to be that person again.

And damn. She missed him already.

Nodding, she left.

Camryn used her spare key to open the door to Maxwell's condo. Knowing he'd be home from the office any second, she poured herself a glass of water and sat on the sofa to wait.

Maxwell's two-bedroom condo was on the eighteenth floor

near the north side of Chicago, and cost more than five years of her salary. He'd hired a decorator when he first bought it. A few weeks ago she thought it modern, but now it just felt cold. Gray walls, black and white abstract art. Not like Troy's house. His was masculine, but showed individuality. Style. Taste.

Maxwell only had one bookshelf. That was a crime in itself. Worse yet, the shelves were lined with non-fiction money-making accounts. Not a single fiction title. She'd bet she'd find a plethora of fiction at Troy's. She grinned. Including romance.

There were also no pictures at Maxwell's. Not of her, his mother, nor friends. If he had any. This could've been her life. Had he not broken off the relationship, they might be sitting together now, probably discussing the fuss of Heather's wedding and how tacky he thought it was.

She wondered if Maxwell really did want her back. She wondered what she ever saw in him in the first place.

The door opened and she rose, setting down her water on a coaster.

"You're here," he said with all the enthusiasm of a slug. He dropped his keys on the counter and walked over to her, running his hands up and down her arms. No kiss on the cheek, no smile.

"You asked me to come."

"Have you eaten?"

"Yes," she lied.

"I'll order from that Thai place you like," he said, as if not hearing a thing she said. He did that a lot, but until two weeks ago, she never cared.

"I said I ate. And I hate Thai food. You're the one who loves it."

He turned, cell in hand, with an expression of shock. It's not like she slapped the guy!

"Okay." He pocketed his cell, smoothing out his features. "I have some interesting news. The firm may be calling you to come back. Fenzer Footwear pulled out when they found out you were gone. The president is coming down on Alicia for letting you go. They want her to shuffle things and..."

"I have a job," she said calmly. Oh, but it felt so good knowing they messed up. Knowing Alicia got reprimanded for a mistake. She wanted to do a happy dance. Instead she stared Maxwell down.

"Since when?"

"Since today. I start next week." She sat on a bar stool by the counter and folded her hands in her lap.

He stared at her like she'd sprouted two heads and spit fire from her nostrils. "Your hair is different. And your clothes." He had the arrogance to smile. "You heard what I said, took my opinion into account."

She always took his opinion into account, even if it clashed with her own. In fact, over the past year and a half, she didn't think she had opinions. She'd been a doormat too long. "Oh, I heard you, Maxwell. I didn't do this for you."

He rubbed his chest like he needed his fiftieth antacid of the day. "Look, I'm sorry for how things turned out. Alicia and I were a mistake. I want to work this out with you. We're the same, you and I."

She stared at the horns on his head, then at his glowing red eyes, noting he didn't say he was sorry for the cruel things he said back in his office, just that he was sorry for how things turned out. He wasn't sorry about the breakup, he was sorry Alicia dumped him. He didn't miss her, he missed their routine.

She didn't know why she agreed to meet with Maxwell, but part of her hoped it was for this reason. Part of her wanted to get back what she once had. To have him admit his mistake and want her back. To miss her.

It felt like a hollow victory.

Troy's words came back to her. The way he pleaded with her to find someone else to love. *True, crazy, can't-live-without-it kind of love.* That was not Maxwell. It had never been Maxwell. Would never be. She'd only loved one person like that, and he was gone. She'd blown that to hell.

"Camryn, you're doing it again. Going off to la-la land and ignoring me."

"You never call me Cam."

His eyes narrowed. "What?"

"You never call me Cam," she repeated. Such a simple thing really. A nickname, an abbreviation. Her family used it a lot. So did Troy. She never noticed until now, but it felt like an endearment. They cared enough to make even a name personal.

"Your name is Camryn. Why on Earth would I call you...Cam?" The last part was said with disgust.

She looked at him, feeling nothing but pity. He didn't have a woman in his life who cared about him like Troy cared for her. Someone to show him life before it was too late. She wanted to tell him that life with him was like being stuck in coach on a twelve-hour flight. And life with Troy was skydiving to escape. She wanted to voice the spiteful thoughts in her head, like telling him he had all the flair of cardboard, while Troy made her laugh endlessly without trying.

But comparing Maxwell to Troy was unfair. She didn't want Maxwell, and she could never have Troy. Stooping to Maxwell's level would solve nothing, and making him feel as badly as she once did would not make anything right.

She hopped down off the stool and slid his key across the counter.

"Camryn, be reasonable."

Unable to control herself, she smiled. "I've been reasonable long enough, and it's gotten me nowhere." She went around him and walked to the door.

"You're making a mistake."

She turned. "I've made plenty of those too. This isn't one of them." She turned the knob as thunder boomed overhead. She paused, remembering the feel of summer rain on her face, the smell of Troy as he held her. "Maxwell, I hope one day you'll learn to dance in the rain."

"What? In this suit? That's the most ridiculous thing I've ever heard."

Her grin widened. "Good, then you can laugh until it hurts. It feels oddly refreshing. Good-bye, Maxwell."

Camryn finished taping the last of her boxes and sat on one with a plop. The movers were coming tomorrow to take her things to storage until her new apartment in Milwaukee became available next month. Tomorrow, she'd finally say good-bye to this dreadful, noisy city and go home. Say good-bye to her old life and start a new one.

Sad, because her old life wasn't a life at all.

She stared out the window at the rising sun, remembering the sunrise in Colorado. So beautiful it was. So ordinary this one seemed.

Troy had wanted her to fall in love. To believe, he'd said.

She had. With him.

The pain erupted inside her chest, like it had every second since they returned home. An ache so deep nothing suppressed it. A can't-live-without-him need.

He'd tried to tell her something back in Colorado before Fisher interrupted. Her mind kept playing the conversation over and over again in her head. For a second, the little girl inside her hoped he would sweep in and declare his undying love. It had sounded like he was leading up to it.

Instead of some silly fairy tale, the man had stood before her, just trying to rationalize the illogical something between them. She wondered what was in his heart. If he did love her in return. She still had trouble trusting herself, and if his possible feelings were genuine. How long would they last in the real world if she had responded to what he said?

She feared the connection Troy felt with her was due to their family. The passion they shared an illusion. Was it something more for him? It felt like more to her. Except when she was alone, with no distractions, she was forced to think over every clause in his words, and was forced to face *her* true feelings.

She loved him more than anything in the world.

Her cell rang, jolting her. Rising, she walked to the counter and checked the caller ID. Fisher. Her mood deflated, not that it should have. Troy hadn't tried to call once in the four days they'd been back.

"Hey," her brother said. "Heather called from Cancun. They'll be back on Friday. Mom wants to have a family dinner."

She sat in a kitchen chair. "Okay, I'll be there."

"I heard you got the job. Congratulations."

She smiled. At least she had that going for her. "Thanks. I think I'll like it there."

"Cam..." He cleared his throat. "It'll be good having you back home."

Aw. Fisher was being genuinely nice. "I love you too."

Pause. "Heather told me about Maxwell, and why you and Troy..." He sighed heavily. She waited him out. "Did you meet with the guy? If you're back together, maybe you could bring him for dinner..."

"We're not back together."

"Oh. Okay."

Thank God Fisher married Anna, because his conversational skills hadn't improved since kindergarten.

"I didn't love him," she said, staring out the window again. The sun shone through the curtains, making little patterns on her carpet. Maxwell didn't make her heart pound and her laugh giddy. The thought of losing him didn't make her feel dead inside. "I love someone else," she whispered.

She bit her tongue and rose, hoping Fisher hadn't heard.

Troy would come to the family dinner on Friday. She'd take that opportunity to pull him aside and talk to him alone. Perhaps asking him to finish his thought from back in Colorado would help her understand what she was feeling and give her clarity. This pain and loneliness was so new and raw.

Emily's voice squealed in the background. A loud muffle followed. Fisher probably hadn't heard. Small miracles.

"Tell her, Daddy!"

"Okay, okay!" he said away from the receiver. "Cam, I'm sorry for how I handled things."

She smiled, picturing her niece bullying Fisher into an apology. "It's okay. I forgive you. Everything worked out for the best anyway."

It was scary how accustomed to lying she'd grown.

Chapter Twenty-Two

Life Lessons According to Camryn:
True love is an electric shock with someone else in
control of the switch.

Troy pulled his truck into the driveway and cut the engine. Fisher was sitting on his front steps, forearms draped over his thighs, looking like he'd slept as little as he had this week. Opening the car door, Troy stepped out into the humidity and up the front walk. Fisher rose.

"What brings you by?"

Fisher rubbed the back of his neck. "Guilt."

Good. He should feel guilty. "Why didn't you use your key? It's hot out here."

Fisher shrugged, looking everywhere but at Troy. "Wasn't sure if you'd want it back after what happened."

Troy watched him for a long minute and nodded. "Want a beer?"

Fisher blew out a breath. "Yes."

He glanced down at Fisher's hand as he unlocked the front door. "What's that?" he asked, pointing to the envelope in his hands. They stepped inside, the AC feeling like Heaven as it cooled his skin.

"I don't know. FedEx brought it by while I was waiting. It's from the Hortons."

Interesting. He shut the door. "Just leave it on the table. I'm going to shower. Help yourself to a beer. I'll just be a sec."

After Troy showered and dressed, he grabbed a beer and sat next to Fisher on the couch in prolonged silence.

"So, um...family dinner on Friday night. Heather and Justin will be back from their honeymoon."

Troy nodded. "Okay."

Fisher looked like a kid who wet the bed. "Camryn will be there too."

Troy almost smiled. "I figured."

"She got the job. She says she thinks she'll like it."

"Uh huh." Now Troy did smile for the first time in four days. Four long, miserable days. "Is that what you came by to say?"

Fisher rolled his eyes. "I'm sorry, man. I really am. I overreacted."

Troy assessed him before answering. "I got used to your impatience and temper long ago." Troy wished he had Fisher's backbone.

Fisher looked at him. "I interrupted something back there, didn't I? This thing between you and Cam wasn't all a lie, was it?"

Troy took a long drink before answering. "Not for me."

He sighed. "If it means anything, she didn't get back together with her ex." A glimmer of hope poked through. "She said she was in love with someone else."

Troy's head whipped up. He stared down Fisher, hoping to God this wasn't some ploy out of guilt.

Fisher stared at his bottle, then drained the contents. Setting the bottle on the table, he rose. "I..." He shook his head. "I didn't mean any of the things I said, Troy. You're family. More than that. No one deserves to be happy more than you. She isn't too good for you."

Troy clamped his jaw down, trying and failing not to react. He shut his eyes, counting his breaths until he reached twenty. When he opened his eyes, Fisher was halfway to the door with his arms crossed as if trying to decide between leaving or staying.

"No one's too good for you."

"Shit, Fisher." Troy ran a hand down his face.

"I gotta go," he said, bee-lining for the door. "Anna's making dinner and I have to pick up Em at Mom's..."

"Fisher." His friend, his brother, turned, refusing to look at him. "Thank you."

"No, thank *you*."

Troy swallowed as the door closed, the pain in his gut growing to monumental proportions. Sucking in a breath, he dropped his head to the back of the couch to stare at the ceiling.

She didn't get back together with Maxwell. Didn't fall into her old pattern or settle.

And she loved him back.

At least, if what Fisher said held any truth, she did. Lifting his head, he looked at the envelope from Colorado sitting on his table.

Leaning forward, he set down his beer and picked up the package. He ripped it open, and let the contents drop to the cushion next to him. Several photos scattered. Troy picked up the note inside.

I just got these developed and thought you'd like copies. After seeing these, your relationship didn't seem fake to me, but what do I know? Anyway, the maid found something under the bed when she was cleaning. I figured you'd want it back. It seemed important. I hope you are well and happy. Come back to visit anytime.

~Bernice

Troy set the pictures aside and froze. Camryn's note she'd

left with the muffin that morning shook in his hand.

You are someone.

He wondered the same thing now that he'd wondered then. Was he just a *someone*, or a someone *to her*? If so, why hadn't she reacted in the Hortons' kitchen? He'd already gone there, already took that plunge in telling her how he felt. If he did it again, would the outcome be different?

Like her definition of insanity.

Hell, he was just crazy enough to declare his love a hundred times if there was even a glimmer of possibility she'd respond the same.

Setting the note down, he picked up the pictures. There were a few of them walking down the aisle, a couple from their karaoke night, and one from the reception of them dancing. In the close up of them looking at each other, her smile was relaxed and happy.

He traced his finger over her image. He'd only seen that smile a handful of times, and each time brought him to his knees. Regardless, he had his answer.

Grabbing his cell, he dialed with impatient fingers. He tapped his foot, pacing until she picked up.

"Mom, I need your help."

After a long drive from hell, with her insides churning into a knot the size of Great Britain, Camryn pulled into her parents' driveway and got out of the car. Judging by the amount of other vehicles, it looked like the majority of the family beat her here. Including Troy.

She stared at his truck. The only way she'd know for sure if he cared about her was to talk to him. But old Camryn wanted to plaster on a stoic face and not confront him at all. Pretend she didn't feel like her organs had been ripped out.

Popping the trunk, she removed her overnight bag and headed up the walkway. She stopped short, seeing Heather and Justin waiting for her on the front porch.

Closing the distance between them, she could smell the roasted lamb and *gibanita* baking. The heavenly, royally fattening scents wafted out through the open kitchen window like a cartoon teasing her to sin. Just smelling the assorted cheeses and pastry from the gibanita had her gaining thirty pounds.

"Hey," she said. "Why's everyone here so early?"

Heather looked at Justin, then back to her. "Um, I don't know."

Camryn's eyes narrowed. The only person worse at lying than her was her sister. "Right. How was Cancun?"

"Oh," she gushed. "It was amazing. The water was so blue. We stayed in this little cabin right on the beach..."

"Heather," Justin interrupted, raising his brows.

"Oh, right," she said, giggling. *Giggling.* "I'll tell you later. Let's go in. Everyone's waiting."

"Waiting for what?" They didn't answer. Great. "What did I do now?" she asked, filtering the recent week through her head. She couldn't think of anything the family could blame on her, like an earthquake or a recent price hike in crude oil.

"Nothing," Heather said quickly. Too quickly. "Troy's inside, though."

"Yes," she said slowly, her sarcasm dripping. "He *is* family. I expected him to be here. And I can see his truck right there in front of my car."

Heather looked nervous. They stood there staring at each other, not a sound but the robins chirping from the pine tree edging the yard. This couldn't be just about what went down at the Hortons'.

Justin rolled his eyes. "Come on, ladies." He took her bag from her and held the door open.

Wondering what all the tension was about, Cam walked inside to find the whole family standing in the living room, staring at her. Halting, she glanced around. "Hello," she said, the greeting sounding more like a drawn out question.

No one moved.

Emily eventually squeezed through the bodies. "Auntie Cam! Spiderman brought Mrs. Horton!"

"Excuse me?"

Anna picked up Emily and set her on her hip. "Not *Spiderman*, a *web cam*, sweetie."

Emily shrugged as Bernice's voice filled the silence. "Hello, Camryn."

Camryn looked around, her gaze finally dropping to the laptop in Fisher's lap. "Uh, hello. I got the pictures you sent. Thank you." Confused, she looked at Fisher. "Why is Bernice on a web cam for our family dinner?"

"I asked her to join us," Troy said, stepping around Yjaka Harold and into her line of sight. "I have something to tell you."

"What is going on?" she asked, starting to panic. Her glance darted around the room. "Where's Nana? Is Nana okay?"

"I'm fine. Quit your fussing."

The view to Nana's chair was blocked by Dad and Mom, but her heart rate returned to normal hearing the crabby old woman's voice. As tactless and cruel as Nana could be, Camryn now understood why she was this way. When Papa died ten years ago, Nana lost the love of her life, along with all her happiness. Loving Troy, even if it couldn't work out, showed Camryn the sheer pain Nana must be feeling every second of every day.

Camryn looked at the faces around the room, all of them staring her down. Something was wrong. "Okay, what's...?"

"I tried to tell you all this back in Colorado," Troy said, cutting her off. "But someone so rudely interrupted me."

Fisher sighed harshly. "I said I was sorry. Can we get over it now?"

Anna made a sound of disgust. "Serves you right for acting without thinking. You're always flapping your mouth."

"I do not flap anything."

Through the bantering, Troy's gaze didn't leave hers. He looked different. His hair was still too long, his eyes still an intriguing dark brown, his body still a solid rock of muscle. But the charming smile was gone. The humor in his words gone. The vitality she so desperately envied was replaced with this subdued, deflated form of Troy. Her heart broke as she looked at him, wondering if she were the reason, and if he could be fixed.

"You are so much more than you think you are, Cam," he said, shaking his head like he was giving a eulogy. "What we had together was real for me. It may have started out as a lie, but it doesn't have to end that way."

Oh, man. Did he just say...?

He took her hand and put something inside, closing her fingers around it. As he stepped back, she opened her hand and looked down at a little blue Matchbox truck.

"Troy," her mother said, her voice tentative and questioning. "This isn't what we..."

"Quiet, Mom," he said, staring into Camryn's eyes.

"Uncle Troy's doing a good job sharing his toys, isn't he?"

"Yes, sweetie," Anna said, patting Emily's back.

Camryn's hand began to shake, her heart pounding so loud her head felt like the ocean. "Troy?"

"Do you remember?" he asked.

Yes, she remembered. How could she ever forget? He'd kept this toy all these years? How could one little thing mean so much to him? When they were kids and she gave this to him, she just wanted to make him feel better, to help him understand things wouldn't always be that horrible.

"You gave that to me once. There hasn't been a day that's gone by I haven't looked at it and thought of you. You saved me. No one knows me like you do. I don't want anyone else but you, or to live one more day without you."

Her heart stopped. Her vision blurred. Her throat closed. "Troy?" she managed to croak out. She used to have the vocabulary of Webster. Apparently now it was reduced to Dr. Seuss.

"Open the truck door," he whispered.

Wiping her palm over her cheeks first, she pried open the little door to the truck. A ring lay inside. "Oh, God," she muttered, tucking her pinkie inside to scoop it out.

As she stared at the single gold band and square-cut diamond, he dropped to his knees. She gasped.

"Troy, it's one knee, not two," Yjaka Mitch said.

"Oh, be quiet," her mother said. "He can do it any way he wants."

"I'm just saying, he's doing it wrong. You propose on *one* knee..."

At the word *propose*, everything else tuned out. The room became a quiet hum of filtered noise. She looked at the ring, so small and beautiful. He would have known she didn't like flashy. He knew her better than anyone else, just like he claimed of her.

And he wanted her. Dear God, he wanted...

"Camryn," Troy beckoned with a firm voice, drawing back the chatter from the room. Her crazy, crazy family. He was doing this right in front of the whole nut farm.

"She should've worn her hair up." From Kuma Viola.

"No, I like it down." From Tetaka Myrtle.

"It's not like she knew this was coming," Heather defended.

"Get on with it." From Nana. "Don't look a gift horse in the mouth, missy!"

"Perhaps we shouldn't say horse in front of her. She may be traumatized." From Dad.

"She's gonna say no. Look at her." From Yjaka Harold. "We should just buy her a dozen cats now."

"I love you." Troy.

He was all that mattered. Troy. Just Troy. The pain in her chest eased. Her stomach settled. And she didn't know true happiness, true love, until right now. Love was everything. Life was nothing without it.

He rose from his knees, took her hands in his. "Don't go off somewhere. Don't tune me out. Stay with me."

"I'm not... I'm here. Troy..."

"I know true love is hard for you to believe in," he said, cutting her off in a panic.

"No, Troy..."

"You are my happy ending, Cam, and I want nothing more than to prove to you they exist."

Well, damn. If that wasn't the sappiest, sweetest darn thing anyone ever said. And he *had* turned her into a gushy female too, because her eyes were welling again.

"Is she crying?" Yjaka Mitch asked.

"No," Nana barked. "She's sweating from her eyes, you idiot! Of course she's crying."

"Naw, can't be," Yjaka Harold argued. "Cam doesn't know how to cry."

"They're happy tears. Right, Auntie Cam?"

"Yes, Emily," she said, wiping the tears, looking at everything she always wanted and never knew. "And they lived happily ever after," she whispered to Troy.

"What?"

She barely saw him through the haze of tears. "I said yes."

The family erupted in cheers behind him. Troy stood there staring, looking shell-shocked, as if she hadn't said anything.

"That was so romantic. I have goose bumps," Kuma Viola claimed. She smacked Yjaka Harold upside the head. "Why didn't you do something that romantic?"

Yjaka Harold rubbed his head. "What was wrong with putting the ring in the mashed potatoes for you to find?"

"I almost choked on it. You didn't even get down on one knee, *prevariti!*"

Camryn couldn't remember what *prevariti* translated to in English, but she hoped it meant fool. She shook her head and started to slide the ring onto her finger when Anna's voice cleared the noise.

"No, Cam. He's supposed to do that. Troy?" They both looked at him, but he hadn't moved.

"Let's eat," Tetaka Myrtle said.

The family muttered to each other and dispersed between the kitchen and dining room since the main attraction was over.

Heather and Justin sat on the couch next to Fisher. Anna set Emily down, and the little girl bounded towards the kitchen.

"Troy," Anna shouted. He blinked and stared at her. "She said yes. Put the ring on her finger."

"Yeah, okay. Right." He closed the distance between them and took the ring, placing it on her finger with all the sentiment of an android. "I thought you were going to say no," he said. "I didn't think..." His hands closed around her wrists. "Did you mean it? Tell me you were serious. 'Cause I couldn't take it if you backed out on me, Cam. You know I can't offer you much. All I have is a three-bedroom ranch and a decent job."

Tugging her wrists free, she cupped his cheeks. She didn't want anything but him. Forever. "You have me," she said. "You'll always have me. I don't need anything else but you. I love you."

He still looked doubtful, a look she remembered from their

285

youth any time someone did something nice for him. Sliding her arms around his waist, she whispered in his ear, "I love you, Troy. Honest. I love you."

One hand came up and clutched her arm, tightening and flexing before drawing around her back. His chest shook. A pent up breath whooshed out. "God, Cam. I love you too."

He lowered his head and closed his mouth over hers. And oh, how she missed this. When the kiss turned from relieved to sweet, she smiled against his mouth. That seemed to drive him crazy. His hold tightened, pulling her flush against his chest. His free hand dove into her hair.

"I'm never, never letting you go," he said.

"I hope you meant figuratively. Things may get a bit awkward otherwise."

He laughed, releasing any trace of residual tension. "I want to take you home, make love to you through the night and..."

She couldn't wait for the *and*. "Later," she said against his lips, a promise if she ever made one.

Something tugged on her skirt. Emily stared up at her. "Can I play with the truck?"

Camryn looked at Troy. "You'll have to ask him, honey."

For a second, he looked torn, trapped somewhere between past and present. But after a moment he nodded, grinning down at her niece. "I don't think I need it anymore. You can keep it."

Enthused, Emily took the toy and ran off.

Camryn looked at her sister. Heather winked back. "Fall wedding?" she asked, linking Justin's fingers with hers.

Leave it to Heather to wait an entire five seconds before demanding the details.

"You could have the wedding here," Bernice said.

"We forgot you were there, Mom," Justin said, laughing at the laptop still in Fisher's lap.

"Figures. Plan a whole wedding and no one can remember you're there afterward. I mean it, though. You could have the wedding here."

Camryn looked at Troy and shrugged. "Or we could leave the family here and elope to Vegas."

Troy laughed. "Tempting."

"I'm going to log off," Bernice said. "Congratulations, you two."

Fisher closed the laptop and set it on the table.

Heather cleared her throat, raising her eyebrows at Camryn. "I told you he'd pass the test."

Camryn smiled and shook her head while her siblings laughed at their inside joke. Troy slid an arm around her waist, drawing her to his side, and looking all kinds of confused. This only caused more laughter.

"What is so funny in there?" her mother demanded.

"Nothing!" they shouted in unison, taking Camryn back to good memories of her youth.

Just as they were settling down, Troy asked, "What test?" and they erupted into hysterics all over again.

"Camryn," Heather said, fanning her face with her hand. "It's time Troy knew our secret. Go ahead and tell him."

Troy's brows rose as he looked at her.

"Well," Camryn started, "once upon a time, three little kids created something called the dysfunctional test..."

Nana's Slavski Kolac Bread

(Nana's Lesson: This is typically made for *Krsna Slava*—the celebration of a Serbian family's patron saint day. However it can be made for *Hristo se Rodi*—Christmas. If made for Christmas, Serbians call this money bread or St. Nicholas bread, they wrap coins in aluminum foil and bake coins inside the bread. Now, get going!)

2 tablespoons active dry yeast

1 teaspoon sugar

3 tablespoons flour

1/2 cup warm water

1 1/2 cups warm water

6 cups bread flour

1 teaspoon salt

1 cup butter, softened

3 eggs, beaten

1/4 cup of lemon juice

1/2 cup sugar

1 egg, beaten with 1 tablespoon water

Mix yeast, sugar and 3 tablespoons flour in 1/2 cup warm water until dissolved. In large bowl, combine 1-1/2 cups warm water, salt, butter, eggs, lemon juice and sugar. Add yeast mixture and the remaining flour gradually. Dough should be stiff. Knead by hand for approximately ten minutes and put in a bowl to rise. Cover bowl with a damp towel. Let sit for 1-2 hours, or until dough rises to twice the size. Knead again for another 5 minutes. Put in a well-greased 9-inch round cake pan. Let it sit for about a half hour, then place in a preheated 350 degree oven. After 30 minutes, brush bread with egg wash mixture and bake for thirty minutes more. Cool on a wire rack.

Mom's Sarma

(Troy's Disclaimer: This may taste good, but it makes the house smell terrible!)

1 large head cabbage

1 pound ground pork

1/2 pound ground chuck

2 large eggs, beaten

1 teaspoon salt

1 teaspoon paprika

1/2 teaspoon black pepper

1 can tomato sauce, plain

5 tablespoons cooking oil

1/2 cup cooked rice

Cut the core out of the cabbage and lightly salt inside. Mix uncooked pork and beef. Add salt, paprika, pepper, eggs and rice. Boil cabbage until pliable, about 15 minutes. Drain and pull leaves apart. Place 3-4 tablespoons of meat mix on a cabbage leaf and roll, folding the corners in. Drip oil into a 13x9 baking pan. Set cabbage rolls on top, pressing together snugly. Pour tomato sauce over rolls. Bake covered in a preheated 350 degree oven for 45 minutes. Uncover and bake an additional 15-20 minutes.

Sweet Cheese Gibanita

(Camryn's Disclaimer: Also spelled *Gibanica*, this can be made with meat or cheese. If made with cheese, it can be made sweet or salty. My family always made it sweet. Your doctor, your hips, your butt, and your cholesterol will hate you after eating.)

1 container of small curd cottage cheese

2 sticks of butter, softened

1 package of cream cheese, softened

3/4 pound of Feta cheese, crumbled

6 eggs

1/2 cup of cream

1 cup of sugar

1 package of Filo leaves, or 1 package of thick dough leaves

Beat butter and sugar until smooth. Add cream, cheeses, and eggs. In a 13x9 greased pan, lay down a thin layer of leaves, covering the bottom of the pan. Spoon thin layer of cheese mixture over leaves. Repeat this process until cheese mixture is gone. It is ideal to have at least 4 layers. Bake in a preheated 350 degree oven uncovered for an hour. Cool 10 minutes before cutting. Serve warm or cold.

Dad's Roasted Lamb

(Dad's Disclaimer: You may also slow cook this on a spit or outdoor rotisserie. Marinate the lamb cut with saucepan directions for an hour or two first.)

1 leg, shoulder, or loin of lamb

1 teaspoon salt

1/2 cup vinegar

1 cups water

1/2 teaspoon of pepper

2 teaspoons of parsley

1 tablespoon of garlic powder

1/2 teaspoon thyme

4-5 slices bacon, uncooked

Rub the lamb with salt and lay it in a deep dish baking pan or roaster. In a saucepan, combine the vinegar, water, pepper, parsley, garlic powder, and thyme. Bring to a boil and pour over the lamb. Lay bacon slices over the lamb meat. Bake in a preheated 375 degree oven. Cook times vary on cut of meat. Typically covered for 30 minutes, then uncover and bake another 10-15 minutes. If you try to pierce the meat and it offers no resistance, or falls off the bone, it's done.

About the Author

Kelly's been known to say that she gets her ideas from everyone and everything around her, and that there's always a book playing out in her head. No one who knows her bats an eyelash when she talks to herself. She began her writing career in the Indie market, becoming the recipient of an *Editor's Choice Award*, a Finalist in the *2008 Best Book Awards*, and a Finalist in the *2009 Indie Excellence Awards* before moving into traditional publishing. Her books not only have honors from the top review sites, but from *NY Times* bestsellers too. She is a respected reviewer and a *Romance Writers of America* member. Kelly's interests include: sappy movies, MLB, NFL, driving others insane, and sleeping when she can. She is a closet caffeine junkie and chocoholic, but don't tell anyone. She resides in Wisconsin with her husband, three sons, and her black lab. Most of her family lives in the Carolinas, so she spends a lot of time there as well.

You can visit her at her website: AuthorKellyMoran.com, Facebook: Facebook.com/AuthorKellyMoran, or on Twitter: @AuthorKMoran.

*Falling for the bad boy is even more dangerous
the second time around.*

Good Girl Gone Plaid
© *2013 Shelli Stevens*
The McLaughlins, Book 1

In high school Sarah fell for her best friend's older brother—one of the sexy, Scottish McLaughlin boys. But a painful betrayal showed her she'd been a fool to give her heart to a bad boy. At least it made it easier to leave him and move halfway around the world when her Navy dad got stationed in Japan.

Eleven years later, the death of her grandmother has forced Sarah back to Whidbey Island for a month. It's the length of time she must stay in her inherited house before she's allowed to sell it, take the money and run. But when she sees Ian, bad as ever and still looking like sin on a stick, she can't keep her mouth from watering.

One look at Sarah stirs up the regret lingering in Ian's heart—and never-forgotten desire lingering in his body. He should walk away, especially since divorced single mothers aren't his style. But when she starts showing up at his family's pub, he can't resist a little casual seduction for old time's sake.

One thing quickly becomes clear, though. The heat between them is causing an avalanche of secrets and betrayal and nothing will ever be the same.

Warning: A bad-boy hero who's good with his hands, a heroine who's trying to be good. Contains liberal consumption of Scotch whisky, a Highland Games competition, men in kilts wielding large poles, and a potential Sarah McLaughlin of the non-musical kind.

Available now in ebook and print from Samhain Publishing.

SAMHAIN

PUBLISHING

It's all about the story...

Romance

HORROR

Retro
ROMANCE

www.samhainpublishing.com